A WARTIME WELCOME AT ROOKERY HOUSE

ROSIE HENDRY

A Wartime Welcome at Rookery House

Published by Rookery House Press
Cover design by designforwriters.com

For David, with love.

Thank you for coming on
this new writing adventure with me.

CHAPTER 1

London, October 1940

Genevieve Hamilton-Jones hurried out of the hospital and headed towards the nearest bus stop. It was half past six and not long before tonight's blackout time when the city would be plunged into darkness. She was later leaving her shift than usual as there'd been several admissions to the ward this afternoon. Now, with her feet throbbing after being on them for hours, all she wanted was to get home before the air-raid siren went off, as it had every night since the Blitz started last month. Night after night, the bombers had returned to pound London with high explosives and incendiary bombs. It was a wonder there was anything left standing, she thought.

Looking over her shoulder, Genevieve spotted a red double-decker approaching and luckily it had her route number on the front. She picked up her pace, running the last few yards along the pavement, reaching the stop as the bus pulled up at the kerb with a choking blast of exhaust fumes.

Climbing on board, she made her way to an empty seat next to a young woman on the lower deck.

'Just made it!' Genevieve smiled at the woman as she stowed her small, brown leather suitcase under the seat before sitting down.

The woman returned her smile. 'Are you going somewhere?'

Genevieve frowned. 'I beg your pardon.'

'Your suitcase.' The woman pointed to where Genevieve had put her case, as the bus pulled out into the traffic with a noisy rev of its engine. 'Sorry, I'm being nosy, only I'm off tomorrow myself. I've got to pack my suitcase when I get home. I'm that excited I can hardly wait!' Her brown eyes danced with happiness as she looked at Genevieve.

'No, I'm not going anywhere apart from home. I carry my uniform in the case, I always change out of it before I leave for home.'

Genevieve knew it wasn't usual to do that – none of the other nurses did – but in her case, it was wise to do so. She couldn't risk being seen wearing it out of the hospital.

'Are you in one of the services?' the woman asked.

Genevieve shook her head. 'No, I'm a nurse. I've just finished my shift.'

'I'll be going into uniform myself tomorrow. I can't wait to wear it and I will be so proud to be seen in it. Don't you want to wear your nurse's uniform out of the hospital – I've seen other nurses wearing theirs?'

'I prefer not to,' Genevieve said matter of factly. She didn't want to explain and was relieved that at that moment the conductor appeared, and they each bought a ticket.

'What are you going to do?' Genevieve asked once the conductor had moved on.

'I'm joining the WAAF!' The woman beamed. 'Today was

2

my last day at my boring office job. I'm so looking forward to getting away and doing something more exciting instead. I'm reporting for my basic training tomorrow, and once that's over I don't know what I'll do, depends on what they think I'd be best at.' She spoke quickly, her excitement bubbling over. 'I fancy being a driver – I've always wanted to learn to drive.'

'Good luck with it, I hope you get your wish, it's important to do what you enjoy.' Genevieve understood the woman's enthusiasm for her new career, and the joy that came from doing what your heart desired. It had taken her so long and much careful planning to become a nurse and now it was absolutely the best thing in her life. It was her secret and she loved it.

'Thanks! John, he's my fiancé, is already in the RAF – he works on planes, keeping them fit to fly. He's as pleased as punch that I'll be a WAAF. We might get lucky and be stationed in the same place.' The woman paused as she opened her wine-red handbag, which was resting on her lap, and took out a photograph, holding it for Genevieve to see. 'This is him.'

Genevieve looked at the photograph of a smiling man dressed in RAF uniform. 'He looks very nice.'

'Oh, he is! He's lovely, I'm very lucky.' The woman gently traced her fiancé's face with the tip of her finger before putting the photograph back in her handbag. 'Have you got a chap in the services?'

Before Genevieve could reply, the air-raid siren suddenly began its eerie wail over the London rooftops and was met by groans from several of the other passengers sitting nearby.

'Can't they leave us alone for one bleedin' night?' an elderly man moaned, loudly. His comment was greeted by nods and sounds of agreement from other passengers.

'The bombers are early tonight!' the woman said as the bus

slowed and pulled over to the side of the road. 'Nightly air raids are something I will *definitely* not miss. I'm hoping to be sent somewhere where I can get a whole night's sleep in my bed and not have to traipse out to an air-raid shelter.'

'Everybody out!' the conductor shouted from the back of the bus as it came to a juddering halt. 'Make your way to the nearest underground station. As quick as you can – if you please!'

The passengers stood up and filed off the bus and Genevieve followed along with the woman. Most of them turned left and hurried down the street, and she was about to do the same when someone grabbed her arm.

'It'll be quicker to go through there,' the woman said, pointing to the opening of an alleyway between two buildings a little further along the street from where the bus had stopped. 'I live not far away from here and know this area like the back of my hand.' She looked up at the sky which had faded from blue to an opaque grey as dusk fell, frowning as the familiar droning of planes' engines grew louder. 'Come on, those bombers aren't far off, we need to hurry.'

'Lead the way.' Genevieve followed the woman into the shadowy alley which cut through to the street running parallel to the one where the bus had stopped. She'd only gone a few yards in when she suddenly realised that she'd left her suitcase on the bus. She halted. 'I need to go back – I've left my case. I need it, it's got my uniform in…'

The woman stopped and turned to look back at her. 'Go on then, but you'd better be quick. I'll save you a space to sit in the underground if you like. I'll see you below in a little bit, don't be long – the bombers are coming!'

'I'll be as fast as I can.' Genevieve ran back along the alley, out onto the street and returned to where the red double-decker was parked. The bus conductor and driver were about to leave and head for shelter themselves. 'I've left my suitcase on the bus – can I get it, please? It's got my nurse's uniform inside it, and I need it for work.'

'Go on then, hurry up!' The conductor rolled his eyes.

'Thank you.' She gave him a quick smile and climbed aboard, quickly retrieved her case from under the seat and had just stepped out of the bus onto the pavement when a whistling scream filled the air, growing louder by the second.

'Get down!' the conductor roared, grabbing hold of Genevieve's arm, yanking her to the ground as he went down beside her, followed by the driver close by.

Landing on the hard pavement with a thud, Genevieve was about to protest at his rough manhandling when there was a loud bang as a bomb exploded nearby. Instinctively ducking her head, she squeezed her eyes shut and covered her ears with her hands as she lay on the ground. Genevieve was aware of a wave of turbulence and falling debris. Dirt and dust pattered down, and an acrid smell of cordite filled the air. She knew that smell from other raids – it was the stench of bombs.

'You all right?' The bus conductor's voice was gruff beside her.

Genevieve opened her eyes, brushing her hands over her dusty face. 'I think so.' She sat up and looked at the conductor and driver, both of whose dark uniforms were now covered in grey dust. 'Where's the bomb? Where did it land?' She peered around her and miraculously apart from another layer of dust and dirt on the London street, there didn't appear to be much damage.

'Must have landed in that alleyway,' the driver said, scrambling to his feet. 'Lucky it did – if it had fallen out here in the street, it would have been a whole different story. Come on, we need to get to a shelter before any more land here.' He looked up, grimacing at the sight of bombers passing over, high up above the city, dark silhouettes against the fading sky.

The alleyway! Genevieve had been there only moments before and had left the young woman there. Had she reached the end and the safety of the street on the other side before the bomb hit?

Genevieve staggered to her feet, her legs struggling to keep her upright as her bones seemed to have turned to rubber. 'I need to go and see... she might be injured.'

'Who?' the conductor asked.

'The woman who I sat next to on the bus. She knew the alley was a shortcut to the underground, we were both going that way but then I remembered I'd forgotten my suitcase.' She glanced down at her case which lay abandoned on the pavement, the brown leather now coated with a film of dust like she was herself.

'We'll go and look – you stay here.' The conductor glanced at the driver who nodded in agreement.

'But...' Genevieve protested.

'Stay there!' the driver's voice brooked no argument.

She did as they asked, watching as they walked the short distance to the alleyway and went in. Her stomach knotted as she waited for their return. Trying to distract herself, Genevieve looked around and noticed a handbag lying on the pavement a few yards further along the street. She hurried over, picked it up and brushing off some of the covering of gritty dirt, saw it was wine-red coloured – like the one the woman had. Could it be hers? She undid the clasp and opened it – inside, along with a purse, powder compact and lipstick, was the photograph of the RAF fiancé Genevieve had seen earlier. There was no doubt that it belonged to the woman from the bus. It must have been blown out onto the street in the blast, she thought, in which case its owner must be in the alleyway, probably injured and needing first aid.

Genevieve hurried towards the entrance to the alley and met the conductor and driver coming out.

'Is she there? I found her handbag.' She held up the bag.

'No one's in there, just some rubble from the bomb blast,' the conductor said. 'And we checked the street at the other end. She's not there either.'

Genevieve frowned. 'But her handbag's here, it was blown out.'

'Oy! You should be in a shelter!' a loud voice shouted.

She turned to see an air-raid warden hurrying towards them, his face scowling under his steel helmet.

'There was a woman in the alley where the bomb fell. This is her bag, the bomb blast must have blown it out,' Genevieve quickly explained.

'But she's not there now,' the driver added. 'No sign of her.'

The air-raid warden frowned. 'Wait there.'

He hurried into the alleyway and returned a few moments later. 'You sure she was there, ain't gone out the other end?'

'We checked,' the conductor said. 'She's vanished.'

The air-raid warden nodded, his face solemn. 'Must have been a direct hit then.' He sighed. 'Nothing left of her...'

Genevieve stared at him, feeling as if a bucket of icy water had been thrown at her. 'You mean she's *completely gone*... just like that?'

The warden nodded. 'It happens sometimes – there's no body left. I'm sorry for your loss.'

'I didn't really know her, I just sat next to her on the bus. You'd better take this.' She held out the handbag to him. 'It will have her details in, her name...' Her voice cracked as she suddenly realised she didn't even know the woman's name.

'I'll see to it so that her family are informed,' the warden said kindly, taking the bag. 'Now get to a shelter, all of you, as quick as you can.'

~

Genevieve couldn't recall how she'd got to the underground station. She must have retrieved her suitcase from where she'd dropped it when the conductor dragged her to the ground. Now sitting on the floor, her case beside her, she leaned back against the cold, tiled wall of the platform and stared around her at all the people settling down for the night. Many were well prepared for a long stay having brought blankets and food parcels with them – no doubt having fled down here often during the past few weeks. Most of them were civilians but there were a few people in uniform too.

Genevieve took some slow, steady breaths to try to calm her pounding heart, her body shivering with shock from what had happened. Sitting here in this stuffy atmosphere that smelled of mouldy bread wasn't helping, but it was safer down here than outside in the streets. A dull crump from above echoed through the platform sending a shower of dust raining down from the ceiling. The raid was still on, and it might be many hours yet before the all-clear sounded.

A sob welled up inside Genevieve and she squeezed her hands into tight fists to try to get a firm grip on her emotions. It was hard to comprehend how the young woman, who'd been so full of excitement and joy at the prospect of her new life, had been snuffed out in an instant. Gone... just like that. With nothing left of her for her family and fiancé to bury. The only thing that had survived the bomb was her handbag which had been thrown clear in the blast.

That could have been Genevieve's fate too. If she hadn't left her suitcase on the bus and gone back for it, then she'd have been there in the alley when that bomb had hit. A moment's forgetfulness leaving her case behind had saved her life. It hadn't been a conscious decision, just simply forgetting it was under her seat in the hurry to get off the bus. That small action had made all the difference between life and death.

Genevieve closed her eyes, wrapping her arms around her body, hugging herself tightly to quell her shaking. Anyone's life could be extinguished in a moment in this war; you didn't need to be a soldier off fighting on the front line in a foreign land to be killed. It was a sobering thought, and after what she'd just witnessed it felt like a wake-up call. *There but for the grace of God go I*, as the saying went. And but for her leaving her suitcase on the bus, Genevieve's life would probably have ended today. It was as if she'd been given another chance, another opportunity to live her life, but this time the way she wanted to. She should grab it with both hands, squeezing out every last drop of enjoyment and doing something worthwhile.

Up to now, her life had largely been one dominated by others – twenty-two years of being told what to do by other people, their choices mapping out most of how she lived. Genevieve might now have a job that she loved, but it had to be carried out in secrecy and with stealth, for fear of what might happen if the truth was discovered. She was living a half-life. Did she want that to carry on?

Her stomach tightly knotted at the thought of what her future might hold. What would her life be after the war ended? Did she want it to return to how it had been before? The answer was an emphatic, no. Life was precious and should not be wasted living in such a way – what she'd witnessed today had shown her that. So where *did* her future lie?

A woman started singing further down the platform, a sweet lilting song and others joined in too. Genevieve opened her eyes and looked along the crowded platform, tears welling up as the notes filled the air, bringing with them a sense of hopefulness and joy despite the circumstances that had driven the people to shelter below ground.

She needed more joy in her life, she realised, to embrace the whole of it with as much enthusiasm as the young woman on the bus had done. But that was impossible if Genevieve continued to live as she had been doing. She had to make a *change*, she needed to escape – but how? And did she even dare?

The answer suddenly came to her. She could pretend that she had been in that alley when the bomb had landed and had suffered the same fate as the young woman. Genevieve Hamilton-Jones could have ceased to exist, disappearing with the detonation of a high explosive bomb, leaving nothing but her handbag to show that she'd been there. There would be no body to identify her: just her handbag with its identity card in, the key to her flat and her purse. She could walk away, start again and no one would know. She could live as Evie Jones, the name she used at the hospital to protect her real identity and keep her secret safe.

The idea of escaping but with no one knowing that she had was exhilarating. The possibility of tasting complete freedom filled her with joy, gave her a sense of lightness. For the first time in her life, she could be in charge of her destiny – she could pursue her dreams without fear of reprisal or punishment.

It would be a lie, though, breaking the law even, a voice in her head reminded her. But the alternative of more years of the same filled her with dread. She couldn't, she wouldn't, go on living like this any more – today had shown her that life was simply far too precious to waste. But did she have the courage to break away?

CHAPTER 2

Norfolk – one week later

Thea Thornton turned the van off the road, passing between the two gate houses and onto the long drive leading down to Great Plumstead Hall. She was on Women's Voluntary Service duty, transporting equipment needed for establishing the Hall in its new role as a Red Cross Military Hospital for convalescent servicemen.

She had swapped her usual WVS uniform dress for a more practical pair of the service's green overalls, replacing the service's felt hat with a red and white polka dot scarf tied around her dark brown bobbed, curly hair, with the bow on top. She might not look so smart, but this outfit was far more suitable for hauling boxes around like a removal man. Today's work made a change from driving the WVS canteen which was a regular job that Thea did each week, and with the hospital due to open in a few days' time, they needed all the help they could get.

A brisk, cold wind sent golden leaves spiralling down to the ground as she drove through the avenue of mature beech trees lining the drive, and the lowering grey clouds were threatening rain. Thea hoped it would hold off until they'd got the van emptied of its load.

Approaching the Hall, which was built of honey-coloured stone, she drove across the wide sweep of gravel that lay in front of the house and pulled up outside the porticoed front door, her delivery not having to go around the back as normal ones would. Now the Hall was being converted into a hospital, things were altering here just as they were in the village. War had brought so many changes to Great Plumstead and not all of them for the worse, Thea thought. It had shaken things up, bringing new people to the village starting with the evacuee expectant mothers' arrival last September – and that in her opinion was a good thing.

Switching off the engine, she got out and went around to the back of the van and was opening the doors ready to begin the task of unloading when the familiar figure of her older brother Reuben came out of the front door ready to help. At fifty-one-years-old, eight years older than herself, his brown hair was threaded with silver, giving him a distinguished look, which suited him, Thea thought.

'Hello.' Thea greeted him with a warm smile. 'How are things coming along?'

'The hospital beds and other furniture arrived this morning,' Reuben said, reaching into the van and taking hold of some boxes. 'It's beginning to look like a hospital, but there's still a lot of work to do before it's up and running.'

Reuben normally worked on Great Plumstead Hall's estate, usually on the farms, but for the past week he'd been brought in to help with the many preparations needed – from taking paintings off the walls, to constructing protective wooden casings around marble pillars in rooms that were to be used as wards. The wear and tear of using the building as a hospital would be much greater than that of living in it as a home. The owners, Lord and Lady Campbell-Gryce, wanted to protect their home and belongings as much as possible.

Thea picked up a couple of boxes and followed Reuben towards the Hall.

'This lot has to be piled up in the hallway until they can be unpacked. Matron's strict orders,' Reuben informed her as they went inside. He carefully put his boxes down on one side of the wide hallway on the chequered black and white tiled floor.

Thea placed her boxes beside his and hearing voices coming from one of the rooms leading off the hall, went to the door and looked inside.

'That was the dining room and is now being turned into a ward,' Reuben said, coming to stand beside her.

Inside, a portly woman in a nurse's uniform with a starched white veil on her head, and a prickly air of authority about her, was ordering several young nurses around as they made up the beds.

'That's Matron Reed,' Reuben whispered, turning his head towards Thea. 'Best keep clear of her! Come on, those boxes won't unload themselves.'

It took nearly fifteen minutes to transfer all the boxes from the van into the hall. Some were heavier than others, and from reading the label on each one to see what was inside, Thea saw that their contents ranged from medical supplies to recreation items to keep the patients occupied. All of it essential equipment for the running of the hospital and the successful convalescence of the patients, both physically and mentally.

'That lot's going to take a while to unpack and sort out,' Thea said placing her final box down and standing back to survey the large pile of boxes in the hallway. 'Setting up a hospital from scratch is no quick task.'

'You're absolutely right about that!' A plummy voice said from behind Thea.

She turned around and saw the poised figure of Lady Campbell-Gryce approaching across the hall, a notebook in her hand. As always, her Ladyship was immaculately turned out. Her short wavy brown hair carefully styled, and her silk dress, one of Marianne's designs Thea noticed, was creaseless.

'Good afternoon, Miss Thornton.' Lady Campbell-Gryce greeted her. 'Thank you so much for helping us by bringing the stores. And yes, there's certainly a lot to be done if we are to be ready for our first intake of patients next week. Reuben has been marvellous making the adaptations to the rooms for us.' She gave Reuben an appreciative smile. 'Although it seems odd to see my dining room being turned into a ward.'

Lady Campbell-Gryce glanced in the doorway of the newly created ward, where Matron Reed spotted her and nodded her head in acknowledgement. Her Ladyship returned Matron's nod, and then turned to face Thea. 'But it's all coming together and I'm sure it will be absolutely fine. There is one problem though, which I'm hoping you might be able to help me with, or perhaps know someone else who can.'

'What's that?' Thea asked.

'We've unexpectedly been allocated another VAD nurse. She's arriving next week but, unfortunately, we don't have a billet for her. Some of our nurses are billeted here, in the old servants' rooms, and others are lodging with Rosalind Platten at The Grange in the village. You've probably heard that Rosalind's taken on the voluntary role of Quartermaster of our hospital, and has provided billets for some of the nurses as well – but sadly she doesn't have room for another one. Is there any chance that you could billet the new nurse at Rookery House?'

Thea considered for a moment. There was of course the room that Anna – a German refugee – had recently vacated having gone to teach at a boarding school. Anna hoped to come back to Rookery House in the holidays, but for the rest of the time it would stand empty... with a nurse needing accommodation, it would be wrong of her not to offer it.

'Yes, I could. Which day should I expect her?'

'On Monday, ready to start work here on Tuesday.' Lady Campbell-Gryce flicked through her notebook, turning over pages until she found what she was looking for. 'Her name is Evie Jones. I can find out what time she's due to arrive and let you know.' She reached out and touched Thea's arm. 'Thank you for your help, both today and with lodgings, it's very much appreciated. Right, I need a word with Matron.' And with a nod of her head, Lady Campbell-Gryce went into the ward.

'Looks like you've got yourself another lodger then. Bet you didn't expect that when you agreed to ferry supplies to the hospital did you?' Reuben chuckled.

Thea turned to her brother, her gaze meeting his. 'No, but it's the right thing to do. Think where else she could have ended up, perhaps even lodging at Prue's and having to live with the dreadful Victor!' She knew her sister Prue would have been welcoming, but certainly not her unpleasant husband.

Reuben grimaced. 'Then you have saved this Evie Jones from a nasty experience.'

CHAPTER 3

Prue Wilson checked her list and was relieved to see that there was just one more stop to make. It had been a long, tiring and very trying afternoon and she was feeling all of her thirty-nine years. She was both frustrated and disappointed to discover the lack of empathy that some villagers still had for others, not caring for those who'd faced worse troubles than any that had fallen upon the residents of Great Plumstead so far in this war.

She'd hoped that after having the evacuee mothers arrive last September, who'd successfully settled into village life, more villagers would have softened their attitudes to helping strangers. But there were still some hard-nosed individuals who'd never have agreed to what Prue asked of them if she didn't have the weight of the law on her side as local billeting officer.

Mounting her bicycle, she headed for her sister Thea's home at Rookery House, where she wouldn't have to battle to get what she needed.

~

'You're just in time for a cuppa.' Hettie gave a welcoming smile as Prue went into the cosy kitchen of Rookery House. 'Thea's just got back and is upstairs getting changed, then we're going to have some fresh-baked scones if you'd like to join us.'

'Oh, that sounds wonderful, thank you.' Prue smiled at the older woman whom she'd known all her life. Hettie had been a good friend of Prue's mother and as good as any aunt to her. She'd worked as cook at Great Plumstead Hall until her retirement last year and anything she baked was always delicious. Tea and one of Hettie's scones would be a most welcome antidote to Prue's difficult afternoon.

'Sit yourself down, you look like you could do with it. What's happened?' Hettie asked putting another cup on the table and pouring out a cup of tea from the large brown teapot which was covered with a colourful knitted tea-cosy.

Prue pulled out a chair at the scrubbed wooden kitchen table and sat down. 'It's been one of those days.' She sighed, smoothing down her ash-blonde hair which was beginning to come loose from its roll at the nape of her neck. 'There are some people in this village who never cease to amaze me. Being billeting officer is *not* one of my favourite roles.'

'Are more evacuees expected then?' Hettie's blue eyes were concerned behind her round glasses.

'Yes, mothers and children who've been bombed out of their London homes. Can you imagine it... your home gone just like that? And with it happening to so many people now, there's a desperate shortage of alternative accommodation for anyone to move into in London.' Prue added some milk from the jug to her tea and stirred it in with a teaspoon. 'That's even if you wanted to stay there with your children with all the bombing going on. If it was me, I'd want to get my children to safety, go as far away from there as I could.'

Hettie passed Prue a plate with a freshly baked scone covered with home-made butter and jam on top. 'Have you got enough billets organised?'

'Thank you. I'm not sure, it depends how many evacuees we're sent. It's always better to have too many billets available than not enough. I'm hoping that Thea will agree to have some.' Prue took a bite of scone enjoying the delicious combination of butter, raspberry jam and Hettie's fine baking.

'Have some what?' Thea asked coming into the kitchen. 'What good works have you been up to today, Prue?' She teased, her blue eyes twinkling.

'Some evacuees,' Prue said. 'I'm here in my role as village billeting officer. I've been told to expect some mothers and children from London any day now and was hoping you'd be able to give a home to some.'

Thea sat down at the table opposite Prue and poured herself a cup of tea from the teapot, then added some milk. 'Well, I would have, but I'm afraid I don't have the room any more.'

Hettie frowned. 'What about Anna's room? She's not using it now that she's away, and when she comes back in the school holidays, we can set up a temporary bedroom for her in the dining room.'

'If you'd asked me this morning, Prue, then I'd have said yes, but I've already promised the room to somebody else,' Thea explained. 'I've been asked to billet one of the nurses from the hospital and agreed to do it. I can't go back on my word.'

'Fair enough.' Prue nodded. 'As billeting officer, I heartily applaud you doing your bit for whoever you take in.' She gave her sister an approving smile. 'A nurse for the hospital is just as important as an evacuee mother and children.'

'Who asked you?' Hettie asked.

'Lady Campbell-Gryce when I was delivering equipment to the Hall. All the other nurses are billeted either in the old servants' rooms at the Hall or at the Grange with Rosalind as she's the new Quartermaster. They're one bed short for the new nurse who's arriving on Monday – so her Ladyship asked me.' Thea took a sip of tea. 'Evie Jones is her name.'

Hettie nodded, her curly grey hair bobbing around her head. 'Well, it will be good to have her here, I miss Anna and like having a full house.'

'How's Anna getting on in her new job?' Prue asked.

'Very well,' Thea said. 'She's enjoying it and happy to be teaching again. After all she went through being imprisoned in Holloway and then on the Isle of Man, she deserves to enjoy her life and be doing something she loves.'

'I'm glad to hear she's doing well.' Prue knew what a difficult time it had been for Thea after German-born Anna had been arrested and imprisoned for being an enemy alien, despite being a Jewish refugee from Nazi oppression. Her sister had tirelessly campaigned to get Anna released and had finally succeeded but only after Anna had endured months of imprisonment.

'I wonder what this Evie will be like,' Hettie pondered. 'I hope she'll fit in nicely with us.'

'I'm sure Evie will soon settle and fit in well.' Thea smiled at Hettie reassuringly. 'So will you be having some more evacuees?' Thea directed her question at Prue.

'Of course, we've got two spare rooms with Edwin and Jack no longer at home.' A dart of anxiety for her sons jabbed Prue's heart as both of her sons were off doing their bit for the war: Jack in the Royal Engineers stationed in the North of

England, and Edwin working for the Friends Ambulance Unit in London and in the thick of the Blitz. They were officially her *step*-sons, but she loved them as much as if she'd given birth to them, thinking and worrying about them both every day.

'And what does Victor say about that?' Hettie asked, her eyebrows raised behind her glasses.

Prue tapped her fingers on the side of her teacup, her gaze meeting the older woman's. 'He doesn't know yet, and no doubt he'll complain about it, but he can't stop me having them. He'll just have to like it or lump it!'

Thea and Hettie glanced at each other and laughed.

'Good for you.' Thea reached across the table and laid her hand on Prue's arm. 'You don't want to take any nonsense from him.'

'Don't worry, I won't be.' Prue's eyes met Thea's, a silent message passing between them.

CHAPTER 4

London

Evie Jones, as she now was, stood in the middle of Tower Bridge looking down into the swirling brown water flowing underneath on its way to the sea. Behind her traffic rumbled across the bridge, but Evie was in a world of her own. Reaching into her coat pocket, she took out a plain gold ring and stared at it as it lay in her palm. To her it represented something keeping her in check, holding her in, beating her down... but no more. Those days were gone. She curled her fingers around the ring and with one smooth motion, launched it forwards, opening her fingers and sending the ring tumbling through the air to fall into the depths of the River Thames. She smiled with satisfaction as she pictured it sinking to the bottom to be forgotten and lost in layers of thick mud.

The act of disposing of the ring was like closing the door on her life here in London. It was almost two weeks since Evie had made the life-changing decision to fake her own death and leave behind a half-life that she could no longer tolerate.

After the all-clear had sounded in the early hours of the following morning, she'd left the underground and had handed her handbag in to a policeman as if she'd found it – just as she'd done with the young woman's from the bus earlier. Evie had explained that there had been two women in the alley when the bomb had hit. With so much chaos going on in the aftermath of another heavy air raid, the policeman didn't question her story, merely telling her that relatives would be informed. Genevieve Hamilton-Jones had become another victim of that night's air raid.

After that, Evie, as she could now fully be, had hurried back to her flat, making the most of the blackout before she had to disappear for good. The key that she'd hidden in case she ever lost hers had enabled her to get in and she'd quickly taken what she needed for her new life: packing some basic clothes, all her nursing uniform and certificates which she'd kept secret and hidden, along with the passbook for the savings account in which she'd secretly squirrelled money away for such an emergency. Evie had hesitated over leaving her beloved books behind; they were precious to her, often providing a temporary escape from her life within their pages. But she'd left them behind in case their absence should raise any suspicion – the flat had to look as if Genevieve had simply gone out and been unfortunate to have been caught and killed in an air raid. No one connected with her who went to the flat afterwards must suspect that she'd made a break for freedom.

Evie had registered to become a mobile VAD, staying in temporary lodgings and carrying on her work at the hospital — where she was already Evie Jones, and where nobody from her Genevieve Hamilton-Jones life even knew she worked — while she waited for a new posting.

Three days ago, her orders had come through along with a travel permit and she was finally leaving her old life behind her. Throwing the ring into the muddy River Thames was her final act. Feeling both excited and scared, Evie picked up her large, brown leather suitcase, took a deep breath of the salty, slightly tarry smelling river air, and walked off the bridge heading for Liverpool Street station. From there she would get the train to Norfolk and to her new, free life.

~

'Great Plumstead's the next stop,' the guard said, as he passed through the carriage on the way to the front of the train.

'Thank you.' Evie smiled at him, and he touched the brim of his peaked cap in response. She'd asked him to tell her when her stop would be when she got on the train at Norwich's City station. With all the station signs taken down now it would have been impossible otherwise for her to know when she'd reached her destination. Coming out to Norfolk was new territory for her, having never been to the county before.

Looking out of the window, she liked what she saw. The woods were painted in rust and gold, the colours bright under today's wide, blue autumn sky. She spotted a gang of land girls busy harvesting crops in a field, bent over in what looked like backbreaking work. Several of them straightened up and waved at the train and Evie waved back.

Knowing the next stop was hers, Evie stood up, took her suitcase down from the overhead luggage rack and made her way along the carriage towards the door so that she'd be ready when the train arrived. Keen as she was to make this new start, her stomach was twisting itself into knots at the thought of beginning somewhere new and not knowing a soul. But that was what she wanted, Evie firmly reminded herself, and the best way to move forward with her life and forget what had gone before.

The train slowed and, looking out of the window, Evie saw they were coming into a village, a tall, square-towered church rising over the rest of the buildings. She'd been informed that someone would be here to meet her and take her to her new billet, so as the train slid into the station, she wondered who it might be.

Stepping down onto the platform Evie looked about her, immediately noticing the freshness of the country air as she breathed it in – it was so much cleaner than the London air she'd been used to.

'Are you Evie Jones?' A young woman with wavy, dark brown, shoulder-length hair who was pushing a pram asked, approaching her.

Evie nodded. 'Yes, I am.'

'Welcome to Great Plumstead. I'm Marianne Fordham.' She held out her hand smiling warmly, her green eyes meeting Evie's.

Evie shook her hand.

'I live at Rookery House where you're going to be billeted,' Marianne said. 'Thea, who owns the house, wanted to be here to meet you herself, but she's been called in to drive patients to the new hospital. She sends her apologies and will meet you later.'

'And who is this?' Evie asked peering into the pram, where a beautiful little girl lay sleeping, her dark hair curling gently about her head and her cheeks rosy with sleep. A pang of sudden longing sliced through Evie and tears prickled the back of her eyes. She swallowed hard to dampen down the unwanted emotion because that was firmly in the past – she needed to focus on the present and the future now.

'My daughter, Emily.' Marianne gently adjusted the blankets around the child, tucking in one of her arms to keep it warm.

'How old is she?'

'Ten months, she's crawling around now and is a delight. Right let's get you home; you must be exhausted from the journey. Can I balance your case over the pram?'

'No, it's fine, thank you. I'm not that tired, although it was a long journey. I didn't expect to have to change stations in Norwich. I never knew there were two, but I'm pleased to be here and I'm looking forward to getting started in my new job.'

Marianne led the way out of the station and through the village, pointing out the row of shops, which Evie noticed were a good selection, including a grocer's, butcher's and a baker's.

'Rookery House isn't in the main part of the village – it's about a half a mile outside,' Marianne explained as they passed the school which was next to the village green. 'It's nice and peaceful there but not too far from the village either.'

'Where's Great Plumstead Hall Hospital?' Evie asked.

'It's a mile out of the village, but on our side so you won't have quite so far to go.'

They went up and over the road bridge which crossed over the railway line and then took a turning down a narrow lane leading out of the village.

'I came to live here last September,' Marianne added as they headed out into open countryside. 'I was evacuated here as an expectant mother and have been here ever since. My husband's away in the RAF, training to be a pilot. It's a lovely village and Rookery House is a special place – I hope you'll be happy there too.'

'Thank you, I'm sure I will be. Is it just you and Thea and Emily who live there?' Evie asked.

'No, there's Hettie, too. She's helping at The Mother's Day Club in the village hall this morning, so you'll meet her later. And Thea's brother, Reuben, lives in a converted railway carriage in the garden. You'll soon get to know us all.'

It sounded so different from her life in London, Evie thought. She liked the sound of the people who lived at Rookery House, and the converted railway carriage home was intriguing.

'That's Rookery House up ahead.' Marianne pointed to a house standing on its own as they rounded a bend in the road.

Evie liked what she saw. The house was a detached Victorian home, built of red brick with a bay window on either side of the front door and three windows on the upstairs.

Marianne steered the pram in through the gateway and Evie followed.

'We come and go via the back door,' Marianne explained as they headed around the side of the house.

Evie liked the look of the large garden where there were many plots devoted to growing vegetables, a greenhouse, and various outbuildings.

Marianne halted and pointed across to the converted railway carriage, complete with a chimney coming out of the top and a veranda built around part of it. 'That's Reuben's house over by the orchard.' Turning the other way, she pointed to a five-bar gate at a field entrance. 'The meadow over there goes with the house as well. Thea's cow, Primrose, grazes in there. Hettie makes wonderful butter and cheese from her milk. Rationing hasn't hit us so hard here as we produce most of our own food. Things aren't so bad in the countryside as in the towns. You can have a proper look around outside later – we'll get you settled in first.'

Evie followed as Marianne pushed the pram into a single-storey annexe at the back of the house.

'This is the scullery,' Marianne said, checking on Emily who was still fast asleep. 'And through there,' she pointed to a door at the far end, 'is the bathroom.'

Evie looked around her taking in the copper for heating water, the sink and a mangle.

'And this door leads into the kitchen.'

Marianne led the way into a homely kitchen where there was a black range sunk into the chimney breast at one end and a large scrubbed wooden table in the middle of the room standing on a floor which was paved with red quarry tiles. A deep stone sink with a hand pump was by the window that looked out into the back garden, and the window was framed by yellow curtains with blue flowers on. There were two dressers lining the walls, holding blue and white patterned cups and plates which looked fresh and cheerful.

'The pantry is through that door,' Marianne indicated a door at the far end of the kitchen. 'And this way leads to the hall and other rooms. And before I forget, I must warn you there's no gas or electricity here, you'll have been used to both in London. Don't worry, you'll soon get used to using a lamp or candle.'

Evie nodded, she liked what she saw – it was completely different to what she was used to, but far cosier and more welcoming. It felt a world away from her London flat and the life she'd escaped.

The hallway led to the front door at its far end, which had colourful stained-glass panelling in it.

'This is the sitting room.' Marianne opened the nearest door and stepped aside.

Evie peered inside to see a long room that ran the length of the house with a bay window at the far end.

'That's the dining room.' Marianne indicated a door on the opposite side of the hall near the front door. 'Though we always eat in the kitchen. I mainly use it for my dressmaking. Right, I'll show you where your room is and then you can settle in.'

Evie followed Marianne up the white painted stairs which had a dark-red carpet runner, secured with brass stair rods, running down the centre.

'That's Thea's room, and Hettie's at the front of the house.' Marianne pointed them out before leading the way along the landing towards the back of the house. 'I'm in here with Emily.' She touched a door on the right, then pointed to another door to the left of her room. 'And this is yours. It was Anna's, but she's gone to teach at a boarding school now.' She opened the door and stepped aside for Evie to go in. 'I'll leave you to unpack and go and put the kettle on, then we can have some tea. Come down when you're ready.'

'Thank you. I appreciate you coming to meet me.' Evie smiled at Marianne. 'It was kind of you.'

Marianne returned her smile, her eyes meeting Evie's. 'I was pleased to. I know what it's like to come and live somewhere new, so if there's anything I can help you with or you need, please don't hesitate to ask.'

Evie nodded. 'I will, thank you.'

Stepping into her room Evie was delighted with what she saw. It was simply furnished and cheerful, smelling of lavender and beeswax polish, but most importantly it was *hers*. She put her case down and looked around – the bed had a black iron bedstead and was covered with a colourful patchwork quilt, there was chest of drawers and a small bedside table. Going over to look out of the window, Evie saw that she had a fine view over the back garden to the meadow beyond where she could see a toffee-coloured cow grazing.

Evie sighed with relief – she'd been lucky to be billeted here. Rookery House felt homely and welcoming, a place where she could finally relax and start her new life of freedom doing what she wanted. She'd be safe here, wouldn't she?

CHAPTER 5

Thea carried an empty stretcher out of Great Plumstead Hall Hospital having just made another delivery there, only this time it was patients rather than supplies.

'I wouldn't want to be working under the rule of that matron,' Thea said to her WVS colleague, Pat, whom she was working with today, as she slid the stretcher into the runners in the back of the ambulance.

'Me neither,' Pat agreed as she returned her stretcher back in to its place in the ambulance.

They'd both just witnessed Matron Reed giving one of the young VAD nurses a withering ticking off over what seemed to be some minor issue. With the hospital's first intake of patients arriving, and with them a huge amount of work to get everyone settled and comfortable, Thea would have thought it more important to get that done, but clearly this matron was a stickler for her rules and regulations whatever the case.

'I think I'll stick to working for the WVS.' Thea closed the back doors of the ambulance and made her way around to the driver's door. She enjoyed this job having been asked to do it because of her experience driving ambulances during the Great War.

With Pat settled in the cab beside her, Thea started the engine and pulled away from the entrance of the impressive Great Plumstead Hall and headed down the tree-lined drive. They'd almost reached the two gate houses where the drive joined the public road, when she spotted two figures walking towards them, one of them pushing a pram. She recognised Marianne, but not the other young woman, who had beautiful long auburn hair – she must be her new lodger.

'There's Marianne.' Thea slowed the ambulance, bringing it to a halt by the young women. She opened the window in the driver's door and called out to them. 'Hello, where are you off to?'

'Hello, Thea,' Marianne said. 'This is Evie. We're on our way to the Hall so Evie knows where to go to when she starts work there in the morning.'

Thea held out her hand through the open window. 'Welcome to Great Plumstead, Evie. I'm sorry I wasn't there to meet you at the station as I'd planned, only I got called in to help deliver the patients you'll be caring for.'

Evie shook Thea's hand. 'Hello, it's fine, Marianne's been very kind. Thank you, for giving me a home at Rookery House – it's a lovely place.' Evie smiled shyly, her blue eyes briefly meeting Thea's.

'You're welcome. I hope you'll be happy living with us all. Were you hoping to go inside the hospital and introduce yourself?' Thea asked.

Evie nodded. 'I'd like to if I can.'

'I wouldn't if I were you,' Thea advised. 'Things were rather fraught when we left. Matron was on the war path giving some poor nurse a thorough telling off. And with new patients just arrived everyone's very busy. If you go in now, you might not get a warm reception.'

Evie's face fell. 'Thank you for the warning. Perhaps it's best just to have a look at the Hall from a distance and arrive tomorrow when I'm due to start work and not before.'

'That matron sounds awful,' Marianne said.

'Some matrons can be tricky,' Evie said. 'I've worked for several in London, and they all have their own particular ways. I'm sure it will be fine.'

Evie's words sounded positive, Thea thought, but the young woman's face now wore a wary look, her blue eyes worried. Thea's experience of Matron Reed so far had shown her to be a difficult woman to work for, but she didn't say anything more; she didn't want to put Evie off her new job. Hopefully everything would be fine for her when she started tomorrow.

'Right, we've got to get this ambulance back, so I'll see you both at Rookery House later.' Thea put the ambulance into gear and with a wave at her lodgers pulled away and headed for the road into the village.

'Your new lodger seems nice,' Pat said.

Thea nodded. 'I'm sure she'll fit in with the rest of us just fine, although it's always a bit daunting when somebody new comes to live in your house. I just hope she gets on all right at the hospital. I don't think anybody working under Matron Reed is going to have an easy time of it.'

'Then you'll need to keep an eye on that young woman, make sure she's happy,' Pat advised.

Thea glanced at Pat. 'I will. I always look out for whoever's living in my house. They become part of my family as much as any blood relative.'

'You're like a mother hen,' Pat said, with a chuckle. 'Taking them under your wing.'

Bringing the ambulance to a halt at the junction with the road, Thea considered what Pat had just said as she checked each way to make sure it was clear of traffic, before pulling out. Perhaps she did look out for her lodgers in the way she would have done for her children – if she'd had any. Only she'd never had the chance.

'Maybe, but I'm not sure if it's mothering them. I don't know what that is exactly, never having been a mother myself.'

Pat reached across and put her hand on Thea's arm. 'You would make a lovely mother – it's not too late you know.'

Thea laughed, glancing at her friend. 'I think that ship has well and truly sailed for me, Pat. I would need a husband to make that happen, and that's something that looks very unlikely.' She sighed. 'Most of the decent men in my generation didn't come back from France.' Including her own fiancé, she thought, a dart of pain reminding her of his loss, which even all these years later still had the power to hurt her.

'There are other ways to become a mother to children; they don't have to necessarily be your own flesh and blood, you know,' Pat said.

'True, but I don't think it's ever likely to happen. I'll just keep an eye on my lodgers, and look out for my niece Alice and my nephews, too.' She glanced at Pat again. 'I've got plenty of people to care for and things to do. Anyway, where would I find the time to be a mother with this war on?'

CHAPTER 6

Prue was in the kitchen of her home in the centre of Great Plumstead village, her hands plunged in hot, soapy water as she washed up after their evening meal while her seventeen-year-old daughter, Alice, dried the dishes.

'Thea's new lodger seems nice, I met her when Marianne brought her back to Rookery House this afternoon,' Alice said picking up another plate to dry. 'She's got rather a plummy voice; she sounds like Rosalind, from the Grange.'

'Where does she come from?' Prue asked.

'London.'

'She's been lucky to be billeted with Thea. I expect we'll get to know her over time, although she'll be busy working long hours at the new hospital.'

Alice worked at Rookery House helping her aunt Thea. She'd left school in the summer and had started helping there while Anna – whose job had been working in the gardens – was imprisoned. Alice had stayed on after Anna had left for her teaching job. It was just a temporary job, but Prue was glad her daughter was working for Thea as it meant Alice still lived at home for the time being. Although Prue knew that sooner or later, Alice would want to spread her wings and leave, go off to do something like her brothers had. Prue was dreading that day coming, and not just because her daughter would be flying the nest, but because it would leave her living here with just Victor. And that wasn't a pleasant prospect.

'I...' Prue began but halted at the sound of the telephone ringing out in the hall. 'Can you get that Alice, please?'

Alice headed for the hall but before she'd reached the kitchen door, the ringing stopped – the phone had been answered by Victor who must have come out of his study, where he always retreated after their evening meal to go through his business accounts.

Prue strained to hear, wondering who it was. Perhaps something to do with Victor's Home Guard duties, council business or one of his many committees. She heard the clunk of the receiver being put down on the table in the hall, and moments later the kitchen door burst open, and Victor appeared.

'It's for *you*, Prudence!' he said glowering at her as if it was her fault that his work had been disturbed and he'd had to answer the telephone.

'Who is it?' she asked drying her hands on a towel as she headed for the door, where Victor stood.

'Something to do with evacuees.' His pale ice-blue eyes narrowed, his mouth pinched into a line underneath his thin moustache. 'What's going on?'

'I don't know yet until I speak to whoever's calling, do I?' Prue met his glare with one of her own as she passed him. 'I am billeting officer for this village, don't forget.'

'Humph!' Victor snorted, leaning against the kitchen door frame, with his arms crossed as he watched her go and pick up the receiver.

'Hello, Prue Wilson here.'

'Good evening, Mrs Wilson. I'm calling to inform you that a group of evacuees from the London bombing will be arriving in Great Plumstead tomorrow, mothers and children – they'll be on the...' Prue could hear the rustling of papers being shuffled. 'They are due on the three o'clock train from Norwich. I hope that billets are organised for them, and that necessary welcoming reception arrangements will be in place.'

'Of course, everything's ready,' Prue said in a cheerful tone, ignoring the way her chest tightened at this news – she'd hoped that the evacuees wouldn't be arriving *quite* so soon. She had what she hoped were enough billets promised, but as for a reception for them... When the expectant mothers had arrived last September, she'd had more notice and the members of the village Women's Institute had rallied round and provided refreshments at the village hall. But with less than twenty-four hours' notice and with rationing now in place, it was going to be impossible to do the same this time.

'Jolly good, good luck!'

'Thank you. I...' Prue began, but the call had been disconnected.

As she replaced the receiver, the weight of responsibility for these new evacuees felt heavy on her shoulders. Could she do what was necessary in such a short time frame – give them the welcome that they deserved and needed?

'Well, what was that about?' Victor's impatient voice interrupted Prue's thoughts.

She closed her eyes and took a steadying breath before she turned to face her husband, pinning a look of confidence on her face and raising her chin. 'The evacuees are arriving tomorrow afternoon, mothers and children who've been bombed out in London and have lost their homes.'

'Have you got enough places to put them?' Victor asked.

'Yes, that's all in order, and of course we have two rooms for them here,' Prue stated matter of factly and then waited for the explosion knowing it would come.

Her husband's eyes glinted with fury. 'I'm *not* having any more evacuees in my house!' Victor's voice went up like a rocket, bringing Alice out into the hallway, her eyes wide as she took in the situation. 'Have you taken leave of your senses, Prudence, volunteering rooms in *my* house without consulting *me* first? You know I don't want any more after that other one we had.'

'You mean Sally?' Prue kept her voice calm. She still missed the lovely young woman who'd been evacuated here last autumn as an expectant mother, but whose baby had sadly been stillborn, after which she'd returned to London. Sally kept in touch and wrote regularly to Prue and to Marianne, whom she'd become firm friends with.

'What's wrong with having evacuees, Father?' asked Alice, her arms folded across her chest. 'If you have any spare rooms in your house, then by law you must provide a billet, that's right, isn't it, Ma?'

Prue nodded, biting the inside of her cheek to stop herself from smiling. She loved the way her daughter had learned to stand up to Victor. 'Yes, householders can be fined if they refuse to take in evacuees when they have the room. And as billeting officer and with you a councillor and local businessman, Victor, then it would look *extremely unpatriotic* if we shirked our responsibilities at this time of need.'

Victor scowled. 'That Sally was bad enough.'

'I don't know why you found her such a problem – you hardly saw her,' Prue said.

'Exactly, and if we have a mother and children, it will be far worse, think of the noise and disruption.' Victor slammed his hand with a bang on the table where the telephone stood making it shudder. 'I won't have it!'

Prue studied him dispassionately for a few moments, taking in his dark brown, shiny brilliantined-down hair, his face blotchy with temper and his cold blue eyes. She felt nothing but dislike for this man, for his selfishness, his need to rule over his empire like some little king, be it at work or at home. Once, she'd been cowed by his attitude, but the years had left her less in awe of him and now she was just biding her time, knowing that as well as being a domineering husband he was also an unfaithful one.

Earlier this year, her younger sister, Lizzie, who lived in Norwich, had seen Victor with his fancy woman. His so-called important meetings each Sunday in Norwich were a lie to cover up meeting his mistress. Prue hadn't yet told him that she knew, holding that information to herself till it proved useful.

'I don't think you have any choice in the matter, Victor.' Prue met his furious glare. 'We *will* be giving a home to some evacuees, and if you don't like it then you can just spend more time at work or perhaps even in Norwich, extend your *Sunday meetings...*'

'I don't know what you mean,' Victor blustered, his neck turning red, betraying his inner discomfort.

Prue narrowed her eyes, meeting his and holding them, until Victor looked away.

Victor glanced at Alice, and Prue knew her words had had an effect, and perhaps even made him feel guilty. Her husband would not want his dalliance with another woman to come out in front of their daughter. He dropped his gaze to the floor for a moment and then looked at her. 'All right, it seems I have no choice in the matter, but I don't want them going in my study, understand?'

'Then lock the door so no one can go in there,' Prue said simply, before heading back into the kitchen, Alice following. Closing the door behind them, Prue leaned against it, her legs shaking. She had just hinted to Victor that she knew something about his other woman, and it had stopped him – she couldn't help breaking into a smile.

'What was that about Father's Sunday meetings in Norwich?' Alice asked.

'Oh, you know him and his many committees and meetings; he spends more time out of the house than he does here, so making a fuss about having evacuees here is ridiculous.'

Prue put her arm around her daughter's shoulders, thinking it wouldn't be right to let Alice find out that Victor was committing adultery. He was still her father, and he did have a soft spot for Alice. And much to Prue's delight, her daughter had worked out over the years the best way to handle him. There was no need to taint that relationship. The adultery concerned only Prue and Victor, it was their business, and theirs alone.

'Right, let's get the washing up finished and then I must think about what needs to be done tomorrow,' Prue said, heading back to the sink. 'It's going to be a busy day.'

CHAPTER 7

When Evie tiptoed downstairs at half past six the following morning – using a candle to light her way – she didn't expect to find anyone up before her. Stepping into the warm kitchen, which was lit by a cosy glow from the lamp on the table, she saw that Hettie was up and setting the table for breakfast.

A damp nudge at her hand made her look down to see that her arrival had been anticipated. Bess, Reuben's border collie, stood looking up at Evie, wagging her tail happily. No doubt Bess had heard her coming down the stairs and come to greet her. Evie reached down and stroked the dog's silky soft ears.

'Good morning!' Hettie greeted her with a welcoming smile, her blue eyes warm behind her round glasses, her curly grey hair neatly brushed. 'I hope you slept well.'

Evie had instantly liked Hettie when she'd met her yesterday, after the older woman had returned to Rookery House after helping at The Mother's Day Club in the village. Hettie was shorter than Evie, barely reaching five feet tall, but had a warmth and inner strength about her and, if last night's meal was anything to go by, she was an excellent cook.

'Not really,' Evie said. 'I'm nervous about today so didn't sleep as well as usual, and with being in a new place, too.'

Hettie nodded. 'Well hopefully you'll sleep like a log tonight. You get yourself sorted and I'll have breakfast ready for you. Is porridge all right?'

'Yes, thank you. I wasn't expecting anybody else to be up yet.'

Hettie chuckled. 'Oh, I'm always up early – after years of having to do it working in the kitchens up at the Hall, it's become a habit. I couldn't sleep in longer now if I tried. The others will be up soon too, and Reuben's coming in for his breakfast. He's been out on duty overnight with the Home Guard, so he'll come in here when he gets back to have something to eat and to collect Bess – she always stays the night in the house with us when he's on duty.'

When Evie returned to the kitchen after using the bathroom, Thea, Marianne and baby Emily were there, sitting at the table, and Hettie was ladling out bowls of steaming porridge.

'Good morning, Evie.' Thea gave her a welcoming smile as she poured out cups of tea from the big, tea-cosy-covered teapot.

'Good morning.' Evie returned Thea's smile.

'Sit yourself down and tuck in. There's some stewed apple to go in your porridge if you'd like some.' Hettie placed a bowl of steaming porridge in front of Evie as she sat down. 'And some honey from Thea's bees to sweeten it.'

'Thank you,' Evie said, gratefully.

'Are you excited about starting your new job today?' Marianne asked, as she mixed some porridge and soft stewed apple together for Emily who sat on her lap, eagerly watching what her mother was doing and clearly ready for her breakfast.

'Yes. Although I'm a bit nervous too,' Evie admitted.

'I'm sure you'll be fine,' Thea reassured her. 'You've already got nursing experience so you're not starting from scratch.'

Last night, Thea had asked Evie about what she'd been doing in London while they ate their evening meal. Evie had told her about her work at the Millbank Hospital but had been careful not to talk about anything more personal, glossing over her home life with vague replies. As far as Evie was concerned, that life was behind her. It was the present and future that concerned her now.

'That's true.' Evie helped herself to some stewed apple. 'I'm sure I'll be fine once I get to know the routines.'

The outside door opened, and Reuben came in and was warmly greeted by Bess who was delighted to see him return.

'Morning all!' Reuben said cheerfully, stroking Bess's head.

'Anything happen overnight, Reuben?' Hettie asked as she spooned a bowlful of porridge out of the saucepan for him.

'No, a quiet night thankfully. Even managed a bit of kip in our HQ.' Reuben sat down at the table and added some stewed apple and honey into his porridge and mixed it all together. 'No enemy paratroopers landing or an air raid – thankfully.'

Evie had met Reuben last night before he'd gone on duty. He, like his sister Thea, had blue eyes – the same colour as bluebells – and had a quiet, steady calmness about him which she was glad of as they were living close by.

Keeping an eye on the clock standing on a kitchen dresser, Evie tucked into her breakfast. The porridge was delicious – the cinnamon-spiced stewed apple and sweet honey combined with the milky oats was tasty, warm and filling and would keep her going all morning.

'Thank you, Hettie, that was lovely.' Evie said scooping up the last spoonful. She got up from the table and took her bowl to the sink.

'You're welcome,' Hettie said. 'Just leave the bowl and I'll sort it out; you go and get yourself ready.'

Evie needed to finish getting ready before she left to cycle to the Hall, Hettie having kindly offered to loan Evie her bicycle as it would be quicker than walking.

'I nearly forgot,' Reuben said, looking at Evie. 'I was asking about a bicycle for you at the Home Guard last night, and one of the men has got a spare one that he's willing to sell; used to belong to one of his daughters who's now married and moved away. I can have a look at it for you, make sure it's in good working order if you're interested in buying it.'

Evie smiled at him. 'Thank you, I'd appreciate that. A bicycle of my own will make getting to and from the hospital so much easier.'

Reuben nodded. 'I'll get it sorted for you then.'

Upstairs in her room, after Evie had finished pinning her long auburn hair into a bun, she checked her appearance in the mirror above her chest of drawers. Wearing her uniform again felt reassuring in this new place. She smoothed down the blue linen dress and checked that her black stockings were straight, and her black shoes polished. Her white apron, with its red cross on the front, white arm cuffs and veil head covering were packed ready in her bag to take with her – she would put them on when she reached the Hall, not wanting to risk getting any dirt on them on the way.

Travelling to and from the hospital wearing her uniform was a massive change for Evie. The thought that she had no need to hide being a nurse here was liberating and filled her with joy.

She took one last look at herself, checking the hairpins that secured her bun at the nape of her neck were firmly in place. Taking a steadying breath to quell her nerves, she reassured herself that feeling anxious was natural when starting at a new hospital. She would still be nursing patients just as she had before, she told herself, but just in a different place. She would be fine.

The sun was rising as Evie peddled towards Great Plumstead Hall Hospital on Hettie's bicycle, the early morning air cool on her cheeks. As the sky in the east lightened it promised to be a beautiful autumn day, with no clouds so far to mar the blue arching overhead.

Turning off the road and onto the long drive leading to the Hall, she passed between the two gate houses and headed down the avenue of tall beech trees. Evie was glad that she'd come this way yesterday so she knew exactly where to go and what to expect when she saw the Hall. She'd been impressed when she'd seen the outside, admiring the large building which was built of honey-coloured stone. It was a beautiful place and she hoped that she would enjoy working there.

Approaching the Hall she steered her bicycle around the back, as Reuben had advised her to, telling her that the other staff parked their bicycles in one of the old stables in the yard behind the Hall.

Bumping her way into an enclosed cobbled yard, she saw a brown-haired nurse who'd just arrived and was making her way towards the back door.

'Hello, you must be the new VAD,' she called spotting Evie, a friendly smile lighting up her face.

'Yes, hello.' Evie dismounted her bicycle, returning the nurse's smile. 'I've been told I should leave my bicycle in an old stable, which one is that?'

'I'll show you. I'm Hazel Robertson.' Her warm, brown eyes met Evie's.

'Thank you, pleased to meet you, Hazel. I'm Evie Jones.'

Hazel led the way across the yard and opened the door of the stable block. 'This is where we leave our bikes, those of us that live out that is. I'm billeted at the Grange with Mr and Mrs Platten — she's the Quartermaster here. There are three of us there altogether, but the other two VADs are on night shift at the minute,' she chatted as Evie followed and parked Hettie's bicycle inside the stable alongside some others.

'Where are you billeted?' Hazel asked as they headed back across the yard.

'At Rookery House.'

'Oh, I know that. I bicycle past it to get here. It looks nice.'

'Yes, it is. I was told to report to the secretary when I got here.'

'That's Miss Howlett, come on I'll take you to her before I go on to the morning briefing.' Hazel glanced at her watch. 'We'd better get a move on, Matron's a stickler for punctuality.'

Evie followed Hazel in through the back door leading to the servants' area of the Hall. Hurrying along a corridor behind her new colleague, she glanced into the kitchen where general service members of the hospital were busy preparing the breakfast.

'That's the old servants' hall which is now the men's dining room.' Hazel pointed to another room as they passed it, where the table was being laid for breakfast. 'You'll soon get used to where everything is.'

After Hazel had shown Evie where to hang her coat in the cloakroom, they both put on the rest of their uniforms. Finally dressed in their aprons, white cuffs and with their veils carefully pinned on their heads, they checked their reflections in the mirror before heading up the back stairs to a ground floor room with a sign on the door announcing, *Administration Office*.

'This is where you'll find Miss Howlett, Mrs Platten and Lady Campbell-Gryce, although not necessarily all at the same time,' Hazel explained, knocking on the door.

'Come in,' a voice called from inside.

Hazel opened the door and went in, and Evie followed her.

'The new VAD has arrived, Miss Howlett,' Hazel announced to an older woman, dressed in a tweedy suit, who sat behind one of the three desks.

'Excellent, thank you Nurse Robertson.' Miss Howlett stood up and held out her hand to Evie, who shook it. 'Welcome to Great Plumstead Hall Hospital.'

Hazel touched Evie's arm. 'I'll see you later.'

Evie turned to her. 'Thanks for your help.'

'You're welcome.' Hazel smiled warmly at her then went out, closing the door quietly behind her.

'Pull up a chair.' Miss Howlett indicated a chair standing at the side of the room as she sat down behind her desk again.

Evie did as she was asked and sat facing the secretary.

'I'll show you around first, so that you get to know the general layout of the hospital and then pass you over to Matron Reed who oversees its day-to-day running. It is to her that you will report at the beginning and end of each shift. Lady Campbell-Gryce is our Commandant, and you will meet her at some point today. Mrs Platten is our Quartermaster. I expect it will feel different to your previous hospital ...' She paused while she checked the file on her desk. 'Ah, yes, The Millbank in London. This hospital takes convalescing patients, its job is to relieve pressure on general hospitals. We take those who are fit enough to travel here by ambulance and, to date, we have ten patients, but with more expected within the week. Our capacity would be fifty. Any questions before I show you around?'

'Not at the moment.'

Miss Howlett nodded. 'Jolly good.' She stood up and made for the door. 'If you'd like to follow me.'

The inside of Great Plumstead Hall was as grand as the outside, Evie thought as Miss Howlett showed her around. She could see its conversion into a hospital had led to necessary changes to protect it from its new role and occupants, plus there was now a pervading smell of carbolic disinfectant typical of all hospitals — which was both familiar and comforting to Evie in this new place.

'This is the Library Ward,' Miss Howlett said as they stepped into a large room overlooking the terrace at the back of the house. It had fourteen hospital beds, seven on each side, but none of which were yet occupied. 'Although sadly you won't see any books. They've been covered over by boarding to protect them, which is a shame, but deemed necessary I suppose.' She stepped to one side of the ward and knocked on one of the wooden boards lining the wall, making a hollow sound. 'The other main ward is in the dining room, where we've settled our first patients. There's also some additional smaller rooms up on the top floor, including the pre-war day and night nursery should we need the space.'

Next they headed for the drawing room which had become the patients' recreation room, with a grand piano, table-tennis table and glass doors opening onto the terrace.

As the tour continued, Evie was shown the Butler's pantry which was now assigned as the surgery, the Butler's bedroom which had become a massage room, as well as the essential sluice, storeroom and bathrooms. She was aware of the comings and goings of other VADs and mobile patients who were heading down to the men's dining room in the old servants' hall for their breakfast. She received smiles and nods of hello from them, as they hurried about their business, and it reassured her that this was a friendly place.

'I'll just show you this last room and then take you to Matron Reed to report for duty.' Miss Howlett opened the door of a cosy room and stepped inside. 'This was Lord Campbell-Gryce's study but is now the nurses' sitting room. It's where you can have a sit-down during breaks and where nursing and administrative staff have their meals.' She indicated the table to one end of the room.

Entering the Dining Room Ward a few minutes later, Evie caught her first sight of Matron Reed, whom she'd already heard about. The woman stood in the middle of the ward with her back to the doorway, her feet planted apart, her back ramrod straight and her uniform dress straining over her portly frame.

'Matron Reed,' Miss Howlett called. 'I have your new VAD for you.'

Matron swivelled around surprisingly lightly on her feet and looked Evie up and down with her beady brown eyes. The welcoming nods and smiles Evie had so far received from other members of staff clearly didn't extend to Matron – the older woman's unfriendly gaze made Evie's stomach knot in instinctive panic.

'I've given Nurse Jones a tour around, so I'll leave her in your capable hands.' Miss Howlett gave Evie an encouraging smile and then left.

Matron didn't say anything for a few moments and those seconds felt like an eternity as Evie was aware she was being scrutinised. Even though she'd checked earlier, she had to fight the urge to look down and make sure that her uniform was as it should be, her shoes polished, her veil straight. This woman clearly had the ability to make those beneath her quake without even saying a single word, something Evie remembered the headmistress from her boarding school being able to do. And later on, so had... She gave herself a mental shake. That was in the past, she firmly reminded herself – it was done, over, gone. She must concentrate on the present.

'Good morning, Matron,' Evie forced her voice to sound calm.

'Welcome to the Dining Room Ward,' one of the bed-bound patients on the ward called. 'Another nurse is always welcome, isn't that right Matron?'

'Best to eat your breakfast while it's hot, Corporal Barkham,' Matron said in a no-nonsense Scottish accent, throwing a quick glance at the man. 'Don't want your scrambled eggs to go cold and rubbery, do you?' Her voice was silky smooth but had a hint of steel underneath it and Corporal Barkham nodded meekly and carried on tucking into his breakfast.

Matron took two steps towards Evie and cocked her head to one side. 'I believe the bed pans need scouring and sterilising Nurse Jones, so to the sluice with you. Double quick, don't dally.'

Evie wanted to protest that cleaning out bed pans was basic work for beginner VADs, not ones like her with months of experience, but the challenging look in Matron's brown eyes told her that questioning orders was not advised if Evie knew what was good for her.

'Yes, Matron.' Evie turned on her heels and left the ward, her heart sinking but doing her best to be stoical because, although cleaning out bed pans was an unpleasant job, it was an essential one for the running of a hospital. And her instinct, which had been honed by her past experiences, told her that on *no account* should she argue with Matron Reed if she wanted to stay longer than a few hours at this hospital. And she did, Evie thought. She hadn't taken such drastic measures to change her life only to stall at the first hiccup. Straightening her shoulders, she headed to the sluice.

By the time Hazel came to find Evie in the surgery, where she was now cleaning out the cupboards, Evie's hands were red and sore. The rough monkey soap, with its tiny pieces of pumice, that she was using to scrub the wooden shelves was hurting her hands. Evie was finding it hard to keep up a positive frame of mind. So far this morning, Matron had given her all the worst jobs, the bed pans had just been the beginning of a long list – it wasn't the new start that she'd hoped for.

'It's time for our meal in the nurses' sitting room,' Hazel informed her. 'All the men have had theirs and are settled again. You'll be glad to know you can stop that for now. It's a horrible job.' Her voice was sympathetic. 'Matron had me doing that last week. I can't see how it would have got dirty again in just a few days, but who are we to question what she tells us.' She rolled her eyes. 'It won't always be like this, Matron will let you do some other nursing work with real patients once you've proven yourself. It's her way of seeing what us nurses are made of – proving we're up to the job. She's done it with all of us, making us do the horrible jobs first.'

'I hope so.' Evie dried her hands. 'I've got plenty of nursing experience and want to be able to use it here.'

Hazel linked her arm through Evie's. 'The important thing is not to question her, and definitely do not argue back if you know what's good for you.'

'I wouldn't dare! I'll do as I'm told,' Evie said trying to sound positive.

CHAPTER 8

Prue was awake long before her alarm clock went off, the loud dinging of the bells on top as the little hammer repeatedly bashed them in turn disturbing the silence of her room. She reached over and turned it off with a heavy sigh, then slumped back into her soft feather pillow – she was tired. Prue seemed to have spent most of the night going over and over the plans for the arrival of the new evacuees due this afternoon, rather than getting much-needed sleep.

Last night she'd made a list of what could be done in the short time they had to prepare. There was no possibility of putting on as good a spread as they'd done when the evacuee expectant mothers had arrived last September. There'd be no sausage rolls and huge slabs of cake this time, or even a *Welcome* banner strung up.

She'd rung around the few members of the Women's Institute who had telephones last night and had been promised some plates of sandwiches. Hettie had also offered to make some of her delicious currant buns for the evacuees. It was the best they could manage today, and hopefully along with cups of tea, it would be something for the evacuees to enjoy after their long journey and before they went to their new billets.

But before then Prue had The Mother's Day Club to attend this morning – it was her turn on the rota to work with the mothers and she didn't want to let them down. It would also be a good distraction from her worries about this afternoon. Throwing back the covers, Prue got up and started her day.

'What? Today?' Gloria, one of the mothers, asked settling her little girl down to play on a rug spread out on the village hall floor.

Prue had just explained to the group of evacuee mothers gathered in the village hall about the new arrivals who were due later that day.

'Yes, and they're due on the three o'clock train. I'll be bringing them here first for some refreshments, before they head out to their billets.'

'How many are coming?' Marianne asked, rocking her daughter Emily in her arms to soothe her – the little girl had a tooth coming through, making one of her cheeks red and turning her usually sunny manner grizzly.

'I'm not sure. I've informed the relevant authorities how many billets we have available.' Prue added another wooden brick to a tower that she was building for a toddler who was sat on the floor. 'I hope we don't get sent too many.'

'Well, I wouldn't rely too much on that,' Gloria said with a chuckle, her bottle-blonde pompadour hairstyle bobbing as she laughed. 'Remember you were meant to get evacuee children and you got us lot!'

The other mothers joined in laughing, filling the hall with a cheerful sound.

Throwing up her hands in mock despair, Prue smiled at the women. 'And all my careful plans went awry that afternoon!' She thought back to the moment at the station when she'd realised that they'd been sent the wrong evacuees – expectant mothers rather than the children. And then being told that the mothers would be staying, and she'd just have to cope with the mistake, which was easier said than done. Prue had had to battle with some of the evacuee hosts who'd only agreed to have *children*, not women in their homes, forcing them to accept the change with the law behind her. But it had turned out fine in the end. Despite their shaky start, the expectant mothers had settled well in the village and become an important part of the community.

'I'm glad it happened, though,' Prue said, sincerely. 'You've all become dear friends and I wouldn't have wanted it any other way.'

'Hear, hear!' one of the mothers chorused.

'What 'ave you got planned for them when they arrive?' Gloria asked. 'We 'ad a lovely spread waiting for us here – very tasty it was too. And much appreciated after the long journey, I can tell you.'

'And that welcome banner was a lovely touch,' another mother added.

Prue nodded, recalling how her daughter Alice had made the banner for them to pin up on the wall facing the door inside the village hall, the word *Welcome* spelt out in bold blue letters. Everything that had been prepared that day had taken time to plan, and those were also the days before rationing had arrived. Sadly, today's evacuees weren't going to be so lucky.

'There'll be some sandwiches, buns and tea, but nothing as

fine as the spread you arrived to, I'm afraid. People are doing what they can but with such short notice and rationing it's impossible,' Prue explained, trying to sound positive.

'What about a banner?' one of the mothers asked. 'Have you still got it?'

Prue shook her head. 'I'm afraid it went for paper salvage and there isn't the paper to spare to make another one like that.'

'We could use newspaper instead, cut letters out of it and pin it up,' Marianne suggested. 'That would be something and I'm sure would be appreciated.'

'Good idea.' Gloria beamed, her lips bright with scarlet lipstick. 'We can get that ready this morning. Would it 'elp if we're all here this afternoon when the new evacuees arrive? We could tell them about the village and how we've got on living 'ere. After all, we know what it's like to arrive here from London – what a shock it is!' She gave a throaty laugh. 'It ain't nothing like the East End that's for sure, but we've grown to love it, ain't we ladies?'

The other evacuee mothers nodded in agreement.

'It took some getting used to, though,' one mother said. 'If it hadn't been for you setting up this Mother's Day Club, Prue, I don't think I'd 'ave stayed. It's given us a place to come to and something to do.'

Prue's eyes suddenly pricked with tears. 'I'm glad you stayed; imagine if you'd gone home and were there now, being bombed every night...'

Gloria shivered, making her ample bosom shake. 'So that's why we've got to give the new mothers and children coming 'ere a warm welcome – a proper Mother's Day Club welcome. Make them feel wanted and 'elp them settle and feel at 'ome.' She reached out and grabbed hold of Prue's hand. 'You can rely on us to help.'

CHAPTER 9

Prue was waiting on the platform of Great Plumstead station for the three o'clock train from Norwich, which was now five minutes late. Beside her stood Gloria who'd come along with her to welcome the new evacuees, leaving her daughter in Marianne's care back at the village hall, where other members of The Mother's Day Club were setting out the refreshments.

'All set then, Prue?' Gloria asked, her voice bubbling with excitement.

Prue met Gloria's gaze. 'As well as I'll ever be without much preparation and planning. It's not how I like to do things.'

'Don't worry, it will be fine.' Gloria waved her hand as if swatting away Prue's worry. 'A cup of tea and a sandwich will be much appreciated by the new evacuees. We all know there's a war on and things ain't how they were before. They'll just be grateful to be out of London and safe…' Gloria grabbed hold of Prue's arm, squeezing it. "ere they come,' she said as the train pulled into the station, blasting out puffs of sooty smoke as it came to a halt alongside the platform. 'Let's give them a warm welcome.'

As the evacuee mothers and children stepped out onto the platform, Prue was immediately struck by the difference between them and the expectant mothers who'd arrived last September. These women had a look of defeat about them. Their faces were grey with tiredness and worry, while their children stuck close by their mother's side.

Prue stepped forward, with a warm smile. 'Welcome to Great Plumstead. If you'd like to gather all your luggage before the train leaves, then we can take you for some refreshments before you go to your billets.'

'This is it; we ain't got no more luggage!' one mother said holding up a small bag. 'Everything we 'ad went up in smoke when our house was bombed.'

'All we've got is what we're standing in,' another mother said. 'No extra clothes to put in a suitcase, even if we 'ad one.'

The other mothers nodded in agreement.

Prue hadn't thought of this. How awful it must be to have lost everything in their homes and have to move somewhere new and start again with just the clothes on their back. This was a wholly unexpected problem which would need to be fixed, and as soon as possible.

'I understand, and don't worry we'll soon sort you out with new things,' Prue reassured them in a positive, upbeat voice. 'If you'd like to come with us.'

'We've got sandwiches and tea ready for you at the village 'all,' Gloria said putting her arm through that of one of the evacuee mothers. 'I'm Gloria and was evacuated 'ere last year. I know what it's like to arrive somewhere new, but take it from me, this is a *good* place to come to.'

Prue watched as Gloria marched the woman and her

children out of the station towards the village hall, grateful to have her and the other women from The Mother's Day Club on board helping her – especially as this evacuation had suddenly become even more challenging than before. Not only did these women need a new home, but they required clothes and shoes suitable for living in the countryside with winter coming on.

First things first, Prue thought. Her priority now was to get these women and children something to eat and drink after their long journey.

'If you'd like to come this way everyone, we can get you a hot cup of tea and sandwich before you go to your new billets.' Prue held out her hand to a little girl whose mother was holding two younger siblings in her arms. The little girl looked up at her mother questioningly, and on receiving a nod of permission, took hold of Prue's hand.

Prue smiled at the little girl. 'We'll lead the way shall we?' With a nod from the little girl, they headed off in the direction of the village hall.

~

'Look at that, Mam!' The little girl pointed at the *Welcome* sign, made from letters cut out from newspaper and strung up in a banner across the doorway, as they went into the village hall. 'Ain't that nice?'

Prue smiled at the little girl. 'I'm glad you like it.'

Once all the mothers and children were settled with food and drink, sitting at tables that had been set up like in a cafe, Prue went over to Hettie who'd come to help.

'It might not be as good a spread as we put on when our expectant mothers arrived, but it looks like it's going down well and is appreciated,' Hettie said, watching as the women from The Mother's Day Club helped the new evacuees, fetching more food and drink and chatting to them.

'Thank you for making the currant buns and bringing some of Primrose's milk for the children to drink – that was a good idea, Hettie.' Prue paused for a moment her mind racing to think how best to fix the new problem. 'We've got to do something about their lack of clothing though. There are some things available in our Mother's Day Club clothing depot here, but that's mainly for babies, toddlers and small children. We need more adults' clothes and for older children.'

Prue passed her eye over the evacuees. There were ten mothers and twenty-five children – that was a lot of extra clothing to find. 'I'll start an appeal in the village. Ask members of the Women's Institute and WVS, put up posters asking for spare clothing and shoes to be donated, books and toys for children as well – they will have lost any they had in the bombing.'

Hettie put her hand on Prue's arm, their eyes meeting. 'If there's anyone in this village who can get them kitted out, it's *you.*'

'Thank you for your vote of confidence.' Prue patted Hettie's hand. 'Though it will be very much a joint effort, with everyone pitching in. I'm sure that our Mother's Day Club ladies will help organise and distribute what we get. But we need to get it sorted as soon as possible.'

Prue was grateful that all the people who'd promised to provide billets for the new evacuees had arrived at the hall on time and had taken the mothers and children to their new homes. She didn't have to cajole or remind any of them about their obligations, unlike when the evacuee expectant mothers had arrived.

Now there was just one mother – a thin, wiry woman – and her two little girls left, and they were coming to live at Prue's. She'd already introduced herself to Nancy, the mother, and her daughters, so that they knew they had a home to go to and hadn't been forgotten.

'Are you all right to lock up the hall?' Prue asked Hettie.

Hettie nodded. 'Of course, we're nearly finished here.' The Mother's Day Club women had cleared away all the empty plates and cups and were in the kitchen washing up. 'You take your mother and children home.'

'Thank you. They look exhausted and ready to go.'

Prue made her way over to where her evacuees sat, Nancy holding one little girl on her lap, while the other stood close by her mother's side.

'Are you ready to go, Nancy?' Prue asked.

'Ready when you are, duck.' Nancy replied. 'Come on girls, it's time to go.'

Prue held out her hand to the older girl, who'd told her earlier that she was eight and her sister was six. 'It's Marie, isn't it?' The girl nodded and took hold of Prue's hand. 'Let's get you home.'

Nancy followed, carrying her youngest daughter, Joan, who was clinging on to her mother.

'I expect you're tired after the long journey and being in a new place,' Prue said as they left the village hall.

'We were tired before we even set off,' Nancy said, wearily. 'Air raids night after night and sleepin' in the underground don't make for a good night's rest.'

'I hope that will soon be remedied,' Prue said. 'You might find it too quiet here at night to begin with. We do have the air-raid siren going off sometimes and have to sleep in the cellar, but it's nothing like what you've been through in London.'

Arriving at her house, Prue showed them their bedrooms first, thinking that it would be important to them to know that they had their own space in the house.

'This room is for you girls.' Prue opened the door of what had been Edwin's room, where she'd organised two single beds, and stepped aside for them to go in. 'Who's going to sleep in which bed?'

Marie headed straight for the bed by the window and sat on it, a beaming smile on her face. 'Is it all right if I have this one, Mrs Wilson?'

'Absolutely. How about you call me Auntie Prue, if that's all right with you Nancy?'

"Course it is,' Nancy said, looking around the room, stroking her hand over the silky eiderdown on the nearest bed. 'It's lovely in 'ere for the girls, thank you.'

'My pleasure.' Prue smiled at her. 'Your room is next door.'

Leaving the two little girls in their room, the pair of them lying on top of their new beds, Prue showed Nancy into her room, where the smell of beeswax polish and lavender from the linen press mingled to make a comforting, welcoming scent.

'This is wonderful.' Nancy circled the room, touching the furniture and then went to the window and looked out at the back garden, before turning round, and smiling at Prue. 'It's a smashing house, thank you for letting us come and stay 'ere.'

'I'm pleased to have you stay,' Prue said returning Nancy's smile.

'Is it just you lives 'ere?' Nancy asked.

'No, my daughter Alice – she's seventeen – lives here and my husband, Victor. Although you won't see much of him; he works long hours and has a lot of meetings to go to.' Prue paused, biting her bottom lip and wondering if she should say something more about Victor and his less than welcoming attitude to evacuees.

'Are they 'appy about having us come and live 'ere?' Nancy asked homing in on what Prue had just been thinking.

Prue wondered what to say but going by Nancy's forthright manner decided it was best to be honest. 'Alice is, but Victor is... less keen. He's a man rather set in his ways and doesn't take kindly to disruption. He won't be rude to you, but probably won't be very friendly either. But as I said, you won't see much of him.'

Nancy gave a laugh, waving her hand in the air. 'Oh, don't worry about that, duck. I've faced Hitler's bombers. I ain't goin' to worry about your Victor being unfriendly. I appreciate you taking us in, I really do, and will 'elp around the house, do my bit, if that's all right. I'm a good cook so can 'elp in the kitchen too.'

'That would be wonderful. I'm often out and about doing things for the WVS or WI and have to rush back to get meals ready, so I heartily accept your offer to help with the cooking – thank you!'

Nancy held out her hand for Prue to shake. 'Here's to a successful partnership then.'

Prue shook her hand thinking that she was going to like having Nancy and her girls living here – they already felt like a breath of fresh air in the house.

CHAPTER 10

Thea reached out her hand, took hold of a rosy-blushed green apple, and deftly twisted it loose from the tree, then carefully placed it in the wicker basket balanced on top of the ladder on which she stood. It was an excellent apple crop this year and it was important to harvest the fruit in good condition so it could be stored to eat in the coming months.

'You should have seen Father's face this morning when he came downstairs and found Nancy cooking some scrambled eggs instead of Ma,' Alice said, from a nearby tree where she was also picking apples.

'I can imagine. I know he wasn't keen on having evacuees.'

Thea was not a fan of her brother-in-law. She'd been astonished when Prue had married Victor, who was not only fifteen years her senior, but totally unsuited to her. It was only because her sister wanted to be a mother to his two motherless little boys, and that the Great War had robbed the country of so many men of their age, that Prue had agreed to marry him. Thea had never got on with him and had merely tolerated him for the sake of her sister.

Alice laughed. 'I think Father might have met his match in Nancy. I don't think she's one for putting up with any nonsense from anyone.'

Thea carefully climbed down the ladder with her full basket of apples, taking care to step to one side as she reached the ground to avoid stepping on a fallen, bruised apple which was being devoured by wasps that buzzed around it.

'Hettie said that most of the evacuees lost everything in the bombing, and only have the clothes they came in.'

'Yes, but Ma will get them kitted out.'

'I'm sure she will. Is your basket nearly full?' Thea asked. 'Then we can take the apples over to the store together.'

'Yes, just room for these last few that I can reach from here.' Alice deftly reached out for the apples and added them to her basket.

As her niece climbed down the ladder with her full basket, Thea glanced around the orchard thinking how much work there still was to do here to harvest all the crop. With rationing in place, it was important not to waste any food. Some of the crop would be stored for feeding everyone at Rookery House, but part of it would be sold to generate income. The sale of fruit and vegetables grown in the garden and orchard here, along with products made from Primrose's milk, was Thea's main source of income.

They placed the full baskets in the wheelbarrow, and Thea pushed it towards the granary store which stood at the far end of the single-storey annexe joined to the main part of Rookery House. Inside, the granary was cool, dry and perfect for storing crops and was filled with the scent of apples that they had already harvested.

Together they began the painstaking process of checking every apple before it could be placed in one of the wooden boxes. Each box had already been prepared with troughs and furrows of newspaper to separate the lines of fruit – it was essential to make sure that none of the apples touched each other. That way if an apple should go bad, it wouldn't spoil others nearby.

'I had a letter from my friend Violet at Ambulance Station 75 in London, yesterday,' Thea said as they worked. 'Things are still bad there with the bombing carrying on night after night. She sounds exhausted but said that she wouldn't want to be doing anything else.'

'Same with Edwin.' Alice spotted a bruise on the apple she was checking, making it no good to store, so put it to one side to be taken indoors and eaten as soon as possible. 'He loves working for the Friends Ambulance Unit – it doesn't seem to bother him being out in the middle of air raids doing his first aid. His letters are full of how much he enjoys his work.'

Edwin wrote regularly to Thea too, but she suspected that his letters to her were more accurate about what he was experiencing working in the East End of London. He didn't gloss over how he felt, how scared he was at times and how he despaired at what man could do to man in the name of war. Thea knew Edwin wanted to protect his sister and his mother, from the reality, focusing on the positives when he wrote to them. He knew how much Prue especially worried about him. But with Thea it was different. They'd been together in London on the day the Blitz had started, and she'd experienced being in the thick of an air raid and helping with the injured. Her work as an ambulance driver in France during the Great War had also exposed her to sights that her sister and niece had no experience of. Thea was glad that Edwin could be honest with her in his letters, and in return she wrote back giving him as much support as she could, knowing how important those letters from home were.

'It's not an easy job, but Edwin's grasped it wholeheartedly and we're all proud of him,' Thea said.

'Not Father, though!' Alice sounded bitter. 'He won't tolerate Edwin's name being said in his presence. If Ma tries to tell him anything about what Edwin's doing, he won't have it. Tells her not to mention Edwin's name in *his* house.'

Thea had to fight back her initial reaction, not wanting to upset her niece. Alice had seen how her father had reacted to Edwin's decision to register as a conscientious objector last autumn after his elder son, Jack, was called up. Victor had been furious and had disowned Edwin, not considering how brave his youngest son was to stand up for his beliefs and to now be working selflessly to help people injured in air raids. Edwin might not be wearing a soldier's uniform, but he was putting himself in danger as much as any serviceman on the front line. His refusal to kill another man hadn't stopped him from helping those caught up and injured in the war.

'Well, he's a fool! He should be proud of his son.' Thea checked the last few apples from her basket and put them in place in a wooden box.

'That's what I tell him, but he won't have it.' Alice shrugged a shoulder. 'There's no shifting his narrow opinion. It's his loss.'

Thea put her arm around her niece's shoulders. 'I agree, but there are some people, like your father, who believe what they think is absolutely right and the only way. They can't or won't bend their opinion, not even to help or support their own family. But Edwin has the support of everyone else in our family, and we are all hugely proud of him.'

Alice laid her head on Thea's shoulder. 'I worry about him though. I'm proud of Edwin, but wish he wasn't working in London with the bombers coming back every night.'

'I know, I worry too about him and Violet. But I know if

we asked them to leave and work somewhere safer, they wouldn't because they believe in what they're doing. I was just the same working in France. I knew it could be dangerous, but it didn't stop me while there were casualties who needed help and driving to hospital. It was my job and as scary as it was sometimes, I enjoyed it. I felt I was doing something worthwhile and making a difference.'

'Do you think that's how Edwin feels?' Alice asked.

'Yes, I do.' Thea squeezed Alice's shoulders and then took a step back to look at her niece. 'I think we should stop for a break now and have a cup of tea before I go into the village to take some supplies to Barker's.'

Alice nodded. 'Sounds good to me.'

Thea stepped out of Barker's grocery shop after making her delivery of fruit and vegetables, as well as some of Hettie's freshly made butter. Closing the door behind her, she caught sight of a poster in the window, appealing for donations of clothes, shoes, toys and books for the new evacuees. No doubt brought in by Prue earlier today – her sister taking swift action to remedy the new evacuees' lack of clothing.

'Hello, Thea,' a voice called, making Thea turn around to see Gloria, who was one of the mothers evacuated here last autumn, walking towards her, pushing her pram, with a wide smile on her red lipsticked lips. She wasn't on her own but accompanied by some women who Thea hadn't seen before.

'Hello Gloria, how are you?' Thea asked, returning the woman's smile.

'Fine thank you. I'm showing some of our new evacuee mothers around.' Gloria turned to the three women with her. 'This is Thea – she's Prue Wilson's sister.'

'Hello,' the women chorused looking at Thea.

'Nice to meet you.' Thea smiled warmly at them. 'Welcome to Great Plumstead, I hope you'll be very happy here.'

'Thank you,' one of the mothers said. 'It ain't nothing like where we came from. A lot quieter.'

'I've told 'em that they'll soon get used to the quiet,' Gloria said, in a cheerful voice. 'Better that, than the air-raid sirens goin' off every night and screaming falling bombs and explosions, eh?'

'Have you been to The Mother's Day Club?' Thea asked. 'Hettie and Marianne are there this morning.'

'We're on our way there now,' Gloria said. 'I've been around to the billets encouraging new mothers to come out so I can show 'em around. I know 'ow it feels to move here, and from experience, how the best thing to do is get involved with what's goin' on. So, come on then ladies, we'll be there just in time for tea if we get a move on. Bye, Thea.' Gloria gave her a beaming smile and led the women off in the direction of the village hall where The Mother's Day Club would be in full swing.

Thea watched them go for a few moments, thinking how well Gloria had settled into village life. She was so different from most of the women here, with her bottle-blonde pompadour hairstyle, her heavy make-up, brightly coloured dresses and high heels, and yet she had embraced life in a country village wholeheartedly. It was good to see her taking the new mothers under her wing, and Thea hoped that in time they'd feel as settled and at home as Gloria did.

Taking her bicycle from where she'd left it leaning against the shop wall, Thea swung her leg over it and pushed off heading back to Rookery House, where more fruit was waiting to be harvested.

CHAPTER 11

'Matron wants to see you in her office,' Hazel announced coming into the sluice on Monday morning.

Evie glanced up from the bed pan she was scrubbing. 'What does she want?'

'I don't know. There's only one way to find out, and best not to keep her waiting.' She gave Evie a sympathetic look. 'Let me finish up in here for you.'

'Thank you.' Evie gladly abandoned her work, having spent far more time in the sluice since she'd started work here a week ago than she liked. Matron had kept her busy doing basic hospital tasks, all of which involved huge amounts of cleaning but no proper nursing contact with patients. It wasn't the sort of work Evie had been used to doing back in London.

'Good luck,' Hazel said.

Evie quickly washed her hands with hot, soapy water and put on a clean apron before heading for Matron's office. She stopped briefly by a mirror in the hallway, checking she was neat and presentable and tucking some stray hairs back inside her veil. She didn't want to give Matron anything to complain about. Pausing outside Matron Reed's door, Evie took a deep breath and then knocked.

'Enter,' Matron's voice called.

Evie went in, clasping her hands in front of her and doing her best to quell the quaking in her stomach as Matron's beady eyes fixed on her from across her desk.

'Nurse Jones.' Matron paused, looking Evie up and down. 'And how do you think you are settling in here?' she asked, her Scottish accent sounding far gentler than her personality actually was.

Evie had the feeling that this wasn't a simple question, and that her answer would be interpreted in Matron's own particular way.

'I'm settling in well, thank you,' she said, playing safe. She'd learned from experience that it was best to tread a neutral path with some people. Always wisest to not to give them any ammunition to use against you.

'And the work?' Matron asked, narrowing her eyes as she waited for a response.

'Fine, it's essential work for the running of a successful hospital.' Evie refrained from adding that it was basic, boring and didn't use the skills she'd acquired over months of nursing real patients.

Matron Reed nodded. 'Absolutely. There is no shame in cleaning bed pans or scrubbing floors. They keep the hospital *hygienic* and that is a key factor in the well-being and healing of patients.' She cocked her head to one side, regarding Evie. 'Tell me about your work at the Millbank Military Hospital in London.'

'I worked there for seven months after I completed my initial training, starting with basic jobs like here.' Matron nodded approvingly. 'And then moved on gradually to working directly with the patients, making beds, doing dressings, temperatures, more general nursing of the patients. I enjoyed the work very much.'

'And what made you become a mobile VAD?' Matron asked.

'I wanted a change,' Evie said truthfully. 'To gain more experience in a different hospital.'

'Well, I'm satisfied with your work so far... so this afternoon I want you to prepare some more sterile dressings.' She raised an eyebrow, looking Evie straight in the eye. 'Another essential job.'

Evie wanted to ask when she'd be allowed to work with the patients but held her tongue, grateful that preparing dressings was an improvement on cleaning bed pans in the sluice. 'Yes, Matron.'

'And after that you can help with cleaning the beds and washing the locker tops on the wards.' Matron nodded her head and turned her gaze to the papers on her desk, clearly dismissing Evie.

'Thank you, Matron.' Evie fled before Matron changed her mind. Outside in the corridor she let out a sigh of relief; at least her new task was an improvement on the last one, and that was something to be grateful for.

Evie was delighted that she wasn't the only nurse who'd been given the job of preparing dressings, as she saw that Hazel had already made a start on the never-ending task when she arrived in the storeroom.

'Hello,' Hazel greeted her with a warm smile. 'Have you been promoted from bed pan duty?'

'Thankfully!' Evie sat down at the table and picked up a

roll of lint and a pair of scissors and began cutting the lint into pieces, folding them into suitable sizes of dressings. Hazel was doing the same from a roll of gauze. 'I'm also being allowed to clean beds and wash locker tops on the ward after I've finished this, so gradually getting closer to patients.'

'That's good – another week or two and you'll be taking temperatures.' Hazel giggled. 'Being a VAD nurse isn't quite the romantic image I had when I first joined. I'd pictured myself wiping the fevered brow of grateful patients, not on my hands and knees scrubbing floors.'

Evie put the pile of lint dressings she'd made into the cylindrical metal drum that stood in the middle of the table, and which would be sealed and sterilised once it was full.

'I've wanted to be a nurse since I was a little girl,' she said. 'I used to have an imaginary hospital treating my toys.'

'Sounds like it's your true vocation then.' Hazel cut through the gauze she was holding with a sharp snip of her scissors.

Her friend was right, Evie thought. Nursing was what she was born to do, and it was the war that had allowed her to fulfil her dream. If war hadn't broken out, then she'd still be living a life of discontent firmly under the thumb of others. War wasn't nice, wasn't pretty, but it *had* brought her freedom.

'You're looking serious,' Hazel commented. 'Are you all right?'

'Yes, I'm fine,' Evie replied. 'Just thinking about being able to be a nurse and pleased to be here at this hospital and preparing dressings!'

CHAPTER 12

Prue's appeal for clothing, shoes, books and toys for the new evacuees had been a great success. Since her posters had gone up all over the village, donations had been flooding into the village hall. This morning's session of The Mother's Day Club, one of the two or three sessions held in the village each week depending on hall availability and what needed doing, was being devoted to sorting through them. Prue, Marianne and Gloria had set up several long tables around the hall ready to begin work when the other mothers arrived at ten o'clock.

'It's a lot more than I expected we'd get,' Gloria said looking at the piles of donations, her hands on her hips.

'It needs to be sorted out into adults and children's clothes first, and then the type of garment – skirt, jumper or whatever,' Prue said. 'We'll have a separate table for the books and toys.'

Marianne picked up a garment from a pile and shook it out to reveal an old-fashioned blue dress which had seen better days.

Gloria winced. 'That must've come right from the back of

74

someone's wardrobe. Probably ain't seen the light of day for years.'

'It doesn't matter.' Marianne felt the soft material between her finger and thumb. 'It's good quality cloth and can be re-used and made into something else. We need to think how to make the best use of what we've got here.'

Prue nodded. 'I daresay some of it needs mending before we can give it out to the evacuees. It can be done at one of our work parties. Perhaps some of the new evacuee mothers are good at sewing and can help make themselves some new things.'

A loud knock on the outside door made Prue glance at the clock on the wall. 'Look at the time, the others are arriving!' She went to the door, opened it, and ushered in members of The Mother's Day Club, who she was pleased to see included many of the new evacuee mothers, some of whose older children now attended the village school.

'Good morning, everyone!' Prue said gaining the women's attention after they'd taken off their coats and settled toddlers on the blanket in one corner where toys were set out and two mothers watched over the children. 'We have an important task to do today – sorting out the generous donations from the village to help re-stock our clothing depot. Marianne, if you can be in charge of the children's clothing which can go on this table.' She pointed to the table on the left. 'And Gloria, if you can do the same for the adult clothes on that table. Nancy, can you sort out the books and toys and put them over there.' Prue carried on giving instructions so that everyone knew what they were doing.

The women quickly got to work. Garments were held up, compared and assessed, before being folded neatly and added to the appropriate table. The hall was filled with a hubbub of noise as they chatted and laughed their way through the donations.

By the time tea break came round, all the donations had been sorted onto the various tables and it was pleasing to see that there was a good selection of clothing for both children and adults, as well as some items like blankets, curtains and tablecloths whose fabric could be used to create whole new garments.

Pushing around the tea trolley, Prue offered a cup of tea to a mother who she hadn't had much of a chance to get to know yet – this was the first time the woman had come to The Mother's Day Club.

'It's Marjorie, isn't it?' Prue asked, holding out a cup of tea to her.

'That's right.' Marjorie took the cup. 'Thanks.'

Prue took a cup of tea for herself and sat down next to Marjorie. 'It's nice to see you here today; how are you settling in at your billet? I hope everything's all right there.'

Marjorie gave a nod. 'It's all right, but it don't feel like 'ome yet. But I'm grateful to Mrs Roberts for taking us in.'

'I can imagine how hard it is to move somewhere so different from what you're used to. I'm sure that if I went to live in the middle of London I'd find it overwhelming,' Prue admitted. 'I hope you'll soon settle and get used to it; the important thing is that it's safer here for you and your children.'

Marjorie nodded and took a sip of her tea. 'I'm not used to having so much time on my hands, to be 'onest. There ain't much for me to do 'ere and now the girls are at school all day, I feel like I'm under Mrs Roberts' feet if I stay at the 'ouse.'

'I understand and that's why we set up this Mother's Day Club last autumn after the expectant mother evacuees arrived. Many of them felt the same way. You should also come to the

Women's Institute meetings; there's one this Thursday evening in the village hall. Lots of the mothers come along.'

'Can I bring my girls?' Marjorie asked.

Prue hesitated. 'Well, we've not had children there before, but perhaps that's something we need to think about – providing somewhere children can go while their mothers attend the meeting if they can't stay at their billet.' Prue patted Marjorie's arm. 'Leave it with me and I'll see what I can do. In the meantime, I hope you'll keep coming here every day. We can keep you busy. Are you any good with a needle and thread, only we've got lots of clothes that need altering?'

'I'm not bad.' Marjorie gave a wry smile. 'I'll be glad to help.'

CHAPTER 13

Evie woke up and lay quietly for a few moments, enjoying being snuggled up warm and cosy under the soft eiderdown, but then panic kicked in as her eyes glanced at the alarm clock standing on her chest of drawers. It was quarter past eight! She'd overslept! She should have been at the hospital forty-five minutes ago. What would Matron Reed say?

Flinging back the covers, Evie swung her feet down onto the rag rug beside the bed and then remembered... it was her day off – the first one since she'd started work at Great Plumstead Hall Hospital.

She sighed and retreated into the warmth of her bed, pulling the covers over her once more, and, as her heart returned to its normal pace, she smiled to herself at her silly mistake. Today was hers to do with as she pleased. There would be no matron telling her what to do and giving her unpleasant jobs. After just over a week's worth of duties – and working days that were twelve foot-aching hours long – she was ready for a day off, although she wasn't sure how she was going to spend it. But beginning with a cosy lie-in while she read was a good start. She reached over, picked up the book she'd borrowed from the bookcase in the sitting room, opened it and began to read, quickly losing herself within its pages.

After Evie had finished her breakfast, which Hettie had left for her in the warming oven having gone out to man the WI store at Wykeham market, she went outside to have a wander around the grounds of Rookery House.

It was a cool late October day, a brisk wind blowing the last of the leaves off the trees and she was grateful for her warm scarf, hat and coat. Having lived most of her life in London, Evie was still getting used to being in the countryside, marvelling at being able to see further off into the distance than the end of the street. She loved the wide skies over Norfolk, how they were ever changing and never the same from day to day.

She was lucky to have been billeted here at Rookery House with its large gardens, she thought as she wandered along, looking at the neat rows of vegetables growing in plots.

Walking past a barn Evie heard her name being called out and peered inside.

'Good morning,' Thea said, shovelling a load of straw and what looked like animal droppings into a wheelbarrow. 'Did you enjoy your lie-in?'

The smell of the dung hit Evie's nose and she took a step back, where the air was fresher but she could still see Thea.

'Yes, once I remembered it was my day off. When I woke up, I panicked thinking I'd overslept!' Evie explained. 'That wouldn't have gone down well with Matron.'

'I can imagine. What are you planning to do today?' Thea asked.

'I'm not sure, I'm just glad to have a day off – it's tiring work. I haven't had a proper look around here yet, so I thought it would be nice to get to know the place better.' Although Evie had been living here for over a week now, most of her daylight waking hours were spent at the hospital and it was dark by the time she returned to Rookery House. Apart from when Marianne had given her a quick tour around the garden on the day she'd arrived, Evie hadn't had the chance to see it properly until now. 'Who lives in here?'

'This is Primrose's byre, where I do the milking.'

Evie nodded. She'd heard more about Primrose, Thea's house cow, from Hettie when she'd praised the delicious yellow butter she'd spread on her toast. Not only did it have a delightful creamy taste but was in much more plentiful supply than could be bought on rations, and Hettie had explained how she'd made it using the cream from Primrose's milk.

'Where is she now?'

'Out in the meadow. Why don't you go and have a look at her, and I'll give you a proper tour around, if you like, once I've finished mucking out in here,' Thea suggested.

'Yes, thank you, I'd like that.' Leaving Thea to finish cleaning out, Evie wandered off in the direction of the meadow which she could see from her bedroom window.

Evie had no experience of cows apart from the ones she'd seen out of train windows, but she had to admit that Primrose was a pretty animal with toffee-coloured fur, large brown eyes and a creamy coloured belly and neck. Leaning on the gate, she watched Primrose, who after giving her a cursory glance, continued to graze, swishing her tail from side to side. There was something very peaceful about watching her, listening to the sound of the cow tearing off grass to eat and taking breathy huffs.

Evie breathed in deeply, enjoying the clean, fresh air of the countryside which was much nicer than what she'd been used to living in London. Everything here was so different – it truly was another world to her and importantly a life where she no longer had to worry and hide.

'What do you think of her?' Thea asked coming to stand beside Evie and leaning her elbows on top of the wooden gate.

'She's lovely, so much prettier than any cow I've seen before, although I haven't seen many, I must admit.'

'Not many cows around in the middle of London!'

Evie glanced at Thea and smiled. 'I like it out here in the countryside, it's peaceful, far less crowded and safer.'

Thea nodded. 'It must be a relief to not have your sleep disrupted by night after night of air raids. I was in London at the beginning of the Blitz – it was shocking and frightening, and to have that happen again and again must be awful.'

'Yes, but in a strange way you come to expect the bombers arrival each night. I always hoped of course they wouldn't arrive, but they did, and they still are coming.'

'My friend, Violet – she's in charge of an ambulance station – says she finds it difficult having to send her crews out in the middle of a raid, never knowing if they'll come back. I worry about her.' Thea sighed. 'But she loves her job.'

Primrose had spotted Thea and ambled over to them, positioning herself by the gate so that she could enjoy some attention. Thea reached out and scratched under the cow's chin, and she responded by sticking out her head like a dog, closing her eyes, clearly enjoying the touch.

Evie tentatively reached out and patted the cow's head.

'You can have a go at milking her sometime if you want,' Thea offered.

'Oh...' Evie hesitated, not wanting to offend Thea. 'Perhaps, one day, when I've got to know her a bit more first.'

'It's all right, you don't have to, but if you'd ever like to try, just say.' Thea said, understandingly. 'Where did you live in London?'

'Not far from Russell Square.' An image of the home she'd left behind flashed into Evie's mind, and she had to suppress a shudder.

'It's a nice area. I lived in London for seventeen years – only came back here to live last year. I heard that Rookery House was up for sale, so I sold my mobile catering business and came home.'

'It must be nice to come back,' Evie said, watching as Primrose wandered off to graze again having had enough attention.

'Yes, it is. What made you decide to leave London?'

'I felt like a change and wanted the chance to nurse patients for longer than just a few days,' Evie said, having already prepared a credible and partly true reason to explain her move to anyone who asked. 'Most patients at the hospital I worked at were moved to safer ones outside the city once they were fit to travel. I decided to volunteer to become a mobile VAD and was posted to Great Plumstead Hall Hospital.' There was so much more that Evie could say, but the past was the past and she didn't want to tell anyone about it. She'd moved on from that, it had no place here.

Thea nodded. 'I can understand wanting to nurse your patients for longer and see them recover, makes the job more satisfying. It must be a relief to be out of the bombing too.'

'Yes, I don't miss it! It's a joy to sleep in my bed all night.'

'Do you have any family still in London?' Thea asked.

'Not any more, my mother now lives in Sussex and my father died several years ago. I have no brothers or sisters. There's no family in London to worry about.'

'I'm sure your mother's glad that you're out of London,' Thea said. 'Right, let me show you around properly, and after that we can have a cup of tea. I believe Hettie left some apple cake in the tin.'

'That sounds lovely.' Evie fell into step alongside Thea, feeling uncomfortable with what she'd said, because the fact was that her mother had no idea she was here – her mother thought she was dead!

CHAPTER 14

The hall of the village school was filled with the happy sound of children giggling as the game of musical statues drew towards its conclusion.

Thea joined in the laughter, having thoroughly enjoyed watching the delight on the children's faces as they took part in the game. She, Alice and Vera, a mother from The Mother's Day Club, had set up a temporary children's evening club at the school, while the children's mothers attended the Women's Institute meeting at the village hall. Prue had persuaded the headmaster to allow them to use the school hall which gave them plenty of space for playing games.

Aware that most of the children here would usually have been getting ready for, or even be in bed by now, with it being just after half past six, Thea decided it was time for a more peaceful game.

'Who knows how to play sleeping lions?' she asked.

Children's hands shot up into the air accompanied by nods and smiles.

'All right then, find yourself a place and lie down. And no peeking, mind.'

'I used to love playing this,' Alice said, as the children laid down on the hall floor with their eyes squeezed tightly shut, some of them laying on their backs, others on their fronts with their heads resting on their folded arms.

'Why not join in now?' Thea suggested, smiling at her niece, 'there's nothing stopping you.'

Alice grinned. 'All right then, I will.' She found herself a space and lay down on the floor alongside the children.

'Do you want to join in too?' Thea asked Vera, who was one of the new evacuee mothers.

Vera shook her head. 'I'll go and make the cocoa. I think they'll be ready for a soothing drink after this.'

'Good idea, and I can read the story while they have it – their mothers are due to pick them up in half an hour.'

Vera headed off to the small kitchen in the staff room and Thea looked around at the waiting children and Alice. The hall was silent except for a few escaping giggles of expectation.

'Remember sleeping lions are *silent*,' Thea said in an exaggerated whisper, as she moved to the far side of the room taking care not to stand on any hands.

She bent down and gently tapped on the shoulder of a little girl, whose eyes sprang open. As she looked up, Thea signalled to the girl to keep silent by putting a finger to her lips. The girl nodded, got up and followed Thea around the hall as she repeated the process over and over, gathering a following of children and Alice behind her, each doing their best to tread quietly, keep silent and smother any giggles with their hands. Eventually, there was just one sleeping lion left. Thea motioned for the children to stand around the last child lying on the floor, pressing her finger to her lips to remind them to stay silent. Then on her signal, all the children called out *'Wake up sleepyhead'* as they patted the sleeping lion, who opened her eyes and beamed at them all, delighted to have been the last one.

'Can we do it again?' A little boy asked, his eyes shining with pleasure.

'Yes please,' other children echoed his request.

Thea looked at Alice who smiled encouragingly at her. 'Very well then.'

After another three games of sleeping lions, the children were settled down sitting cross-legged on the floor drinking their cups of warm, milky cocoa ready for a story.

Thea had found a copy of *Adventures Of The Wishing Chair* by Enid Blyton in a bookcase in the corner of the hall. She began to read, aware of the children's eyes fixed on her as they listened to the story, some of them starting to suck their thumbs after finishing their cocoa. Alice and Vera went around collecting the empty cups as a sense of peace and relaxation fell over the children.

Turning the page, Thea glanced at the children, her heart squeezing at the thought of what many of them had been through before they were evacuated here. Living in Great Plumstead must feel like a world away from their homes, but she hoped that they were happy and settled. And at least for the moment they could lose themselves in the joy of listening to a story that whisked them away into a happy land of adventure. Tonight had been fun, for them and for her too.

CHAPTER 15

Tonight's talk at the Women's Institute meeting had been a great success, Prue thought, sipping her tea during the break. The speaker, Mrs Bukowski, who was a Polish refugee, had given an interesting talk about her homeland, describing its customs and ways of life in peacetime which made the thought of the current situation there even more terrible.

'You all right Prue, you're lookin' very thoughtful?' Gloria asked, sitting down beside her.

'Yes. I was just thinking about what Mrs Bukowski told us – and how dreadful it must be to have your country overrun and your family put in camps.'

'And that's what we are fightin' for, to stop it happening 'ere as well, and to free those countries already invaded like Poland.' Gloria laid her hand on Prue's arm. 'Anyhow, the new evacuee mothers seem to be enjoyin' themselves.' She gestured to where a group of mothers were gathered chatting happily to other Women's Institute members as they all had their tea and biscuits.

'It's good to see them here. I hope they'll keep on coming

to our meetings and joining in with the other activities we do. I know it's not easy for them – or for any of you.' Prue sighed and then put on a bright smile, her gaze meeting Gloria's. 'But we have to make the best of things.'

'Exactly! So what have you got planned for us for after tea break then?' Gloria asked, her eyes wide with expectation.

'Would a game of musical chairs followed by a sing-song suit you?' Prue asked.

Gloria beamed, her red lipsticked lips forming a wide smile. 'Sounds good to me.'

The social half-hour at the end of the Women's Institute meetings was always popular. For each meeting, Prue planned something fun and light-hearted which would send the women home full of good cheer. Its aim was to allow members to let their hair down a little which was especially important these days, with so many worrying reports on the wireless and in the newspapers and the uncertainty of living in wartime.

The riotous game of musical chairs was down to the last two players, having caused a great deal of laughter and brought out a surprisingly competitive spirit amongst some of the women.

Prue took one of the two remaining chairs away and stepped to the side of the hall joining the rest of the women watching. Only two people were left in the game – Nancy who lived with Prue, and Jess Collins, who was also an evacuee mother. Both women had wholly embraced the game and from the determined look on their faces wanted to be the winner.

Rosalind Platten, who was seated at the piano, turned her

back and began to play a jaunty tune and Nancy and Jess circled around the last remaining chair.

'Who do you think will win?' Hettie asked, standing next to Prue.

'I wouldn't like to say.' Prue glanced at Hettie and grinned. 'They both look so determined.'

Rosalind carried on playing, and both Jess and Nancy continued to circle the chair. Then suddenly the music stopped and Jess, being on the right side of the chair to plonk herself down onto its seat, pipped Nancy to it, a look of triumphant delight on her face.

The room burst into a round of applause and cheering. The game was a huge success and had brought a sense of fun to the meeting.

Smiling happily, Jess joined in the clapping after holding out her hand to shake Nancy's — both women had thoroughly enjoyed themselves.

'I think we can safely declare that Jess is our winner!' Mrs Baden, who was President of their WI said. 'Now let's all join together for some singing to end our meeting. Ladies if you'd like to arrange yourselves by the piano, we will begin.'

Everyone did as Mrs Baden asked, and Rosalind began to play the first notes of a song that needed no introduction – *If You Were the Only Girl in the World*.

As Prue began to sing the familiar words, joining in with the other women, their voices mingling and filling the village hall with sweet music, a shiver of delight ran through her. She loved it when they had a sing-song at the end of meetings. There was nothing quite like singing together with other people – as their voices mingled in harmony it made the song even better, bringing a sense of real joy to her. And looking around at the other women's faces as they sang, it clearly had the same effect on them too.

After Rosalind had played the closing notes, she swivelled on her chair to face the women. 'Any requests?'

Several song titles were called out and Rosalind chose one. 'Thank you, let's start with *Daisy Bell*.' She turned and began to play, the notes she was coaxing from the old piano sweet sounding, the women silent as they waited for the right moment to begin singing.

Prue was very fond of this song. Beside her Hettie's fine voice began to sing the familiar words and Prue joined in, singing happily as the swell of voices surrounded her.

By the time the clock hands had crept their way around to nearly seven o'clock, they had sung several more songs – *Danny Boy*, *Take a Pair of Sparkling Eyes* and finishing off with the popular *You are my Sunshine* which was often heard on the wireless these days.

It was a wonderful end to the meeting, Prue thought, and would send everyone off with a cheerful heart after they'd had the chance to step out of their normal life for a short while. It had certainly given her a much-needed boost and she hoped everyone here felt the same – especially the new evacuee mothers.

CHAPTER 16

Prue checked that her green felt WVS hat was straight in the hall mirror, then let herself out of the front door and stood waiting in the covered porch for Thea to arrive with the mobile canteen. She was looking forward to this morning's work, going around to various scattered places where troops were stationed far from facilities.

In the months since she'd started working with her sister on the canteen, Prue had grown to love the job and always enjoyed talking to the servicemen and women they served. It felt like a worthwhile way to spend her time, and the hot drinks, food and other items they provided were always most welcome. She'd been amazed when she'd discovered how much else the canteen stocked for the troops. As well as providing hot drinks and food, they sold goods such as stationery, matches, soap, stamps, candles, pencils, even razor blades – items that servicemen and women stationed in isolated spots would find hard to get. Her voluntary work on the canteen helped make the lives of the troops a little bit easier, contributed to the war effort, and was enjoyable too.

A toot of a horn sounded, and Prue saw Thea pull up by the gate in the canteen, which had been converted from a delivery van. She hurried out to join her through the drizzly rain which had been coming down since she'd got up, and made for a dreary, grey day.

'Good morning,' Prue said as she climbed into the cab.

'Morning! It may be nothing...' Thea said, her face concerned, 'but I just passed Vera and her children heading towards the station with what looked like all their belongings. Do you want to go and see what's going on?'

Prue stared at her for a moment, taking in the news. 'What? I can't believe they're going back to London, none of them have said anything to me about it. It would be madness taking children back to the bombing.' She threw her hands in the air in exasperation. 'We must go and find them. Quick!'

'I know, but let's not panic, it might not be that. They might just be going to Norwich for the day or something.' Thea sounded dubious as she put the canteen into gear, and they headed for the station.

They'd almost reached Great Plumstead's village station when Prue spotted Vera and her two young boys. She'd thought Vera was settling in well as she came along to The Mother's Day Club and her boys went to the local school but going by the bags Vera was carrying, it looked like they were leaving.

Thea pulled up at the station and Prue leapt out before her sister had turned off the engine. She had to handle this carefully because, if it was as Prue feared, this was a delicate situation. If she was going to persuade Vera to stay, then she must not show her annoyance at what she considered the stupidity of taking children back to what had become a war zone. Many of the evacuee mothers were fiercely proud and devoted mothers, and Vera wouldn't take kindly to being spoken to in a patronising or authoritative way.

'Good morning, Vera, boys,' Prue said, pasting a smile on her face as she went to meet them. 'Where are you off to? Can we give you a lift in the canteen?'

Vera looked taken aback by Prue's sudden appearance, no doubt hoping to leave without being spotted.

'We're going 'ome to London,' Vera said, firmly, meeting Prue's eyes. 'I appreciate everythin' you've done for us here, but I'm that worried about my 'usband being there on his own. It ain't good for him. I had a letter from him yesterday and he ain't managing without me. He works hard at the docks and needs feeding properly and looking after to do a day's work.'

'But what about…?' Prue began but was silenced by a hand on her arm and turned to see Thea looking pointedly at her, giving a slight shake of her head.

'Come on boys, come and have a look in the back of the canteen – you wouldn't believe how much we've got packed in there. If that's all right with you for a minute or two, Vera?' Thea asked.

Vera nodded. 'Go on then, boys, two minutes that's all.'

Prue watched as her sister led the boys to the canteen and opened the back for them to climb in and have a look around, grateful that Thea had thought to take them out of earshot for what she had to say.

'Vera, I appreciate that you're worried about your husband, but what about the boys' safety? Those bombs don't discriminate between adults and children – they kill and injure anybody who gets in the way. You've seen it, you've been bombed out already, it's madness to take those boys back into that. Please stay here, if not for your sake…' She glanced at the canteen where she could hear exclamations of delight as they explored. 'Then for your *children's*.'

Vera crossed her arms and raised her chin. 'Don't you think I'm worried about them too? It ain't a decision I've taken lightly, but I just can't leave my Reg there on 'is own, he can't look after 'imself properly and I'm that worried about him.' She paused for a moment her lips pressed into a thin line. 'Besides, this place don't feel like 'ome to us, it's too quiet, it ain't what we're used to. I want to go back to London, it's my 'ome.'

Prue's eyes held Vera's who stared back at her stubbornly. She could see that there was no shifting the woman, her mind was made up. 'Then please leave the boys here if you must go back – they'll be safer here.'

Vera shook her head, droplets of rain splashing down onto her coat from her hair. 'I can't. They go where I go. We're a family, and we stay together and...' her voice wobbled, 'if that means we die together, then so be it. At least we'll 'ave been with each other, not hundreds of miles apart.'

Prue squeezed her hands into fists in the pocket of her green tweed WVS coat. She wanted to shout at Vera, scream at her that she was mad to possibly be leading her children to their deaths. She hoped it wouldn't prove to be the case, but by returning to London and the Blitz, inevitably their chances of being injured or worse by a bomb were massively increased compared with staying here in the village.

Prue forced her voice to remain calm. 'Is there *anything* I can do to make you change your mind, a change of billet, anything?'

Vera shook her head. 'There ain't a thing. You've been very kind to us, and I appreciate all you've done for us, but we need to go back 'ome.'

A thought suddenly struck Prue. 'But you were bombed out; you haven't got a home to go back to.'

'Reg has found a new place to stay and there's room for us too.'

Prue fixed an understanding look on her face. 'Then I wish you well, Vera. Remember, if you change your mind there's *always* a place for you here in the village. Don't be afraid to come back.'

'Thank you.' Vera's voice was gruff. 'Right, we'd better get a move on, don't want to miss the train.' She held out her hand to Prue. 'Goodbye.'

Prue shook her hand. 'Good luck Vera.' She hoped that the woman would not end up paying a very heavy price for her devotion to her husband's welfare.

~

Back in the cab of the canteen, Prue sat staring glumly out of the window as they drove out into the countryside heading for their first stop. The grey heavy clouds drizzling out rain looked miserable and matched how she felt.

'You did all you could, you know.' Thea reached across and touched Prue's arm. 'Vera's a grown woman and had made up her mind – she was doing what she thought was the right thing for her family.'

'But it's *madness*!' Prue's voice came out shrill. 'Who would take children back to a place which is being bombed night after night? You were there at the start of the Blitz, Thea, you've seen it.'

'Yes, I know. But Vera obviously thinks the risk is worth it to be with her husband and have her whole family together.'

'Then I hope she doesn't live to regret it.' Prue folded her arms across her chest, blinking back tears. 'Those two young boys don't deserve to be injured or worse because of their mother's decision.'

'No, they don't, but she *is* their mother and is entitled to make decisions about them.'

'I tried to persuade her to leave them here, but she wouldn't. I would *never* have taken my children back to such danger to be with my husband.'

'What would you have done with the boys if she'd left them here?' Thea asked.

'Well, if they couldn't have stayed on in the billet they'd been in, then I would simply have found another one. That wouldn't have been a problem.' Prue sighed heavily. 'What worries me is that with Vera gone, it might open the floodgates and others will follow. I need to be prepared for that, and if the mothers insist on going back, try to persuade them to at least leave the children here where it's safer.'

They drove along in silence for a while, Prue's mind going over and over what had happened, and what might happen with the other evacuee mothers. It had been bad enough when some of the expectant evacuee mothers had returned to London after just a short while here last autumn, and that was before there'd even been any bombing. But now there was no doubt about the danger with the city coming under nightly attacks.

'Would *you* be prepared to have some evacuee children if their mother returned to London without them?' Prue asked.

Thea glanced at her. 'I'm not sure, I'd need to think about it. Anyway, I don't have a spare bedroom any more now that Evie's moved in.'

'But surely you could squeeze some beds for children in somewhere?' Prue asked.

'Perhaps, but to be honest, Prue, I'm not sure that I have the time to care for evacuee children properly – I'm busy enough as it is. Besides it wouldn't just be *me* who'd be affected, there's everyone else at the house to think of.'

'But you will think about it, though?' Prue urged her. If her sister would be prepared to take in some child evacuees, it might be a good lever to persuade another departing evacuee mother to leave her children here. She knew Thea would provide an excellent home for them, and that prospect could be tempting to any evacuee mothers wavering over whether to leave their children or not.

'All right. But I'm making no promises, so don't go expecting me to say yes, Prue, because there's a good chance that I can't take any.'

Prue nodded, satisfied that at least Thea would think about it. 'All right, thank you. And I do hope there won't be any other mothers deciding to go back. I need to talk to them at The Mother's Day Club tomorrow – no doubt word will have gone around about Vera leaving.'

'Good idea, nip it in the bud.' Thea slowed the canteen down as they approached their first call – a searchlight detachment which was several miles out from the nearest village, and whose servicemen were always glad to see the arrival of the WVS canteen.

CHAPTER 17

Thea leaned her head against Primrose's flank, breathing in the warm smell of cow and sweet hay as she pulled rhythmically on the teats, sending streams of creamy milk into the metal pail. She always enjoyed milking sessions at the beginning and end of each working day – they gave her a chance to mull things over while she worked.

Since yesterday's incident, when Prue had tried to persuade Vera to stay in the village, or at least leave her boys here rather than taking them back to London, Thea hadn't been able to get what her sister had asked out of her mind. Could she have some evacuee children come and live here at Rookery House if necessary? After all, that's what she'd been expecting to happen last September when Marianne had arrived here. She'd happily agreed to give a home to an evacuee child then, but a mistake in sending on evacuees in Norwich had brought her an expectant mother instead. What difference would it make to have some evacuee children now? Wouldn't it be more important than ever – keeping them from returning to a city under daily attack from enemy bombers?

Thea sighed. The problem was that her life was different now to what it had been back then. She had more work to do, more responsibilities and was often out doing things for the WVS. She couldn't be here all the time to look after them, so how could she possibly think about giving a home to children who needed someone there for them? She was already doing plenty to help with the war effort – from growing food to her WVS work and filling her home with lodgers – there was no need to feel guilty about her decision. Her reasoning made sense, but it didn't stop a prickle of unease and questioning doubt from settling heavily in her chest.

~

'Vera leaving has caused quite a stir at The Mother's Day Club,' Marianne said as she spooned some mashed vegetables into Emily's mouth. 'It was all people seemed to talk about this morning.'

'I'm not surprised. The woman was mad to take her little lads back to London.' Hettie shook her head, pursing her lips. 'But where one has gone, others might follow.'

'Prue tried to stop her. She did her best,' Thea said, gathering up a forkful of delicious shepherd's pie from her plate. The three of them were sitting around the kitchen table having their tea, the room cosily lit by the lamp on the table, and the range at the far end throwing out a welcome warmth. 'She was adamant she wanted to go back to her husband.'

Hettie tutted. 'Then she should have left them little boys here, I dread to think what might happen to them now.'

'Prue's worried that more mothers might leave – she said so at the club this morning. And that if anyone else is tempted to go then they should please think of the children and leave them here where they're safe,' Marianne explained. 'She reassured the mothers that any children left here would be well cared for.'

'I suppose Prue will be looking for more billets who can take just children then. Looking after children is a bigger responsibility than having a mother in your house who can look after herself and her children. Children need more care, time and effort,' Hettie said cutting up a piece of carrot. 'Though I think the village is getting fit to burst with so many new people having already arrived and needing billets.'

Thea prodded at her food with her fork, the niggling weight of her sister's request still needling at her despite her earlier decision. 'Prue asked if I'd be prepared to take some children in if another mother went back and left them here.' The words spilled out of her before she could stop them.

Hettie and Marianne stared at her for a moment.

'Where would you put them?' Hettie asked, her eyes concerned behind her round glasses. 'With Evie here now, we don't have a spare bedroom any more.'

'There's my sewing room.' Marianne said. 'It's not that big, but there's room for a single bed in there. I could move the sewing machine downstairs and work in the dining room – if that would be all right with you, Thea?'

Thea nodded. 'Of course.' Marianne already used the large dining room table to spread material out on when she was cutting out fabric and patterns – it wouldn't be a problem to put the sewing machine in there, and it would free up the smallest bedroom. But why was she even thinking about this? Thea wondered. It was irrelevant because she simply didn't have the time now to look after one child or more, properly, with everything else that she had to do.

'If they were small, they could share a single bed,' Hettie said. 'Sleep top to toe.'

'That wouldn't be any different from what many children

do back home in London. It could even be more familiar for them, from what I know about how some families live there,' Marianne added.

Thea put her knife and fork down and looked at her friends. 'But I *can't* give a home to any children.'

Hettie frowned. 'Why not? You were going to do *exactly* that last September when the village was expecting evacuee children. And the need is even greater now with the bombing.'

'I know.' Thea sighed, fiddling with her fork as it rested on her plate. 'But I've taken on a lot more responsibilities since then – I'd have much less time to care for them. It wouldn't be right to give a home to a child if I'm not here to look after them.'

Hettie chuckled. 'And who says you'd have to do it all yourself?' Hettie shot a look at Marianne who gave a nod of her head. 'You're not the only one who lives here, don't forget. Between us – me and Marianne, and you – we could *all* look after them, make sure there's always someone here with them when need be. If they were old enough, they'd be away at school for part of the day anyway. You wouldn't have to do it all on your own, Thea.'

'We'd all help,' Marianne added.

Thea couldn't believe she hadn't thought of that – she'd been so wrapped up in thinking it all had to be down to *her*. What was the saying, *It takes a village to raise a child*? Well, if everyone at Rookery House was willing to play their part if needed, then perhaps they *could* give a home to a child or even more than one.

Her face broke into a smile. 'I hadn't looked at it that way. You're right of course. Thank you, Hettie, Marianne.'

'So, you'll tell Prue, "Yes" then, will you?' Hettie urged, her face hopeful.

Thea nodded. 'Definitely, although that doesn't necessarily

mean we will have any children come to live here. I hope that no other mothers do decide to return to London for their sakes, but if they do, then I hope at least they'll have the sense to leave their children here and we can offer them a home.'

'Good.' Hettie stood up. 'Now I'd best get that apple crumble out of the oven – don't want it to burn.'

Thea picked up her knife and fork again and began to eat, knowing that they'd made the right decision, and together could provide a warm and welcoming home to some children if the need arose.

CHAPTER 18

Loud barks penetrated Evie's dream, and she woke with a start, her mind taking a few moments to catch up as it was muzzy with sleep. Was that Bess? Reuben had left her here in the house tonight as he was out on overnight duty with the Home Guard.

Someone knocked on Evie's bedroom door and before she could answer, it was opened and Thea looked in, her face lit from the glow of the torch she was holding.

'Evie – are you awake? The air-raid siren's going off in Wykeham. The wind's blowing in the other direction so it's barely audible, but Bess heard it. We need to get to the shelter.'

'I'll be right there.' Evie swung her legs out of bed as she heard Thea move on to Marianne's room. This wasn't the first time she'd been woken in the night by an air raid since moving to Great Plumstead. Annoying as it was losing some sleep, so far, the raids had been nowhere near as bad as the ones she'd experienced in London – just disturbing their sleep and thankfully no bombs falling nearby. Pushing her feet into her soft slippers, she grabbed her thick woollen dressing gown over which she'd put on her coat before going outside.

Downstairs in the kitchen, Evie picked up one of the baskets of provisions they always took to the shelter with them – pillows, blankets and a flask of hot tea – and followed the others outside. The cold night air was a shock after her warm bed but at least made her feel slightly more awake as she walked across the garden towards the Anderson shelter. Looking up, she saw that the sky was a clear inky-black and pin-pricked with thousands of stars. It looked beautiful. It was hard to comprehend that there were bombers flying up there against that beauty – bombers who'd come with the intention of causing injury and death to innocent civilians.

Once everybody was settled inside the shelter, including Bess who lay beside the door as if on guard, Evie settled back on one of the benches which ran along each side. Marianne had placed a still sleeping Emily in the makeshift bed at the far end, the little girl oblivious to their night-time flee to the shelter.

'Who's for a cup of tea then?' Hettie asked taking cups from the basket she'd carried out and placing them on the bench beside her, then unscrewing the lid of the flask.

'Yes please,' Evie, Marianne and Thea chorused, then grinned at each other.

'How long do you think we'll be in here this time? Marianne asked taking the cup of tea that Hettie handed to her.

'Your guess is as good as mine,' Hettie said. 'We have no control over it, but I hope it's not too long. I'm on duty at The Mother's Day Club in the morning and need some more sleep before then.' She handed Evie her cup of tea. 'Here you go – you look like you could do with that.'

'Thank you.' Evie cradled the cup in her hands glad of the

warmth seeping into her fingers as it was chilly in the shelter, their breaths pluming in the cold air lit by a tilly lamp hanging from a hook in the roof. 'I was in a deep sleep when Bess's barks woke me – I feel like I haven't quite caught up with myself yet.'

'Same with me,' Thea agreed. 'It's been a busy day for all of us and the last thing we need is to spend half the night out here.'

'I dread to think how many hours of sleep people are losing altogether every night across the country, because of air raids,' Hettie said, shaking her head. 'And yet we're expected to carry on as normal, do our jobs on not enough sleep. Of course, I know it's much worse in places like London than here. But then you know all about that love, from being in the Blitz.' She reached across the shelter and patted Evie's arm. 'There are more women having to be out at work now and on not enough sleep. This war has brought so many changes to our lives.'

'You're sounding very philosophical tonight, Hettie.' Marianne said.

Hettie gave a wry smile. 'Well, it's true. If you went back even two or three years, most women's lives were different to what they are now. Ours certainly were. I was working as a cook at the Hall, Thea you were still living in London running your business. Marianne you were dressmaking in London. I don't know what you were doing then, Evie, and tell me if I'm wrong – but I expect it was different to now.'

Evie nodded, gazing into her hot tea from which wisps of water vapour spiralled upwards like tendrils. Her life had been hugely different back then. 'You're right, Hettie. I wasn't a nurse then.' *Because you'd never have been allowed to be one*, a voice in her head reminded her.

'What job did you do?' Marianne asked.

What could she say? Evie thought. That she hadn't been *permitted* to have a job, that her place had been in the home. Even before that had become her role in life, she'd been limited in what she could do, depending on what was deemed suitable. Only she couldn't tell them that. She'd escaped that life and didn't want knowledge of it to taint what she now had here.

'I did voluntary work and helped in my mother's home.' That much was true, Evie thought. 'And when the chance came along, I took classes with the Red Cross to learn to become a nurse. I did first aid, nursing and hygiene courses, which led to me to becoming a VAD. I was glad of the chance to do that.'

'Just like in the Great War, this war has given women opportunities to do things they otherwise wouldn't have had the chance to do,' Thea said. 'From that perspective it's not all bad.'

'I know, but there's a lot more expected of us now,' Hettie added. 'But then we are a country at war and fighting to keep our land free from invaders.'

Bess suddenly leapt to her feet and started barking, and when Thea put her hand on the dog's head to quieten her, they could faintly hear the sound of the all-clear coming across the four miles of countryside from Wykeham.

'There you go, Hettie.' Thea smiled at the older woman. 'Thankfully it was just a short stay in here tonight – we can all go back to our beds and hopefully get some sleep.'

As they gathered up the things to return to the house, Evie thought about what they'd just been discussing, about how their lives had changed from before the war. Back then, she could never have believed she'd be where she was today. Evie was grateful for where her life had brought her. Although she wished that she could be more open with these warm-hearted people who'd taken her into their home, showing her nothing but kindness and consideration. Evie felt guilty that she hadn't been completely honest with them, omitting things about herself and her past, but it was the price she had to pay for starting afresh, for her freedom and her safety.

CHAPTER 19

Prue stood outside the village hall surveying the pile of salvage that had been collected by members of The Mother's Day Club this morning. Now that they were running weekly collections, there wasn't as much as had been collected on the first salvage drive back in the spring, but every bit helped.

Today's collection of paper and bones would bring in more precious money for the wool fund and help keep the villagers knitting garments for the troops. The socks, scarves and gloves they'd be working on at this afternoon's knitting bee would be made from wool paid for by these weekly collections. It gave Prue great satisfaction that they were turning what would otherwise be waste into money for the wool, which the women's knitting skills then transformed into clothing for the troops defending the country. The women might not be on the front line, but so much of what they did these days was part of a bigger picture working towards the war effort.

'Are you comin' in to open the parcels?' Gloria called as she came out of the village hall and marched over to Prue. 'Only some of the others are hoppin' about in there as if it was Christmas morning with wanting to know what's inside them.' Her red lipsticked mouth broke into a wide smile, as she gestured back towards the open door of the village hall with a wave of her hand.

'I'll be right there,' Prue said. 'I just want to put what we've collected into the shed in case it rains – otherwise the paper will be a soggy mess.' She picked up some of the bundles of newspaper that were tied with string and took them into the shed standing at the side of the village hall, where the salvage was stored until Prue took it to the collection depot.

'I'll give you a hand.' Gloria picked up some bundles and followed.

It didn't take them long to move the paper. The last thing to go inside was the metal dustbin in which the bones were stored, with its heavy lid to keep the smell firmly inside. Prue plonked it down with a clang as the bones jiggled about inside it.

'There's enough for a carload now, so I'll take it to the depot tomorrow,' Prue said casting her gaze over the rest of the salvage that had been collected over the previous couple of weeks. She always waited until she had enough to pack her little car to the brim with salvage before taking it, not wanting to waste a drop of precious rationed petrol. Everything these days had to be stretched as far as possible, nothing wasted or squandered.

'Right, let's go and see what's inside those parcels then.' Prue linked her arm through Gloria's.

Inside the hall, the mothers had set up a line of tables as Prue had asked them to, and the pile of parcels stood waiting at one end. They'd come all the way from America, donated by the American Red Cross, and would be a welcome addition to their clothes depot. Following Prue's appeal for clothing and shoes after the new evacuee mothers and children had arrived, their stock of clothing had expanded, but much of that had now been loaned out and once again the depot was running low.

'We'll sort the clothes out as we did before – adults can go on that table and children's on there.' Prue pointed to the tables. 'Gloria if you can oversee the adult clothes and fold them into piles of each type of garment, skirt, jumper or whatever, and Jess, if you can do the same for the children's clothes. The rest of us can open the parcels and do the initial sorting out. And remember to fold up the paper from the parcels to reuse.'

The next half an hour passed with a lot of chatter and excited exclamations as the women opened the parcels to reveal their contents.

'Look at this!' One of the mothers held up a pretty cotton frock against her, stroking the soft fabric. 'It's lovely – I'd never 'ave given this away if it was mine.'

'We're lucky the Americans are being so generous and helping us out in this way,' Marianne said, shaking out a pair of blue boy's trousers from the parcel she was sorting through.

By the time all the parcels had been opened and the clothes sorted into different piles on the tables, there was a good selection of sizes and types of garments to swell the stock of their clothes depot.

'We've done very well,' Prue said. 'The clothes might not be brand new, but they're all in good condition and will be well used here. These are especially needed.' She put a hand on the pile of children's coats. 'We'll open up the clothing depot on Saturday morning so children can come along to try things on for size. I know yours need bigger coats, Jess.'

Jess Collins, who was one of the recently evacuated

mothers, nodded. 'I can't believe how much my two 'ave grown since we got here – it must be all this fresh air!'

'And getting a proper night's sleep too. Staying all night in their own beds is what children need,' Gloria added. 'And there's better food here as well. All the children are looking rosier cheeked than when they arrived. But then we all are!' She laughed her throaty laugh and the others joined in.

'Well, whatever it is that's working, it's wonderful to see,' Prue said. 'Right, who's ready for a cup of tea?'

CHAPTER 20

Evie could feel Matron Reed's eyes watching every move she made. Taking slow, steady breaths to calm her nerves which were jangling inside her like a loud doorbell, Evie took a pair of forceps out of the jar of disinfectant and used them to slightly open the lid of the metal drum, quickly removed a sterilised dressing and closed the lid again. Finally, two weeks after starting work here, Matron was giving Evie the chance to change the dressing on a patient's wound, all the while being scrutinised by the older woman's eagle eyes.

Evie had done this task many times before in London. She was confident that she could do a proper job, but with Matron breathing down her neck, it felt as if she was doing it for the first time. She must get this right or the nearest she'd get to dressings for the foreseeable future would be cutting them up and packing them into the grey metal drums ready for sterilising – and she'd done plenty of that in the past week.

'Don't look so worried, nurse,' Corporal Barkham said, cheerfully. 'I'm used to this now. I promise I'll keep still.'

Evie smiled reassuringly at the young man who lay looking

up at her with a grin on his face. 'Thank you, this won't take long.'

She was grateful for his words as they helped to ease the tension in her shoulders a little. Concentrating on what she was doing, she deftly put the new dressing on his leg, taking great care to ensure it was tidily done, giving him as little discomfort as possible. Evie was satisfied that she had done a good job, but would Matron think so?

'How was that Corporal Barkham?' Matron asked as Evie tidied away the equipment on the dressings trolley.

'Absolutely perfect,' the soldier said. 'I'll willingly have Nurse Jones change the dressing again if she's that good at it.' He winked at Evie and her cheeks grew warm.

She knew the patients were aware of Matron Reed's iron rule over the nurses, and they always did what they could to support the young women who cared for them.

'Well, Nurse Jones, you clearly know how to deal with changing dressings as well as packing them.' Matron's shrewd brown eyes met Evie's. 'You can be responsible for taking care of Corporal Barkham's dressings while you're on duty, and the rest of the men in this ward who need them too.'

'Thank you, Matron,' Evie said, not daring to look at Corporal Barkham who was giving her a thumbs up behind Matron's back.

Matron gave a nod of her head, turned on her highly polished shoes and headed out of the ward.

'Congratulations! You passed the test.' Corporal Barkham beamed at Evie. 'Her eyes were watching every move you made.'

Evie nodded. 'I could feel them, but thankfully I've proven to her that I'm capable of changing dressings.'

'Was that your first time?' he asked.

'Not at all, I've done hundreds of them where I used to

work – you were in safe hands, as long as I didn't drop the dressing through nerves! I...' She began but halted as an anguished cry came from a bed further down the ward.

'It's young Sullivan, nurse,' Corporal Barkham said, his face concerned. 'Another nightmare.'

'I'll go and see to him.' Evie hurried to the far end of the ward where eighteen-year-old Private Sullivan lay sleeping, but from the sheen of sweat on his forehead and tortured expression on his face, it wasn't a peaceful slumber.

His face contorted and he let out another yell. Evie took hold of his hand which was scrunched into a fist.

'Private Sullivan, it's all right, you are safe.' She spoke softly, gently stroking his hand, watching as his eyelids flickered open and he looked around him, a startled expression on his face, his breathing fast. 'You're in hospital back in England.'

Registering that he was indeed where she said, the young man's eyes met hers and his breathing eased, the tense look on his face slowly dissolving away.

'It was a dream,' he whispered. 'Just a dream.'

Evie nodded. 'Yes, just a dream.' She'd seen this happen many times – men reliving the horrors of what they'd been through, thrashing about in their beds and crying out. It was heart-breaking to see, and especially in one so young as Private Sullivan. He was the youngest patient on the ward and sadly the only one of his unit who'd survived an attack. Whatever had happened to him was something he often revisited in his dreams. Evie had seen some of the older men talking to him, no doubt being able to understand what he'd been through far better than any of the medical staff here. She hoped that with time and patience the dreams would fade.

'Can I get you cup of tea?' she offered.

He shook his head. 'No thank you, I'm all right now I'm awake.' He managed a smile.

'Well, in that case, you can be next to have your dressing changed. I've just got Matron's approval to do the dressings on this ward.'

'And she's good at it too,' Corporal Barkham called from the other end of the ward, where he lay watching what was going on. 'I was the test guinea pig watched over by Matron, so I can vouch for Nurse Jones' steady hand and gentle manner.'

'Go on then,' Private Sullivan agreed, 'might as well get it over and done with.'

Evie squeezed his hand. 'I promise to be gentle.'

She appreciated that changing dressings was not always pain-free for the men and was something they dreaded, but it was essential for the healing of their wounds. This young man was wounded in not only his body but in his emotions as well, and it was likely that his outer injuries would heal long before his mind and heart. While he was here Evie would do all she could to help him. 'I'll just go and wash my hands and be right back.'

With freshly washed hands and without Matron breathing over her shoulder, Evie began to do what she usually did while changing a patient's dressing, knowing that it helped to distract them from their discomfort – she talked to them.

'So where is home for you?' she asked the young soldier, who was watching her every move as she began to remove the soiled dressing from the wound on his leg.

'North Yorkshire, in the Vale of York.' Private Sullivan looked far away for a moment, his eyes shining. 'It's a grand place.'

'And what did you do there before you joined the army?'

Evie asked, inspecting his wound and glad to see that it was healing well, with no sign of infection.

'I worked in my father's nursery, helping with growing plants... I loved it, but fool that I was, I wanted to do my bit and joined up as soon as I could,' he explained as Evie swabbed and cleansed his wound. 'I lied about my age. I was seventeen and would have been old enough to join up in six months, but I didn't want to wait that long.' He sighed. 'I thought the war might be over by the time I was old enough and didn't want to miss out.'

Evie carefully began to apply a clean dressing to his wound. 'You've certainly done your bit now, once you're discharged from here, you'll be able to go home and back to the nursery.' She knew his injuries were enough to have him medically discharged; he'd never be fit enough to be a fighting soldier again.

'I can't wait to get back amongst all the plants, the birds and the insects. Its peaceful there but it took me going away to fully appreciate it.' Private Sullivan paused briefly, a wistful look passing across his face. 'But I do now.'

'It's often the way – we don't know the value of what we have until it's taken away from us.' Evie checked the new dressing was correctly in place and then began to wind a new bandage around it. 'You'll be glad to go home.'

His face lit up. 'I picture it in my mind, think myself there. It's keeping me going until I get back – helps to chase away the nightmares.'

'Good idea, keep focusing on the good, what you love and what's to come.'

'Is that your recommended treatment, Nurse Jones?' Private Sullivan said, cheekily.

'Absolutely!' Evie grinned at him. 'Along with a regular change of dressings.'

'Not so keen on that bit, but it's not as bad as it used to be, and you have a gentle hand doing them.'

'I'm glad to hear it.' Evie tidied the dressings trolley, glad to see Private Sullivan looking much happier and more relaxed than he had when he'd woken from his nightmare. She doubted that it was the last one he'd have, but if he could keep focusing on his future then, hopefully, he'd be able to banish the demons that haunted his dreams. Now knowing more about his home life and hopes for the future, she'd be sure to talk to him about it again, encourage him to look to the good things, not remember the bad. It was something she practised herself so knew it helped.

CHAPTER 21

Prue was sitting in an armchair enjoying a hot cup of tea and relaxing reading through the latest edition of the WI's *Home and Country* magazine. It was Saturday morning, and she was glad to have a quiet day for once. It had been a busy week with her work at The Mother's Day Club and volunteering for the WVS, so now having time to sit quietly and enjoy catching up on WI news was a treat. Nancy was in the kitchen with her girls doing some baking, Alice had gone into Wykeham to meet up with a friend and of course Victor was at his beloved business.

Taking a sip of tea, Prue started to read through an article about a group of WI members taking over a neglected allotment, successfully clearing it and putting it into food production. It made her think about the possibilities of doing something similar with their village WI on some unused land. Her thoughts were interrupted by a loud, insistent knocking at the front door, and she stood up about to go and answer it when she heard Nancy call out from the hall, 'I'll get it.'

Prue sat down in the chair again, her ears straining to hear who it might be. She wasn't expecting anyone this morning. It might be someone leaving some paperwork for Victor about one of his various committees, or even the postman. Prue returned her attention to her magazine again but had only read a few words when the sitting room door burst open, and Nancy came in.

'You better come, Prue.' Nancy's face was grim.

Prue stood up and headed to the door. 'What is it?'

'It's Jess Collins – she's come to tell you that she's going 'ome.' Nancy shook her head, her mouth a thin line.

Prue's heart sank. First Vera had gone back last week, and now Jess. Prue had thought that Jess was settling into village life well; she came along regularly to The Mother's Day Club and had attended the WI meeting, so why was she leaving now? And if she was, what about her children?

Prue sighed – so much for her quiet morning.

'She's crazy to 'ead back into the Blitz!' Nancy hissed.

Prue nodded and touched her friend's arm. 'I think so too. I'll try and persuade her to change her mind. You get back to the girls and the baking.'

'All right but give us a shout if you need me,' Nancy said heading back to the kitchen.

Prue braced herself with a couple of deep steadying breaths, then walked along the hall to the front door where Nancy had left Jess Collins waiting on the doorstep. Prue's heart sank at the sight of her two young children standing beside her, six-year-old Betty and five-year-old George.

'Jess, what's going on?'

Jess raised her chin and met Prue's gaze. 'I'm going back to London. I can't leave my husband to fend for himself any longer – I was that shocked how he looked last weekend, he's lost weight because he ain't feeding 'imself properly and working all hours on the docks.' Prue knew that Jess's husband had come to see her and the children on a short visit. 'He ain't capable of looking after himself. He needs me to be there.'

'But what about your children?' Prue looked at the pair, who stood quietly, hand in hand, dressed in warm coats, knitted hats and scarves which had been supplied to them from The Mother's Day Club clothing depot. They, like most of the other families, had arrived here in the village with very little, having lost almost everything in the bombing.

'That's why I'm 'ere and didn't just go straight to the station.' Jess put a hand on Betty's shoulder as she stood near to her mother. 'I want to leave them here where they'll be safe. Can you find them a new 'ome? Mrs Dawes, where we've been staying, is nice enough, but she's elderly and she ain't keen on having two small children to look after. It's been all right for her while I've been here to care for them but now I'm going back to London…' Jess's voice wavered for a moment, and she quickly suppressed the emotions which churned across her face. 'I know you offered to do the same when Vera took her boys back to London.'

Prue nodded. 'Of course, they can stay.' If there really was nothing that she could do to persuade Jess to remain here, then Prue was grateful that the woman was thinking what was best for her children. There was no question about which was the safest place, a city still under nightly attacks or a Norfolk village. 'But it would be better if you stayed too,' Prue urged her.

Jess folded her arms across her thin frame. 'I can't. But if I know that they'll be safe 'ere and well looked after, then I'm 'appy to leave them in Great Plumstead.'

'Mam?' Betty said, her bottom lip wobbling.

'We've already talked about this,' Jess said firmly to her daughter. 'It's the best thing for you both – I'll write to you every week and come and see you when I can. It won't be for long.'

Betty's blue eyes were bright with tears and Prue's heart went out to the little girl who was trying to be brave and strong.

'These are their things.' Jess picked up a wicker basket standing by her feet, which contained clothes and some toys, and held it out to Prue. 'If you can let me know where they're billeted so I can write to them. This is where I'll be staying.' She pulled a slip of paper out of her coat pocket and passed it to Prue. 'Right now, you two, you do as Mrs Wilson tells you and be good for whoever's going to be lookin' after you, all right?'

Jess bent down and kissed each of her children on the cheek and then pulled them both into a long hug. She looked over their heads at Prue and managed a watery smile, her eyes brimming with tears.

Prue's heart squeezed in sympathy; she appreciated how hard it must be for Jess to leave her children behind, but it was the right thing to do. Prue didn't agree with Jess's decision to return to London, but if she was determined to go she admired the woman's courage in putting her children's safety first, even though it clearly was hurting her.

'I promise you that they'll be well looked after here – I have a home ready for them, with my sister, Thea. She'll take great care of Betty and George.' Prue reached out and took hold of the children's soft hands in hers as their mother released them.

'Thank you.' Jess picked up her bag. 'I appreciate it, I really do.' She took a deep breath and straightened her shoulders. 'I need to go, mustn't miss the train. Goodbye then, Betty, George.' She reached out and gently touched each of them on the cheek and then turned on her heels and walked down the path to the gate, where she turned and gave them a last look, blowing them a kiss before hurrying off towards the village station.

'Mam! Come back!' George wailed, tears running down his face as he pulled at Prue's hand trying to follow his mother.

Prue crouched down so that her eyes were level with his. 'It's all right, George, we'll look after you and you'll be with Betty. Shall we go in and see what's going on in the kitchen? Nancy and her girls are baking some buns – they'll be ready soon. Let's go and have a look.'

He looked in the direction that his mother had gone and then at his sister who gave him a swift nod.

'Come on then.' Prue stood up and lead them both inside, feeling a mixture of emotions swirling through her. She was disappointed that another mother had decided to return to London, but also grateful that she'd had the sense to leave her children behind, even though it had clearly cost her to do so.

In the kitchen, which smelled of delicious baking, Nancy's two girls, Marie and Joan, were washing up at the sink while Nancy was clearing up the table where they'd done the mixing. At the sight of Prue and Jess's children, she stopped wiping the wooden table and stared at them.

'You couldn't persuade her…' She began but halted as Prue shook her head.

'Betty and George were hoping to try one of your freshly baked buns when they're ready,' Prue said in a cheery voice.

Nancy smiled at the children. 'Of course, they'll be done in a few minutes and once they're cool you can have some. Leave the washing up girls,' she said to her daughters, 'dry your 'ands and you can get out some toys and play with Betty and George in the meantime.'

Her daughters did as they were asked, clearly delighted to

take the younger children under their wings, and swiftly leading them off to find their toys.

'What are you going to do?' Nancy asked once they were out of earshot.

'I'm going to ring Thea,' Prue said.

CHAPTER 22

Thea paced up and down the kitchen of Rookery House, checking the clock on the dresser again, but it hardly seemed to have moved since the last time she'd looked.

'Why don't you go outside and find something to occupy yourself with rather than wearing a path in the kitchen floor?' Hettie asked, her eyebrows raised behind the frames of her round spectacles.

Thea sighed, her shoulders dropping. 'Maybe I should – it's ridiculous being so nervous.' She gestured with her hands. 'I'm overreacting and not sure why. We were ready to have an evacuee child last September and I wasn't as anxious about it as this.'

'No, but that was different.' Hettie said sympathetically as she checked the crumbly consistency of the flour and butter she was rubbing into breadcrumbs in a bowl, making the topping for an apple crumble for their tea. 'We'd more time to prepare ourselves then, whereas this is sudden. We've only had a few hours' notice to get organised and turn our minds to having children to care for.'

Thea nodded in agreement. After Prue had telephoned this morning, they'd carried out the necessary preparations, making sure Marianne's former sewing room was ready for Betty and George. Now they were just waiting for them to arrive.

'It feels like there's more at stake this time,' Thea said. 'After the poor things have been deserted by their mother. It's not like when thousands of children were evacuated last autumn – they were all in it together then. These two are probably feeling especially lost and abandoned. What happens if they don't settle here?'

'Let's not put the cart before the horse,' Hettie said, firmly, her gaze meeting Thea's. 'Our job is to offer them a calm and caring home, that's what they need. Any problems we'll deal with along the way. Now go outside and do something useful.' She smiled encouragingly, her blue eyes kind. 'I daresay you can find a job to do.'

Thea returned the older woman's smile. 'Always. There's never a shortage of jobs to do around here. Thank you for calming me down, Hettie.'

'You're welcome. I'm looking forward to having some more children about the house and it will be good for little Emily to have some playmates.' Hettie motioned towards the door with her eyes. 'Off you go then.'

Thea added another armful of fallen golden oak leaves to the wheelbarrow, glad that she'd taken Hettie's advice to get outside and do something. Being busy outside in the cool, fresh air was helping to steady her. Picking up the rake again she continued her task of clearing up the leaves that were scattered across the lawn at the front of the house. It was a job she'd been planning to do, and it allowed her to be here ready to meet Prue and the children as soon as they arrived.

The wheelbarrow was almost full when she heard Prue's voice coming from the lane on the other side of the hedge bordering the road. Thea's heart quickened – they were here. Moments later, her sister came in through the gate, the little boy walking between Prue and his sister, holding on tightly to each of their hands. The sight of the two small children, looking so unsure and worried, touched Thea's heart. The urge to scoop them up into her arms and hug them, tell them everything would be fine, filled her, but it wouldn't be the right thing to do. Not now. The children had only seen her once before when she'd looked after them the night their mother had gone to the WI meeting. It would take time for them to get to know her.

'This is my sister, Thea Thornton,' Prue introduced Thea to the children. 'Do you remember her from the children's evening club?'

They both nodded, looking at Thea, their blue eyes anxious.

Thea crouched down so that she was eye level with them and smiled warmly. 'Hello, George, Betty. Welcome to Rookery House. We're pleased that you're going to stay here with us.'

'Hello Miss Thornton,' Betty said, in a quiet voice.

'Why don't you me call Auntie Thea?' Thea suggested, knowing that the evacuees in Prue's house referred to her as auntie, which was so much nicer than being addressed more formally.

'That's a good idea,' Prue said. 'Shall we go inside and get you settled. You can see your new room.' She looked questioningly at Thea who nodded.

'We've got it ready for you.' Thea stood up. 'Can I take

that?' She held out her hand to take the basket from Prue, which she could see was packed with some clothes and a few toys.

'Thank you.' Prue handed the basket over.

Thea led them around the house to the back door which they always went in and out by, aware that the two children were holding on tightly to each other and George was clinging to Prue as well. They were clearly worried, and her heart went out to them thinking how awful it must be to suddenly be left here in the village with their mother gone, and only each other left together of their family.

Stepping inside, the warmth of the kitchen was welcoming and the smell of the evening meal cooking in the range's oven was mouth-wateringly delicious. The children stared around them, wide-eyed.

'This is Hettie, you'd best call her Auntie Hettie,' Prue said introducing the children to the older woman who was peeling potatoes at the sink.

'Hello, my dears,' Hettie said, smiling warmly at them. 'Welcome.'

'Hello,' the children chorused, Betty in a much louder voice then George's, his little more than a whisper.

'Let me show you your bedroom.' Thea led the way across the kitchen, into the hall and up the stairs to the room she and Hettie had prepared for them.

'This is lovely,' Prue said, standing in the doorway of the children's room as Betty and George looked around it. 'It's nice and cosy in here.'

'We've only got the one spare bed at the moment, so I've made it up so that one of you can sleep one end, and one the other,' Thea said gesturing towards the iron-framed bed. 'My brother Reuben said he could make you a bunk bed if you'd like.'

Betty and George looked at each other, the pair of them still tightly holding hands.

'Can we both sleep in the same bed and the same end, please?' Betty asked sticking her chin out, although her eyes looked less certain.

Thea nodded. 'Of course you can, if that's what you prefer. I'll redo the bed later so it's ready for you at bedtime.'

A look of relief washed over both children's faces.

'Thank you,' Betty said. 'We always slept like that at home.'

'Then that's what you shall do here,' Thea reassured her. 'We want you to be comfortable and happy. Let's leave your things here and we can sort them out later.' She put the basket she'd carried upstairs beside the chest of drawers. 'I'll take you outside and introduce you to Primrose and the chickens next.'

'Who's Primrose?' Betty asked.

'She's a cow.' Thea was pleased to see the look of interest on George's face, the little boy having been so quiet and reserved, his sister doing most of the talking. 'Have you met many cows before?'

George shook his head. 'Is she a big one... With horns?'

'Well, she has got horns and is cow sized, but don't worry Primrose is very gentle. Come and see for yourself.' Thea held out her hand to George.

He glanced at his sister, who gave him a little nod, and letting go of Betty's hand, George took hold of Thea's and went with her as they headed outside.

'If you rub under her chin like this,' Thea demonstrated what to do to the children, as Primrose stretched her chin forwards exposing more of her neck, 'she'll enjoy it.'

George tentatively reached his arm through the bars of the

gate and gently stroked the cow's soft fur, his face serious with concentration.

'That's it! You're doing a fantastic job,' Thea said, her heart warming as the expression on the little boy's face changed to one of delight.

He looked at her and grinned. 'She's like a cat that likes being stroked.'

'She's a lot bigger than a cat,' Betty said, hesitantly reaching through the bars to touch Primrose herself.

George looked at his sister and rolled his eyes. 'I know that! I never thought you could stroke cows. She's lovely though, ain't she?'

Not to be outdone by her little brother, Betty joined in with stroking Primrose's chin, gradually growing in confidence as Thea watched over them thinking that this was a good first step in helping the children settle in. Introducing them to Primrose had been a good idea as animals had that special way of helping people feel calm and relaxed – even some cows.

Thea cradled her cup of hot cocoa in her hands as she sat by the range in the kitchen.

'Do you think the children will be all right and that they'll settle and be happy here?' she asked Hettie who sat opposite her, having pulled a chair up by the stove as they often did when they had their evening cocoa.

'Of course they will. Just give them time to get used to another home and new people – we've got off to a good start today,' Hettie reassured her. 'Children are very adaptable. Remember, thousands have been evacuated and are living away from their families and home.'

'I know, but Betty and George did have their mother here with them to start with, and now she's gone.'

'Her being here to begin with will have helped them settle into the village when they first arrived.' Hettie reached over and put her hand on Thea's arm. 'I can see you're worrying about it but try not to. We just need to take it a day at a time – there's bound to be some hiccups along the way, but nothing we can't manage. Every parent has them, and we're standing in for the children's mother and father while they're here living with us.'

Thea nodded and took a sip of cocoa. She couldn't help worrying that Betty and George would miss their mother too much to settle here. *But was she over thinking things?* she wondered. They'd only been here a few hours and she shouldn't expect too much, too soon, only she desperately wanted them to be happy here. As soon as she'd seen them walk through the gate this afternoon they'd captured her heart – stirring maternal feelings that she'd suppressed because there'd been no point in indulging thoughts about such things with no husband to be a father.

'You're right, Hettie, I know.' Thea managed a smile. 'I'll try not to worry.'

'Good. Look on the positive side – they both ate a good tea and were soon asleep after you read them a story.' Hettie put her empty cup down and picked up her knitting. 'Tomorrow they can get outside in the fresh air and have a good run around. You could take them to gather some chestnuts for tea – there's plenty come down now after that wind and rain the other day.'

'Good idea.' Thea had always loved going chestnutting as a child – she hoped Betty and George would too.

Leaning back in her chair, Thea recalled how she and her brothers and sisters had always been fiercely competitive in their foraging expeditions – challenging each other to see who could get the most chestnuts to take home for their tea or pick the most blackberries. She and her brothers, Reuben and William – who'd been killed in the Great War – and sisters Prue and Lizzie, had spent many happy hours foraging for food in the woods and fields around Great Plumstead, helping to supplement their family's food supplies.

The sound of the door from the hall opening brought Thea's attention back to the present and she sat up straight at the sight of Betty and George standing in the doorway, the girl holding a bundled-up sheet in her arms, both of them with anxious faces.

'George 'as wet the bed.' Betty said, biting her bottom lip. 'I'm ever so sorry.'

Thea's heart squeezed at the sight of George, his hands clasped tightly together and his eyes wide as they looked at her.

'It's all right, don't worry.' She stood up and went over to them, putting a hand on the little boy's shoulder, smiling at him. 'Let's get you both washed and changed into some dry night clothes and we can change the bed and get you settled again – it won't take long.'

'I'll go and sort the bed out,' Hettie said getting to her feet.

Thea glanced at Hettie who nodded encouragingly at her. The older woman had been right to suggest they put a rubber sheet on the bed when they'd made it up earlier, just in case of such events. They had hit their first hiccup, Thea realised, but like Hettie had said earlier, it was nothing they couldn't manage – night clothes and sheets could be changed and washed. The important thing was that the children didn't feel they were in trouble.

'Let me take that.' Thea held out her hands to take the wet, balled-up sheet from Betty. 'We'll soon have you both clean and changed and by the time that's done, you'll be able to snuggle up in bed again and get back to sleep.'

George looked up at her and nodded, his eyes less worried than when he'd come in. 'I'm sorry, Auntie Thea.'

'It's all right, George, it was an accident and probably because you're in a new place,' Thea gently reassured him.

'That's what Mam said when he did it after we first moved here at the other billet,' Betty informed them. 'But you soon stopped didn't you George?'

He nodded.

'It doesn't matter, the important thing is to get you into some clean, dry things and back to bed, or you'll be tired in the morning, and we've got someone coming to stay with us for the day who'll be keen to meet you both.'

'Who?' Betty asked.

'Bess, she's my brother Reuben's dog – remember I showed you where he lives in the little railway carriage house?' Both children nodded. 'Well Reuben's on Home Guard duty tomorrow so Bess will spend the day with us, and she'll be delighted to have someone new to play with.'

George looked at Thea, his blue eyes wide. 'Can I play with her?'

'Yes, of course.' Thea put her arm around his shoulders. 'The quicker we can get you both sorted out, back into bed and to sleep the sooner tomorrow with come.'

The following afternoon, Thea and Marianne took the children – Betty, George and Emily – out for a walk with Bess in the nearby woods just down the lane from Rookery House. After washing up the things from a delicious Sunday dinner, they'd left Hettie dozing in an armchair by the warm fire and come out to enjoy the crisp, late autumn afternoon.

'Bess has made a new friend,' Thea said watching George and her brother's dog running together through a drift of fallen leaves. After last night's bed-wetting George had been a bit subdued this morning despite Thea's reassurances. Bess had picked up on the little boy's emotions and had stuck to his side like glue since Reuben had left her with them this morning. It had been wonderful to see how George had responded to the dog's gentle nature, his initial worried manner from this morning changing to a more relaxed and happier look.

'It's good to see,' Marianne said, walking beside the pram where Emily was sitting up, smiling her gummy smile at Betty who was helping Marianne to push it.

'George 'as always wanted a dog,' Betty said. 'Only Mam said he couldn't cause it ain't allowed in the flats where we live.' She frowned. 'Where we used to live before they was bombed.'

Thea put a hand on Betty's shoulder. 'It's good that George can play with Bess here then.'

Betty looked up at her and nodded. 'And I can play with Emily.'

At the sound of her name, Emily beamed another gummy smile at Betty, the pair of them quite taken with each other. Since Betty had met baby Emily, she'd been keen to help Marianne with her and play with her. Thea hoped that like Bess with George, Emily would help Betty to soon settle in and feel at home.

'Let's see if we can find some chestnuts for tea,' Thea said as they neared the place where some tall, sweet chestnut trees grew. The leaf-strewn ground under the tree canopy was littered with spiny nut cases that had fallen, some of them splitting open to reveal the glossy brown chestnuts nestling inside the creamy inner shell.

Marianne unclipped the reins that secured Emily safely in her pram so that she didn't fall out if she tried to climb the sides, and carrying her in her arms joined in with the search.

George, with Bess still close by his side, began to pick up plump chestnuts and, when he had a handful, added them to Thea's basket.

'If you scuff leaves aside, you can often find some nuts underneath them.' Thea demonstrated, poking some of the fallen brown chestnut leaves to the side, sending an earthy smell into the air and revealing glossy nuts underneath. 'And you can always have a look in any cases that haven't split open.'

George looked her, frowning. 'But they're all prickly.'

Thea smiled encouragingly at him. 'It's all right if you use your feet instead of your hands, like this.' She positioned a closed spiny green nut case between the inside edges of her booted feet, and with gentle sideways movements prised open the prickly case to reveal the plump nuts inside. 'Now you have a go.'

Both children copied what she'd shown them and exclaimed with delight when they managed to prise apart the nut cases with their feet, revealing the hidden treasures within.

'This is fun,' Betty said as she put another handful of chestnuts into the basket. 'We ain't ever done anything like this before.'

'There's more opportunity to do this sort of thing in the countryside,' Thea said. 'We can forage for food out in the woods and fields.'

'You'll be able to join in the blackberry picking next year as well,' Marianne said.

Thea recalled how the evacuee expectant mothers had joined in blackberrying expeditions with enthusiasm, and how it had helped them adjust to life in the countryside. There was no doubt that life here was a sharp contrast to what it was like in the city, and it was best to embrace those differences if the evacuees were to settle in and live here happily.

Thea couldn't provide the home that the children had been used to with their parents in London, and there was no point in even trying – but what she *could* do was give them a new home that was kind, caring and reflected the countryside ways around them.

'Just you wait until you taste these chestnuts later,' Thea said. 'They'll be even more delicious for having picked them yourself.'

'Are we having some for tea?' George asked.

'Definitely!' Thea laughed. 'So let's collect enough and then we can go and see if we can find any conkers to have a game with later.'

'What's conkers?' Betty asked.

'They are the seeds from the horse chestnut tree – they're bigger than these ones, and you can't eat them, but you can play a game with them,' Thea explained. 'I'll show you. I used to love playing conkers when I was small.'

Having children to look after was giving Thea a chance to revisit things she hadn't done for years. Never having had children of her own she'd missed out on this, but now with George and Betty to care for, she could. It would be fun to show them and play again. Taking on the evacuee children wasn't just about the extra work and responsibility – it was also an opportunity for them all to have fun together, as she would have done if she'd had children of her own.

CHAPTER 23

Evie and Hazel were working together changing the bedding in Dining Room Ward. It was quiet in here as the mobile patients were either in the recreation room or had gone out for a walk making the most of the fine November day. Matron Reed encouraged those men who were able to get outside to go for some exercise and they sometimes ventured into the village, where they were always made welcome, standing out from the locals as they wore their hospital blue uniform.

'Are you going to the social afternoon at the village hall tomorrow afternoon?' Hazel asked, pulling off a pillowcase and throwing it into the wicker laundry hamper, then reaching for a clean case and slipping it on to the pillow.

'Yes, I'm planning to. I've heard lots about it from Hettie who I live with – she's helping organise it and it sounds like it should be a good afternoon. I'm lucky it's my day off so I can go.' Evie tucked in the clean bottom sheet she'd just spread over the bed, making sure it looked neat, with hospital approved corners, as she knew Matron would be checking later when she inspected the ward.

Hazel sighed. 'I wish it was my day off too. I'm hoping Matron will allow me to accompany some of our patients to the social.'

Evie smiled sympathetically at her friend. 'I hope you can come along. It should be fun.'

At the sound of chesty coughing from the far end of the ward, Evie turned to look at Private Sullivan who still spent most of his time in bed due to his injuries. She didn't like the sound of that cough and he didn't have it yesterday.

'I'll be back in a minute, just want to check he's all right,' Evie whispered to Hazel before heading over to the young soldier's bed.

He lay with his eyes closed, his covers tucked tightly around him. Despite that, he was shivering. Alarm bells sounded in Evie's head – she didn't like the look of him – his face had a ghostly pallor, apart from a pink splotch blooming on each cheek, and a film of sweat slicked his brow.

Evie reached out and touched his forehead. It was hot.

Private Sullivan opened his eyes and looked at her, managing a weak smile.

'It's time to take your temperature and pulse,' Evie said even though that wasn't due for a while yet.

Private Sullivan obligingly opened his mouth as Evie gently placed the thermometer under his tongue, and then she took hold of his wrist to take his pulse while his temperature registered. His heart rate was much faster than normal. After recording it on the chart at the end of Private Sullivan's bed, Evie removed the thermometer from his mouth and saw that his temperature was high, as she'd suspected.

'How are you feeling?' she asked as she plotted his temperature on the chart, where she could see that it had gone up since this morning.

Private Sullivan frowned. 'Not so good, to be honest, Nurse.' He coughed, wincing as he put a hand on his chest.

'Are you in pain?' Evie asked, as Hazel came and looked at Private Sullivan's chart.

He nodded. 'My chest's feeling sore, hurts when I cough.'

'I think we ought to get the doctor to come and have a look at you.' Evie glanced at Hazel who nodded in agreement. 'Matron will need to telephone for him to come,' she added. The hospital didn't have its own in-house doctor but called in the local one when needed.

'Shall I go and ask Matron?' Hazel asked. 'Or do you want to go?'

'No, you go. I'll get a cloth and some tepid water to bathe Private Sullivan's forehead and try and get his temperature down.'

When Evie returned to the young soldier's bedside a few minutes later with a bowl of water and a cloth, he was still shivering and yet sweating, his body wracked with fever. She dipped the cloth into the tepid water, wrung it out then gently placed it on his forehead.

'Thank you,' he croaked. 'Sit down.' He patted his bed motioning for her to sit beside him.

'We're not supposed to sit on patient's beds,' Evie said.

'Please, just for a minute or two, otherwise I'm having to look up at you and my neck aches.'

Evie looked around and checked, but she was the only nurse on the ward. 'All right then, but not for long.' She perched on the side of his bed and took hold of his hand, which felt hot in hers.

'Do you like being a nurse?' he asked.

Evie nodded. 'Very much, and now I'm allowed to nurse patients again, like I used to back in London, I'm enjoying it much more than my first weeks here. It's a happy place to be, lots of laughter and banter amongst you men and good-hearted teasing of us nurses.'

Private Sullivan managed a smile and then began to cough again, his face wincing in pain.

'Nurse Jones!' Matron's loud voice made Evie jump and she glanced over her shoulder to see the older woman standing in the doorway with Hazel beside her. 'What on *earth* do you think you are doing?'

Evie leapt to her feet. 'I'm bathing Private Sullivan's head to bring his temperature down.' Her stomach clenched tightly as Matron marched down the ward towards her, her eyes flashing with anger. The look of fury on the older woman's face triggered memories of other times Evie had been looked at that way, turning her legs to jelly and making her heart pound.

'Go to my office at once! I'll deal with you later,' Matron ordered, then turned to speak to Private Sullivan in a much softer, caring voice as she checked the chart on the end of his bed. 'Let's have a look at you, young man.'

Evie caught Hazel's eyes, her friend silently mouthing the words *Good luck* to her.

Evie nodded briefly and fled, glad to put some distance between her and Matron, and give herself some time to calm down. This wasn't like those other times, she reminded herself. She had just been sitting on a patient's bed, which Evie knew she shouldn't have done. It was bad luck to have been caught by Matron but she needed to focus on the important thing which was that Private Sullivan should be seen by a doctor and as soon as possible. Whatever Matron had to say to Evie about breaking the rules, she would deal with it and not blow it out of perspective by comparing it with what had happened in the past because that had been personal.

Waiting outside Matron's office, Evie received sympathetic looks from other nurses and staff who passed by, all of them having been on the receiving end of Matron's wrath at one time or another. By the time she heard Matron's footsteps coming along the hall, Evie felt calmer, her memories banished to a deep recess of her mind. She was a professional nurse, she kept reminding herself, who had stepped out of line and would be reprimanded. Evie smoothed down her apron and stood up straight ready to face Matron.

'Follow me.' Matron opened the door and went into her office. She sat behind her desk and fixed her beady eyes on Evie.

Evie linked her hands behind her back, squeezing them together as she braced herself for what was to come – all the while painting a neutral expression on her face. She'd learned in the past that it was safest thing to do in these situations.

'I don't want *any* excuses or reasons why you were sitting on a patient's bed, Nurse Jones, and breaking one of our essential rules. The fact is that a nurse should *never*,' Matron raised her voice emphasising the last word, 'sit on the bed. Not only is it unprofessional, it's unhygienic. I will *not* have it in my hospital, do you understand?'

Evie nodded. 'Yes, Matron. It won't happen again.'

'I have a good mind to put you back on bed pan duty in the sluice for a week to give you time to think over your lack of professionalism…' She narrowed her eyes as she glared at Evie. 'But doing so would make us short-staffed on the wards, and for that reason alone, I am prepared to give you another chance. However, if you put one foot out of step, I'll have you back in the sluice before you know it.'

'Yes, Matron.' Evie paused wondering if it was wise to ask

the question she wanted to but deciding to risk it. 'Is the doctor coming to see Private Sullivan?'

'Yes, I telephoned as soon as Nurse Robertson told me about Private Sullivan's fever.' Matron looked concerned. 'You had best return to the ward and continue to attend to him until the doctor arrives.'

'Yes, Matron. Thank you.' Evie turned and quickly left the room, grateful that she wasn't now heading for the sluice and that Matron's wrath had been purely professional and a reaction to the breaking of a hospital rule which existed for a good reason.

Arriving back at Dining Room Ward, she could hear Private Sullivan coughing.

'How is he?' Evie asked Hazel who was changing a nearby bed whilst keeping an eye on the young soldier.

'About the same,' Hazel whispered, her eyes meeting Evie's and sharing a look of concern. Fevers could so easily make a patient seriously ill.

Private Sullivan opened his eyes as Evie approached his bed.

'I'm sorry I got you into trouble asking you to sit on the bed.' His voice was raspy. 'I told Matron it was me that asked you to sit down on account of my aching neck. What did she say?'

'It was fine, I was just reminded of the rules.' Evie touched his shoulder. 'And the doctor will be here soon to have a look at you.' She took the damp cloth off his head, dipped it into the bowl of water standing on top of the bedside locker, squeezed it out and then gently laid it on his feverish forehead again.

'Thank you,' he whispered, then closed his eyes again.

When the doctor arrived nearly an hour later, Matron Reed ushered him onto the ward and instructed Evie and Hazel to leave while the examination took place.

'Doesn't she realise we could learn something by watching the doctor at work?' Hazel muttered, as they headed off to the nurses' sitting room to have a short break.

'We'll find out what he says later.' Evie put her hand on her friend's arm. 'The less time I spend in Matron's company the better.'

'What did she say in her office – did she give you real ticking off?' Hazel asked as they headed along the corridor.

'Luckily for me it would have made the ward short-staffed, otherwise I'd have been back on bed pan duty in the sluice for a week – giving me time to reflect on my error of sitting on a patient's bed,' Evie explained. 'I'll be sure to stick to that rule in future.'

'It was just bad luck she caught you,' Hazel said sympathetically as they went into the nurses' sitting room. 'Right, I need a cup of tea.'

'Private Sullivan has pneumonia and will require careful nursing,' Matron Reed informed Evie and the other nursing staff on duty after the doctor had left.

Evie's stomach clenched at the news – pneumonia was a serious condition.

'Plenty of sleep and rest are essential for his recovery so I've instructed orderlies to move him to the quieter Library Ward. Alongside other treatments, we'll be using poultices to relieve the pain and ease his breathing. He'll need plenty of fluids, light, nourishing food at regular intervals, as much as he will take. The next week or so will be critical for him but

I'm optimistic that we can nurse him through this.' She looked around at them, taking in nods of agreement.

'Nurse Jones and Nurse Robertson, can you see to it that a screen is put up around Private Sullivan's bed once he's settled in Library Ward?'

'Yes, Matron,' Evie and Hazel chorused.

'I will see to a poultice for him. Nurse Heath, you can help me.'

With a nod of her head, Matron Reed turned on her heels with Nurse Heath following.

'Poor lad,' Hazel said, 'pneumonia's the last thing he needs after everything he's been through.'

Evie nodded. 'We'll get him through this.' Although her words were positive, a heaviness filled her heart because pneumonia was a serious illness, and Private Sullivan was still recovering from his injuries, physically and emotionally. Would he have the strength to fight it? The only certain thing was that she would do all she could to nurse him back to health — or at least all she was allowed to do by Matron.

'Come on, let's go and get that screen ready.'

Evie should have gone off duty ten minutes ago but she wanted to check on how Private Sullivan was doing before she left, as it was her day off tomorrow. Walking softly into Library Ward, where only three of the beds were occupied, she headed towards the screened-off bed where the young soldier was being nursed. Peeping around the side of the screen, she saw to her surprise that Matron was sitting beside Private Sullivan's bed, holding the young man's hand.

The older woman must have heard her approach and turned to look at her.

'Shouldn't you be off duty now, nurse,' Matron said softly.

Evie nodded. 'I'm about to go home but I just wanted to check how he is.'

'About the same.' Matron glanced at the sleeping figure of Private Sullivan, whose flushed face clearly showed he still had a fever. 'It's early days yet, but with careful nursing there's no reason he shouldn't recover. You'd best get along now, nurse. Goodnight.' Matron turned back to watch over her patient, dismissing Evie.

'Goodnight.' Evie crept away, amazed at what she'd just witnessed. For all her brusqueness, Matron Reed showed great care for the patients. She could have ordered one of the other nurses to sit with him but instead was doing it herself. And judging by the look on the older woman's face, Evie would say that she was extremely concerned about Private Sullivan. If anyone could get him through this illness, Evie thought, then Matron Reed would. Her strict adherence to nursing regimes and treatments would give him the best possible chance of recovery.

CHAPTER 24

As she turned the page of the book, Thea glanced at Betty and George who lay snuggled up together in their bed, their eyes fixed on her. In the week since they'd come to live here, reading to the children before they went to sleep had quickly become something Thea looked forward to doing each night. She loved the quiet, cosy calmness as they shared the story in the soft light from the lamp.

Prue had given Thea some books that had been donated for the evacuee children and this Enid Blyton story, about three children who'd moved to the country and had adventures with a magical tree, had entranced Betty and George. And Thea was enjoying it very much herself.

'Don't stop!' Betty said, and then smiled encouragingly. 'Please read some more, Auntie Thea.'

She smiled back at the little girl. 'A few more pages and then it's time you went to sleep. It's going to be a busy day tomorrow and you don't want to be tired.'

Tomorrow afternoon The Mother's Day Club was running a social afternoon in the village hall for the evacuee mothers and children, as well as villagers and mobile patients from the hospital up at the Hall. From what she'd heard from Hettie and Marianne, who were involved with the organising, it should be a fun occasion for all ages.

Thea read on, thinking how she'd have enjoyed this book when she was a child — she'd always loved tales of adventure and magic. Now having Betty and George to care for she had a chance to enjoy such things herself.

Reaching the end of the chapter, and a natural point at which to stop although she could so easily have gone on reading right to the end of the story, Thea closed the book. George's eyes were flickering open and shut, as sleep was pulling him in.

Putting the book on the chest of drawers, she quietly kissed first George's and then Betty's cheek. 'Goodnight, sleep tight,' she said softly.

'Night,' George mumbled, his thumb in his mouth.

'Goodnight,' Betty said, snuggling further under the blanket.

Thea pulled the covers further up to their shoulders, then picked up the lamp and headed to the door. She paused and looked back and saw that George was already asleep and Betty not far off.

How her life had changed since this time last week, Thea thought, and yet in a strange way it felt as if the children had always been here. Her worries about how she would manage looking after them with all she had to do had proved fruitless. Even George's bed-wetting, which had lasted for a few nights after he'd arrived, had stopped. It had caused a lot more laundry washing, but everyone had treated him with kindness and understanding and that had reassured him. Now he was dry overnight again which was a sure sign, Hettie said, that the little lad was feeling happy here at Rookery House.

Between them she, Hettie and Marianne were always here or where they needed to be for the children. Today, for instance, Thea had been out with the WVS canteen, so Marianne had met the children from school and brought them home. It was as if they had three extra mothers to care for them here at Rookery House. It wasn't the same as having their own mother with them but, by working together as a team, Thea was happy that they were doing a good job of caring for Betty and George.

Closing the door behind her, Thea headed downstairs to the kitchen where Hettie was sitting in a chair by the warm range, her fingers busy knitting a sock.

'All settled?' Hettie asked, looking up but not stopping her knitting.

'Yes, although we could have carried on with the story, but they're tired and need to sleep.' Thea pulled up a chair from the table and sat near the range opposite Hettie.

'They were pleased with their mother's letter,' Hettie said. 'And it was nice of her to put one in for us as well.'

Thea had helped the children to write to their mother earlier in the week, letting her know where they were living and that they were settling in. Jess had written back to them, and it had arrived in the afternoon post, along with a letter for Marianne from her husband, Alex. Letters were so important these days, keeping those far apart in touch. Thea knew how much Marianne treasured hers, the young woman having only seen her husband once since their marriage back in March as he'd been posted to the other end of the country while he completed another stage of his pilot training.

'I was a bit worried that hearing from their mother might unsettle them,' Thea admitted. 'But they seem happy enough.'

'I think the fact that it's so different here helps,' Hettie said.

'And that they've got several of us looking after them. I do enjoy having them here.'

'So do I. And there I was getting myself worked up about them arriving last weekend.' Thea looked at Hettie and gave a sheepish smile.

'I told you it would be all right.' Hettie chuckled. 'These might be funny old times but there's been a lot of good come from it as well. This old house is full, and the village has blossomed in my reckoning. A dose of new people has shaken up the old stick-in-the-muds for the better. And who knows what else will happen here before the end of the war.'

The door from the hallway opened and Marianne came in.

'Is Emily sleeping again?' Hettie asked.

'Yes, I think she's got another tooth coming through which is bothering her,' Marianne said. 'But she's drifted off now. Shall I put the milk on for some cocoa?'

'Yes please,' Thea said getting up from her chair. 'I'll get the cups ready. I want to hear all about what's happening at the social afternoon tomorrow.'

CHAPTER 25

'Is everybody ready?' Prue asked looking around at the members of The Mother's Day Club who, like her, had spent the morning at the village hall preparing for this afternoon's social event.

'As ready as we'll ever be!' Gloria called from beside the hoopla game which she was in charge of. 'Open the doors and let 'em in.'

'Stand back everyone, watch out for the stampede!' Nancy added with a cheeky wink to Prue.

'In that case...' Prue headed for the door. 'Let the social begin! Have a good time everyone.' She opened the front door of the village hall and was pleased to see that a queue had formed outside. Not only were there evacuee mothers and their children waiting, but members of the village's Women's Institute and other local residents.

'Welcome!' Prue said, throwing the door wide. 'Come in and enjoy yourselves.'

When Evie arrived at the village hall with the others from Rookery House, and peered through the open doors, she was delighted to see that some of the patients from the hospital were already there. Dressed in their hospital uniform – blue woollen jacket and trousers, white shirt and red tie – they stood out from the rest of the villagers. Even better was that the nurse who'd accompanied them was her friend Hazel and Evie was keen to ask her how Private Sullivan was doing.

'Will you look after Emily?' Hettie asked Evie as she took the little girl out of the pram that she'd just parked in the porch. Hettie, Thea and the children, along with Evie, had walked into the village together – Marianne having gone in earlier to help get things ready. 'Only I've promised to help in the kitchen but can't do that with this little one.' Hettie handed over Emily, before Evie could protest. 'I'll see you later, enjoy the afternoon.' She gave Evie an encouraging smile and headed off to the kitchen.

Evie held Emily awkwardly in her arms, not knowing the best way to carry her and scared that she would drop her. The little girl didn't seem bothered by her inexperience and reached out a soft, starfish hand and touched Evie's hair.

'You'll be fine with her,' Thea said, reassuringly. 'If you get in a muddle, Marianne's over there helping with the refreshments.' She nodded to where the end of the hall nearest the kitchen, had been set up like a little teashop, with chairs around small tables. These were already busy with people chatting while they enjoyed tea and buns. 'But I'm sure you'll be fine. If I were you, I'd take Emily around to look at what's going on. I think we'll have a go at the games first, shall we?' Thea directed her question to Betty and George who were patiently holding her hands but looking longingly over to where several of their fellow evacuees from school were laughing as they tried out different games. The children nodded at her eagerly. 'Let's go then.'

Evie watched as Thea and the children headed to the games, wondering what she should do first. She wasn't used to small children like Emily, who was still patting Evie's hair, perhaps because it was so different from her mother's curly brown hair.

'Who's this little one then?' A familiar voice made her turn around to see the smiling face of Corporal Barkham looking up at her from where he sat in his wheelchair, with Hazel pushing him.

'This is Emily – her mother lives at Rookery House where I live. I'm just looking after her for a bit,' Evie explained.

'Can I hold her?' Corporal Barkham asked. 'She reminds me of my little niece, Gracie.'

Evie hesitated 'I'm not sure… What if she knocks your wound?' She gestured towards his injured leg which was hidden under a blanket.

'It will be fine. I'll hold her so she can't touch it and it will do me the world of good to hold a little one for a bit.' He held up his arms to take the little girl and Emily reached her arms out to him.

'Looks like Emily wants to sit with Corporal Barkham,' Hazel said.

Evie gently put Emily onto his lap and stood back to check that the child was well away from his injuries.

'Don't look so worried,' Corporal Barkham said, as Emily grabbed one of his hands and held onto it tightly, while his other arm cradled her securely against his chest. She looked quite comfortable there and began to investigate the red tie of his hospital blue suit, pulling it out from underneath his jacket.

'I'm glad you could come this afternoon,' Evie said turning to Hazel while keeping a watchful eye on Emily.

'So am I,' Hazel agreed. 'It's lovely to get out and about and away from the hospital for a while and it's clearly doing the men good...'

The sound of laughter from one of the mobile patients, who was having a go on the hoopla game, caught their attention for a moment.

'How's Private Sullivan today?' Evie asked, keeping her voice low.

'About the same, no better, but no worse either.' Hazel's eyes met Evie's and a look of understanding passed between them. 'It will take time and he's getting the best care possible. Matron's been doing a lot of the nursing for him.'

'She was with him when I went off duty last night,' Evie said.

Hazel nodded. 'She's very devoted. If anyone can see him through this, it's her.'

Evie had expected Matron to order the nurses to do it while keeping an eagle eye on them and Private Sullivan, but her devotion to doing the nursing herself showed Matron's caring nature beneath her gruff exterior. Knowing that Matron Reed was personally looking after the young soldier was reassuring and for the first time since Evie had left the hospital yesterday, she allowed herself to stop worrying so much.

'Shall we have a go on some of the games?' Evie asked. 'Is there anything that you want to try Corporal Barkham?'

'I'll have a go at the hoopla,' he said looking towards where some of his fellow patients were still enjoying it. 'And you can help me, Emily.'

'Very well then, let's go try your luck,' Hazel said pushing his wheelchair towards the game.

Thea smiled fondly at the look of concentration on George's face, the tip of his tongue peeping out, as he manoeuvred the fishing line into place – moving it slightly this way and that, the string with the hook dangling underneath swinging in a circle, as he tried to catch a bigger fish in the pond marked out in chalk on the floor. Betty was doing the same and had already managed to catch one fish in the game so far.

'Hello, caught any big ones?'

Thea turned to see that Nancy, who lived at Prue's house, had come to stand beside her.

She greeted her with a smile. 'Hello, just the one so far, but we're determined to catch more.'

'It's a good game, provin' popular with the children. So 'ow are you getting on with your new charges?' Nancy asked.

'Good, they've settled in well and we're all getting used to each other. It's not just me looking after them – Hettie and Marianne help too, otherwise I couldn't have managed on my own.'

'You're in the WVS ain't yer, like Prue? She's always busy as well.'

'Yes, we man the mobile canteen together and I do other driving jobs for them as well when needed.'

'I'm glad you could take them in.' Nancy put her hand on Thea's arm and gave a nod of her head indicating that she wanted to say something out of earshot of the children. Thea stepped away from the game to hear what Nancy had to say. 'They've got a good 'ome with you all. Although...' Nancy shook her head and lowering her voice added, 'I think Jess was mad to go back to London. You wouldn't catch me goin' back there – not while the bombers keep on comin', night after night.'

'At least she had the sense to leave the children here.'

'Yes, but she's putting herself at risk to keep an eye on her old man, who otherwise would be goin' astray while 'is wife and children are away in the countryside.' Nancy frowned, folding her arms firmly. 'I wouldn't put myself in danger like that, not for some fella who don't respect me enough to keep to 'is marriage vows if I'm not around to keep an eye on 'im.' She pursed her lips. 'It was worrying about what he's been getting up to behind 'er back that sent Jess back there, and if she comes to any 'arm because of that, leaving them children without a mother…'

Thea put her hand on Nancy's shoulder. 'Shush!' She nodded towards Betty and George, who probably couldn't hear above the hubbub of chatter and laughter in the hall but she didn't want to risk it. 'I didn't know that, but this isn't the place to talk about it.'

Nancy nodded, mollified. 'I know, but it makes my blood boil – I'm worried about her. Have you 'eard from Jess since she went back?'

'Yes, a letter came for them yesterday. We wrote to her at the beginning of the week so the children could tell her where they were and what they've been doing. She wrote back quickly; she hasn't forgotten them.'

'Good. I've written to her as well, but ain't heard nothing yet.'

'Are you happy living here?' Thea asked.

Nancy nodded, a smile lighting up her face. 'I am and so are the girls. We're stayin' put until it's completely safe again to go back. I wouldn't risk it and I know I could trust my 'usband if he was there on his own, which he ain't because he's away in the army – and he's pleased that we're 'ere and safe.'

'I've got one!' George's shout of delight drew Thea's

attention back to him, as he held up the paper fish in his hand, a huge beaming smile lighting up his face.

'Well done, that's marvellous!' Thea patted his shoulder, smiling with him, and delighted to see that he and Betty were enjoying themselves so much.

～

'Ladies and gentlemen, boys and girls, can I have your attention please!' Prue shouted from her position standing on the low platform at one end of the village hall.

'Let the woman speak!' A man's voice called out, one of the patients from the hospital who from the tone and volume of his shout was probably used to bellowing at soldiers.

The hall quickly fell silent, all eyes turning to look at Prue.

'I hope you've all had an enjoyable and fun time at our social afternoon, the first of many I hope.'

Cheers filled the hall, echoing a shared sentiment that there should be more such events.

'I want to thank the members of The Mother's Day Club for their hard work organising this afternoon. It's very much appreciated.'

'Three cheers for The Mother's Day Club ladies,' one of the patients from the hospital called out. 'Hip hip...'

'Hooray!' Everyone chorused back.

When the last of the cheers had died away, Prue continued. 'We'd like to end this afternoon's event with a sing-song. Mrs Platten, whom some of you will know is Quartermaster at the hospital, has kindly offered to play for us.' Prue swept her arm in the direction of Rosalind Platten, who was seated at the piano.

Rosalind smiled graciously, then turned and began to play a tune that needed no introduction.

As everyone began to sing the familiar words of *Daisy Bell*, their voices mixing – the deeper men's, higher women's and children's – it created a delightful sound that swirled and filled the village hall to the rafters. Looking around the faces as they sang, Prue was pleased to see the look of enjoyment everywhere. She loved the way singing had that almost magical property of rousing spirits and lifting singers out of their everyday life for a short refreshing while. It was the perfect ending to a successful afternoon, which she very much hoped would be the first of many more, bringing together so many people from the village, both long-time residents and newcomers too.

CHAPTER 26

Back at Great Plumstead Hall Hospital after her day off, Evie hurried along the corridor to the morning briefing where the incoming day-shift nurses would receive their orders and be updated, ready to take over from the night shift. She'd just reached the door of the nurses' sitting room when she heard Matron's quick footsteps clicking along the corridor's tiled floor and slipped inside, grateful that she was just in time.

Inside the room, Evie was instantly aware of the sombre mood of the other nurses – she'd grown adept at picking up these signals having come to rely on them in the past. They'd often given her warning of what was to come and occasionally had allowed her to avoid difficult situations. But before anybody could say anything the door opened and Matron Reed came in.

'Good morning.' Matron glanced round at them all, checking everyone was present who should be. She paused for a few moments, a shadow passing across her tired face before she quickly regained her usual professional composure. 'For those of you who don't yet know, I'm sorry to report that Private Sullivan died half an hour ago.'

Evie couldn't stop the gasp that escaped her. She clamped her hand over her mouth and looked down at the floor, fighting back tears. He'd been stable yesterday when she'd asked Hazel about him at the social afternoon. Evie had been thinking about Private Sullivan during her day off and had been relieved to hear that he was no worse.

Matron ignored Evie's reaction and added, 'His condition was serious but stable until a little after midnight when it began to deteriorate. We did everything we could but...' She sighed heavily. 'The pneumonia was too much for him.'

Evie forced her face into a suitable expression, one that showed sorrow but kept her tears in check, letting only her hands, tightly clasped together behind her back, express how she felt. Looking around at her fellow nurses, she could see that the young soldier's death had affected them too. He'd been a lovely young man and everyone was saddened by his untimely death.

'We need to perform the last offices for Private Sullivan so does anyone here have experience of laying out a deceased patient? I need someone to help me who already knows what to do – I'm too tired to have to teach anyone how to do it this morning.' Matron gazed at them and nodded when one of the night nurses raised her hand.

Evie didn't want to but it wouldn't be fair to ask a colleague who'd just done a twelve-hour shift to stay longer so she raised her hand too. She had experience of laying out patients who'd died from injuries sustained in air raids when she was working in London.

'Right, Nurse Jones, you will assist me then,' Matron said nodding at her, and then quickly ran through the update on the rest of their patients and assigned the other nurses coming on duty their tasks for the morning.

∼

Matron Reed was waiting in the doorway of Library Ward when Evie arrived with a trolley set up with equipment a short while later. The older woman's eyes quickly scanned over everything Evie had set out and, satisfied that everything they'd need was present, led the way to where Private Sullivan's bed was screened off from the rest of the bed-bound patients in the ward.

She braced herself as Matron moved one of the screens aside so that Evie could wheel the trolley into the closed-off area. She had seen dead patients before but the sight of the young soldier's still form, shrouded by a sheet, shook her. Aware that Matron was behind her, drawing the screen closed, Evie forced herself to appear calm and professional, ignoring the churning of her stomach and the heavy weight that had settled in her chest since hearing the news of his death.

'A terrible waste of a young life.' Matron shook her head and then looked at Evie, their eyes meeting. 'We have to control our emotions and be strong. It's no good breaking down.' Her tone was soft and gentle. 'Let's do our best for this young man.'

Evie nodded, glad to see this glimpse of a softer person. 'Yes, Matron.'

Together they worked in silence, gently doing the necessary tasks to prepare the young man for burial – washing him, combing his hair, trimming his nails and applying clean dressings to his wounds.

As she did each task, images of Private Sullivan alive

flickered through Evie's mind like a film at the pictures. She'd never known him in full health, only as a wounded patient, but he had been a gentle soul traumatised by his experiences. She'd hoped that he would heal and be allowed home, his fighting days done… but pneumonia had put paid to that and now it would never happen.

'There.' Matron's voice brought Evie's thoughts back to the present as they finished dressing him in a clean gown. 'We've done all we can for him.' She drew a clean sheet up over him.

No more nightmares for him, Evie thought as Matron covered his face which would be for ever still and at peace.

'Thank you, Nurse Jones, you did a good job. I'll wait here with him until the orderlies come.' Matron nodded at Evie and moved a screen aside for her to leave.

Evie glanced at the shrouded figure for the last time and then wheeled the equipment trolley out through the gap in the screens, biting her bottom lip to keep tears at bay – there was no place for them here – she must be professional.

Evie stood in a line of nurses, watching with heads bowed as Private Sullivan was carried out of the ward, past bed-bound patients who saluted their lost comrade as best they could. The stretcher on which he lay was covered with a Union Jack flag and a forage cap was laid on his chest. The orderlies walked slowly, their leather boots creaking with each step, the ward otherwise silent, patients and all the staff showing their respects.

Evie blinked away the tears that stubbornly still smarted in her eyes, despite the way she clasped her hands tightly behind her back. And from the sharp intakes of breath from either side of her, she was not the only one feeling such emotions.

Once the cortège had passed by and out into the hallway and the front door was heard closing behind it, Matron addressed them all. 'It's been a sad day for us, but we are professionals and must carry on. You will have jobs to do.' With a curt nod of her head, she turned on her heels and headed for her office.

Evie glanced at her fellow nurses who, like her, stood still for a few moments longer before Nurse Heath broke the silence.

'We'd better get on.' Nurse Heath sighed heavily, then headed off to begin her next task.

Evie pulled herself together: she had dressings to see to, tending to living patients who still needed her care. Life went on within the hospital, as it always did after a patient died, but the memory of them would remain. Private Sullivan may be gone, but he would live on in her memory and that of all who had known and liked him here.

CHAPTER 27

Thea pulled the sheet and blankets up, tucking them around Betty and George who lay snuggled up together, fast asleep, their breathing soft and steady. The eiderdown had slipped halfway off the bed, and she gently repositioned it, so that it covered them once more. Stepping back, she looked down at the two young evacuees, who'd insisted on sleeping together, not wanting to lay top to toe, or even have a bunk bed made for them, which Reuben had offered to do. The pair gained comfort from being together as it hadn't been easy for them with their mother leaving, but they were settling in well and growing in confidence each day. Their mother still wrote to them regularly and the children, with Thea's help, wrote back to her.

Satisfied that they were fine, Thea tiptoed out of the room, closed the door quietly behind her and headed for her own room as it was getting late. She was tired and ready for some much-needed sleep as she'd had a busy day working in the garden. Passing by Evie's room, she thought she heard sobbing, and halted to listen. It was definitely coming from the young nurse's room; Evie was clearly upset. Thea had noticed she'd looked pale when she'd returned from her shift earlier and had only picked at her evening meal which was unlike her. But she'd offered no explanation when Hettie had asked her if anything was wrong, merely saying she had a headache and was heading up to bed early.

Thea tapped lightly on Evie's door, not wanting to wake the others in their rooms.

She waited, aware that the sobbing had stopped but Evie hadn't answered the door. Debating whether to knock again or leave Evie for now, Thea's decision was made for her when the door opened a little way and Evie's face peered out, lit by the soft glow of Thea's candle.

'Are you all right?' Thea asked. 'Only it sounded like you were crying.'

Evie didn't answer straight away. 'I was,' she whispered, averting her eyes.

'Can I help you? Is there anything I can do?' Thea paused. 'Do you want to talk about it?'

Evie hesitated and Thea thought she was going to decline, as the young woman, although always polite and pleasant, had a reserved manner about her.

'Thank you.' Evie opened her bedroom door and motioned for Thea to come in, then closed the door behind them.

'What's happened, what's wrong?' Thea asked.

'One of our patients died today,' Evie said, her voice catching. She pushed her hands deep into her woollen dressing gown's pockets and began to pace around the bedroom which was now bathed in pale candlelight, making shadows flicker on the wall.

'I'm sorry to hear that. It must be hard to lose a patient,' Thea said sympathetically.

'It is... but with Private Sullivan it feels so...', Evie stopped pacing and threw her hands out wide, shaking her head. 'He was only *eighteen* and had been through so much – he was the only one of his unit who survived an attack. Whatever happened to them haunted his dreams.' Evie sighed heavily. 'It wasn't his injuries that killed him – it was pneumonia.' She dashed away tears with the back of her hand. 'It was so unfair. He should have recovered and gone home, his war over.'

Thea stepped towards the young woman and put a hand on Evie's arm. 'After all he'd been through, he deserved to go home.'

Evie nodded. 'Life is so bloody unfair sometimes.' Her voice was gruff with emotion.

Thea put the candle holder on the bedside table, gathered Evie in her arms and held her while the young woman sobbed.

'I'm sorry.' Evie stepped back after a while when her sobs had subsided, grabbing a clean handkerchief out of her chest of drawers, and wiping her face. 'You must think me terribly silly. It's not as if I knew Private Sullivan very well, or that he was family… but sometimes it's hard to bear the way life twists and turns. It often doesn't deal out the fate people deserve and especially now in this hideous war.'

'I don't think you're silly at all,' Thea said gently. In fact, she thought seeing Evie showing more emotion was a good thing, although Thea wouldn't ever say that to her. 'And you're right, life doesn't always deal out the hand that people deserve, quite the opposite in fact in my experience. In wartime that sadly becomes more frequent.'

Evie plonked herself down on her bed, making the springs creak, and clasped her hands tightly on her lap.

'I was caught out in an air raid and the young woman whom I'd been sitting next to on the bus was killed by a bomb, a direct hit… She was on her way to the shelter…' Evie paused for a few moments, biting her bottom lip as more tears slipped silently down her face. 'She'd been so full of *joy* and excitement on the bus, telling me how she was leaving London to join the WAAF the next day... but then her life was senselessly wiped out in an instant.' Evie took a deep breath. 'I could easily have been killed too – you see I was with her heading for the underground, but then I remembered that I'd left my case on the bus and went back for it. The bomb fell on her while I was gone... and there was nothing left of her except her handbag.' She fell silent for a few moments before carrying on. 'It wasn't fair what happened to that young woman. It made me realise how precious life is and how it shouldn't be wasted.'

'I'm sorry, that must have been terrible,' Thea said, going to stand next to the bed and putting her hand on Evie's shoulder. 'It's just chance where somebody is and where the bomb falls – it makes the difference between life and death in an air raid.'

'I would have been killed that night too if I hadn't forgotten my case...' Evie twisted the handkerchief in her hands. 'It felt like I'd been given another chance and made me think about what I *really* wanted to do with my life. It was then that I decided to volunteer to become a mobile VAD, which brought me here and to a new job.'

'None of us know how our life will twist and turn and in which direction it will take us,' Thea said. 'All we can do is learn from our experiences, the good ones *and* the bad, and make sound choices based on them. I'm glad that you made the decision to come here. I hope that you're happy living at Rookery House.'

Evie looked up at Thea, their eyes meeting. 'I am, I love it here at Rookery House with you all... I feel like I've finally come home. I enjoy working at the hospital, mostly, apart from what happened today. But none of this would have happened if I hadn't caught that bus, sat next to that woman, if the air-raid siren hadn't gone off when it did and so on…' She motioned with her hand.

'Something good came from something bad,' Thea said, then added kindly, 'I'm always here to talk to if you want.'

'I appreciate that.' Evie smiled gratefully at her. 'Thank you for listening to me.'

'Anytime. But if you're all right now then I should get to bed.'

'I feel much better now,' Evie said.

Thea picked up her candle holder and headed for the door. 'Goodnight then.'

'Goodnight and thank you again.'

As Thea made her way along the landing to her own room, she was glad that Evie had opened up to her a little. She had the feeling there was still much more to Evie Jones than she had let on, although quite what it was, Thea didn't know. Perhaps with time the young woman would grow confident enough to share whatever it was that kept her so reserved and wary looking sometimes.

CHAPTER 28

'Ugh! I'm not eating that!' Victor declared loudly.

Prue spun around from the sink where she was filling up the kettle in time to see Victor shove his bowl of porridge into the middle of the table.

'What's wrong with it?' she asked.

'It's got salt in it again!' Victor snapped. 'That blasted woman's been making the porridge again. I told you, Prudence, No... Salt... In... The... Porridge.' He punctuated these words with staccato stabs of his index finger on to the kitchen table, his cheeks and neck growing mottled with red splotches.

Prue had an urge to laugh at his behaviour, which was more on par with a toddler having a tantrum than an adult. It was an improvement she supposed on the normal rage which he'd have flown into before Nancy had come to live here. These days he tried to make his outbursts of temper quieter, though they were absolutely clear in their meaning.

Alice leaned across from her side of the table and took his

bowl. 'Well, if you don't want it, then I'll have it.' She used her spoon to scrape his porridge into her own bowl. 'I'm surprised you could even taste the salt with the amount of honey you've put on it.'

'I didn't know it was salty then.' Victor reached over and grabbed the breadboard with the loaf on top. 'If I'd known *that woman* had made the porridge this morning, I'd never have touched it. I don't know why she has to put salt in it – it's horrible.'

'Nancy's mother was Scottish,' Prue explained, relieved that Nancy was upstairs getting her girls ready. 'So it's how she grew up eating it.'

'I rather like it, especially with some honey, makes a delicious sweet and salty combination,' Alice said, scooping up another spoonful of porridge.

Victor harrumphed as he attempted to saw a slice off the loaf, making a mess of it.

'Give it here, I'll do it.' Prue took the bread knife from him and deftly sliced the end Victor had been hacking at from the loaf, and then cut another neat slice, placing them both on a plate and passing it to him.

Without a word of thanks, he spread some of Hettie's home-made butter, followed by some jam, on both pieces and began to eat noisily, slurping at his tea between mouthfuls.

Dishing up a bowl of porridge for herself, Prue sat down at the table and added a spoonful of honey from Thea's bees and mixed it in. She really didn't mind whether the porridge was salty or not – she was just grateful that Nancy helped with the cooking, especially on days like today when she was going out with the WVS canteen. Victor had never helped her with the cooking, not once in all the years they'd been married.

As she ate, Prue was thankful that Nancy and her

daughters had missed witnessing Victor's little outburst over the salty porridge. Not that it would have particularly upset Nancy, who was more than capable of dealing with Victor. Although since she'd come to live here, Nancy and Victor had had very little to do with each other, partly Prue suspected because Victor, like all bullies, knew she wouldn't put up with any nonsense from him. These days he spent less time in the communal areas of the house when he was at home, only coming into the kitchen for meals and for the minimum amount of time – the rest he spent holed up in his study. Prue was quite happy with this arrangement, the less time she spent in her husband's company, the better.

It didn't take Victor long to eat his bread and jam and slurp his tea. 'I have a meeting tonight, so won't be home for tea,' he said standing up.

'Very well,' Prue said.

Not bothering to say goodbye Victor stalked out of the kitchen, and a few moments later Prue heard the front door bang behind him, and she sighed with relief.

'I don't know why he hasn't learned to try a small spoonful out of the saucepan first — check he likes it before he helps himself to a bowlful.' Alice grinned.

'I have told Nancy about the salt, but I suppose she forgot – it's the way she's been making it all these years.' Prue took a sip of her tea. 'I quite like it for a change, we don't have it that way every day, it depends on who's making it and if they forget the salt or not! I just appreciate someone else making it instead of me having to do it all the time.'

'Perhaps Father should take a turn making it then,' Alice suggested.

Prue raised her eyebrows. 'That would be a sight worth seeing. Though I suspect if he did, then it would taste burnt rather than salty.' Prue glanced at the clock on the dresser. 'I need to get ready. I'm going out with Thea in the WVS canteen so mustn't be late.'

She got up from the table and put her bowl in the sink, Nancy having said that she'd see to the washing up later.

Passing by Alice, she stopped to plop a kiss on her hair, resting her hands on her daughter's shoulders for a moment. 'You handle your father very well, you know. He's not an easy man to deal with.'

Alice turned in her seat and looked up at Prue. 'I'm glad he doesn't get to you so much any more Ma. Why's that?'

'I suppose I'm busier these days and have more important things to think about – no time to dwell on his silly ways.' That was partly true, Prue thought, but also his betrayal of her with his mistress in Norwich had deflated his power over her and it was truly liberating after years of worrying and treading on eggshells around him. There was no way that Prue was ever going back to that. 'I'll see you later then, have a good day.'

'You too, Ma,' Alice said.

'Salty!' Thea burst out laughing. 'I bet Victor wasn't amused.'

Thea took the tray of delicious-smelling meat pies that Prue handed up to her and stowed it safely in the back of the WVS canteen, with the freshly made sandwiches and currant buns they'd already loaded aboard. They were at the depot in Wykeham, provisioning the canteen ready to take it out.

'No, he wasn't.' Prue's face broke into a grin. 'But I was. It's not the first time it's happened. If only he'd bothered to check first before he helped himself to a large serving, then he wouldn't get in such a temper about it.'

'Not a great start to the day for you then – Victor blowing his top.' Thea looked at her sister who was, like her, dressed in her green WVS uniform. Prue had climbed inside the canteen and was now topping up one of the urns with fresh water.

'The only person he upset was himself. Victor getting cross doesn't bother me the way it used to – I'm more immune to it these days.' Prue put the lid back on the full urn. 'There, that's done.'

Thea leaned back against the counter running along one side of the canteen and regarded her sister. 'You've come a long way since last autumn, you know. You've changed and it's good to see.'

Prue's eyes met Thea's. 'In what way?'

'You're like a different person in some respects, and the best thing is that you're... well, sort of free of Victor's domineering ways. I know he's still your husband and you live in the same house, but he doesn't seem to affect you the way he used to.'

Prue nodded. 'You're right, he doesn't, not after what he did to Edwin and after Lizzie discovered his dirty little secret. He can shout, stamp, poke his finger at the table like he did this morning, but it feels like water off a duck's back to me these days.' She reached out and touched Thea's arm. 'And you're right, I do feel free of him. I only wish it hadn't taken me this long.'

Thea put her arm around her sister's shoulders. 'We can only do what we can at the time – it's what you do now and in the future that's important. The past is gone, you can't touch it or change it, only learn from it.'

'You're right, thank you.' Prue leaned her head against Thea's shoulder for a moment. 'I'm glad you came back to live at Rookery House.'

'So am I.' Thea blinked away sudden tears, recalling that

one of the reasons for coming back to live in the village was to keep an eye on Prue as she was worried about her. 'Right, we need to get this canteen on the road – there are troops expecting us.'

~

Arriving at their first stop of the day, a searchlight detachment which was sited several miles from the nearest village, Prue waved out of the passenger window as they drove in through the gateway of the field. She signalled to the servicemen, by holding up her outstretched hands, that it would be ten minutes before they'd be able to open the canteen ready for business. The soldiers knew the routine and would always be there waiting outside the hatch when they opened up.

'Here we are again,' Thea said, pulling on the handbrake and switching off the engine. 'Let's get to work.'

Between them they quickly prepared to open, putting pies in the oven to warm through, turning the urns on for hot water, one for making tea and the other for soup. Plates and cups were taken out from the drawers where they were stored in little compartments for travelling.

'I had a letter from Edwin yesterday,' Prue said, adding cubes to one of the hot water urns to make tomato-flavoured soup. 'He sounded cheerful and is still enjoying what he's doing.' She sighed. 'It should help that he's happy, but it doesn't stop me from worrying about him. I wish he was working somewhere else than London, somewhere much safer.'

'I know,' Thea said, sympathetically, as she set cups out along the counter. 'But he's happy and purposeful. And even if a conscientious objector like Edwin, or a serviceman, is stationed out of a danger zone, it's no guarantee that they're completely safe from harm.'

Prue put her hand on Thea's arm. 'What do you mean?'

'Well, there are no guarantees in life are there? Regardless of whether enemy bombers are dropping bombs over where you are or not.' Thea shook her head. 'One of Evie's patients at the hospital died yesterday morning.'

'Oh no! Did he come to the social afternoon?' Prue asked.

'No, he was too ill to go. He was in the hospital because of his injuries but, unfortunately, he caught pneumonia and died. He was only eighteen.'

Prue gasped, putting a hand over her mouth. 'Oh, that's awful, to survive being injured and then…'

'Yes, Evie was very upset about it. I imagine his family would have thought he was safe now he was back in England and in hospital, so to have him snatched away so cruelly…'

Prue looked serious. 'It makes you think, there are no guarantees in life for any of us – we need to stop more and appreciate each day we're given, celebrate what we have.' She paused for a moment. 'We should do something.'

'What do you mean?' Thea asked.

'We need to celebrate the good in our lives more, not just carry on day after day. We haven't seen Lizzie since she got her new job working at the Land Army office – it's been several weeks now. That deserves celebrating.'

'I know, but she's been too busy to come over – she has to work on a Saturday because it's market day when a lot of the land girls go into Norwich and need help.'

'Well in that case, we should go to her. We can go to Norwich and celebrate there; it would be a day out for us and be fun.'

Thea smiled at her sister. 'All right then, why not? I'll

telephone Lizzie and arrange something. Now...' She cocked her head to one side listening. 'Unless I'm very much mistaken, we have customers waiting outside. Check the water's boiling in the urns and I'll open up the hatch and get this canteen ready for business.'

CHAPTER 29

Thea climbed into the train compartment, closed the door and sat down next to the window opposite Prue. She was looking forward to a day out in Norwich – it was ages since she'd last been there. Leaning back against the springy seat, she sighed.

'What was that for?' Prue asked looking at her, as the guard's whistle blasted outside on the platform of Great Plumstead's station, and moments later the train began to move, smoke billowing past the window as it picked up speed.

'Just feeling happy to be having a day off and be going out,' Thea said. Her eyes met her sister's. 'It feels wonderful.'

Prue nodded. 'I know what you mean; it's been a busy time. We've all got lots going on in our lives. But we can forget about that for today – we're off to enjoy ourselves, have a wander around the shops and then afternoon tea with Lizzie to celebrate her new job. I'm very impressed that she's moved jobs to do something more important for the war effort than working in the accounts office of Curls department store.'

'She seems to be liking it so far – it's a big change for her.' Thea was glad that Prue approved of their younger sister's new job. Prue and Lizzie had a rocky relationship, the pair of them often clashing as they were so different, and Thea had found herself acting as peacemaker between them many a time.

They fell silent each looking out of the window at the passing landscape, which had a stark winter beauty under a clear blue sky, the leafless trees reaching upwards, the countryside settled into its dormant phase.

Thea loved observing the passing of the seasons – it was something she'd missed while she was living in London. Of course, seasons still occurred in the city, but there they seemed incidental, unlike here in the countryside where the changes went on all around you and couldn't be missed. Looking back, she sometimes wondered how she'd managed to live there for so long, but then she'd been busy, building up her business which had occupied so much of her time.

The gentle rhythm of the train lulled Thea into a sleepy state, her eyelids growing heavy. The week's busy work, combined with a couple of nights' disturbed sleep when the air-raid siren in Wykeham had gone off in the early hours, sending them traipsing out to the Anderson shelter only for the all-clear to go again half an hour later, had left her feeling weary. Every time that happened it was always hard to get back to sleep again. So now, sitting comfortably and having nothing to do but gaze out of the window, the train's gentle motion rocking her towards sleep, Thea gave in and let herself drift off thinking a nap would set her up for the day in Norwich.

'Wake up!'

Prue's shrill voice seeped into Thea's sleep, and a rough shaking of her shoulder brought her back to consciousness.

Blinking her eyes, she frowned at her sister whose look of

terror acted like a splash of cold water on Thea's face. 'What's the matter?'

'That!' Prue pointed out of the window to where a plane was banking around in the distance, low over the fields. 'It's an enemy plane and it's coming back for another go at us!' Prue shrieked.

The sound of the plane's engines grew steadily louder and there was no doubt that it was heading towards the train. Moments later they heard bullets pattering down outside and instinctively ducked, throwing themselves onto the floor into the gap between the two rows of seats in their compartment. Thankfully the bullets had missed the train, as the track had snaked around a bend in the line. The sound of the plane grew louder and with a rushing roar of throbbing engines it tore overhead.

'What happened before? Did it shoot the first time?' Thea asked raising her head to look at her sister.

'Yes. It happened so quickly, caught us unaware. I was surprised you slept through it!'

Thea pulled herself up to a crouching position, peeping out of the window, where she could see the plane banking around in a wide arc – it clearly wasn't done with them yet.

'We're stopping!' Prue's eyes were wide with alarm as the train jolted to a halt with a squeal of brakes and hiss of steam close to where the track was bordered by woodland. 'We'll be like sitting ducks.'

'Not necessarily,' Thea said spotting doors either side of their compartment opening and people climbing out. 'If the plane is aiming for the train, then we'd be better out of it.' She scrambled to her feet, pulled Prue up, then pushed open the compartment door and climbed out, jumping down onto the stony ground of the railway track. Reaching out to take Prue's hand as she leapt down behind her, she was aware of the plane's engines in the distance as it circled round ready to begin its next attack.

Around them other passengers were scrambling down, and Thea noticed the guard helping a mother with three small children out of the next compartment. The mother's face was etched with fear as she hurried her children along, with one in her arms, the other two stumbling down the embankment beside her. Thea imagined how it would feel if Betty and George were with her... Her chest tightened... she had to help them as there was no way they could reach the safety of the trees before the plane returned. The wood was only a matter of twenty yards away, but the plane's engines were growing louder – it could fly much faster than the children could run.

Thea rushed over and picked up one of the children, Prue did the same, and with the mother following close behind carrying the smallest child in her arms, they ran for safety.

'Get into the wood, and *hurry!*' the guard bellowed to the fleeing passengers.

The hairs on the back of Thea's neck stood up, and her heart banged hard in her chest as she stumbled over the uneven ground, holding on to the little girl whose arms were flung tightly around her neck as she buried her face against Thea to block out what was happening. Thea was aware of her sister running close by, along with many others from the train.

Never had Thea been so grateful to step into woodland before – she kept going until she was a good way in, putting as much distance between her and the train target as she could.

'Get down!' A man's voice roared, and Thea dropped to the ground, shielding the little girl in her arms as the staccato rattle of the plane's machine gun strafing the train with bullets echoed around. Lying on the floor of the wood, Thea smelt the earthy scent of fallen leaves and noticed a beetle scuttling around the base of a nearby tree, quite oblivious to the terror in the sky.

Once the plane had passed over, the sound of its engine receding, someone shouted out, 'Is anyone hurt?'

Thea sat up and looked around her, others were doing the same. Thankfully none of the bullets had hit anybody, the pilot had been aiming for the train.

Scrambling to her feet, Thea led the little girl over to her mother, who sat cradling her other two children in her arms.

'Thank you,' the mother said, her eyes brimming with tears as she opened her arms to welcome the little girl who had started to sob. 'I'd still have been out there in the open with them if I'd had to get them in here on my own.'

'I'm glad we could help.' Thea smiled at the mother and then went over to where Prue sat leaning against the trunk of a beech tree. 'Are you all right?'

Prue nodded, although the expression on her face didn't match her actions. Her bottom lip was quivering, her face pale and drawn.

Thea sat down beside her sister and put her arm around her. 'This isn't what we planned for our trip to Norwich.'

'It's coming in again, get down!' someone shouted as the noise of the plane's engines grew louder and once again Thea lay on the floor of the wood, this time holding on to Prue's hand as her sister lay beside her.

The enemy plane had six more goes at attacking the Norwich train before it was chased off by the arrival of two Spitfires, the roar of their throaty engines met with cheers of relief from the passengers.

'I hope they shoot the bugger down,' an old man shouted, shaking his fist in the air as people began to head back towards the train.

'Hear, hear!' Several other passengers called in agreement.

Thea tucked her arm through Prue's as they made their way out of the wood to where the passengers were gathering on the track.

'The fireman's been hit by a bullet, but he's all right,' the guard said passing along the length of the train checking that everybody was in one piece. 'We'll get you all back on board and get to Norwich.'

It took a while for everyone to clamber in again, it being harder to board a train from the low level of the track compared with stepping in from a platform. Older and younger passengers needed help, but once everybody was safely on the train once more, the guard blew his whistle, and they resumed their journey to Norwich.

Back in the compartment where they'd abandoned their bags in the hurry to escape, Thea looked at her sister, whose face had regained its colour, and whom she noticed had a swipe of earth across her cheek from the woodland floor.

'How are you feeling?' Thea asked.

Prue took a deep breath before replying. 'Shaken up...' Her voice wobbled. 'We could all have been killed.'

Thea nodded. 'But we weren't. I know it was scary, Prue, but let's not allow it to spoil our day. You probably just want to go home as soon as possible now, but I think we should carry on and do exactly as we'd planned. We should *celebrate* the fact that we came through it, we survived and so did everybody else on this train. If nothing else, it should teach us to enjoy every day that we have.'

Prue's eyes brimmed with tears, and she pulled a clean handkerchief out of her handbag and used it to dab at her eyes. 'I can still hear the sound of the plane's engines coming in, and the spray of its machine-gun bullets...'

Thea reached across and took her sister's hand in hers. 'It will get easier with time, I promise you. I had a few memorable and hair-raising moments in France during the Great War. We won't forget what happened today, but you'll learn to move on from it.'

Prue sniffed, nodding her head. Sticking her chin out she said, 'If I let it spoil today and keep on upsetting me, then that's like letting the enemy win and I'm *not* having that. I've got too much to do.' She managed a watery smile.

Thea squeezed her sister's hand. 'I'm glad to hear it. So let's enjoy the day we'd planned.'

~

'Blimey!' Lizzie said, putting a hand over her mouth after Thea and Prue had finished describing their eventful journey into Norwich. 'Nowhere is safe these days! I'm glad you're both all right and that no one was badly hurt or worse.'

They were sitting in a busy tea shop in the centre of Norwich having met Lizzie on her afternoon off.

'It would probably have been a different story if we'd stayed on the train,' Prue said. 'There were bullet holes in the carriages.'

'Let's not dwell on what could have happened – let's just be grateful it didn't!' Thea reached for a sandwich off the tiered stand the waitress had brought them. 'Tell us about your new job, what's it like working as County Secretary for the Land Army?'

Lizzie's red lipsticked lips broke into a wide smile. 'Marvellous. I'm really enjoying myself. It's hectic and I have a lot to organise, people to keep busy, but it's refreshingly different from what I was doing before, and it's directly involved with the war effort. I'm usually out and about in the county for a couple of days each week, which makes a nice change from being in the office.' She fiddled with her teaspoon. 'You know, I was feeling guilty that I wasn't doing much compared with you two, but now I can hold my head up high.'

'You certainly can,' Prue said, reaching over and patting Lizzie's arm. 'It's an important and responsible job you've got. I'm proud of you.'

'Why thank you.' Lizzie caught Thea's eye and grinned. 'That's lovely to hear.'

Thea took a sip of tea to stop herself from laughing – it was a rare thing for Prue and Lizzie to agree about something.

'So how is dear Victor?' Lizzie asked. 'Have you told him that you know about his *Sunday meetings* here in Norwich?'

It had been Lizzie who'd discovered what Victor was up to when he came to Norwich each Sunday for his so-called important committee meetings, when in fact he was having a meeting of an entirely different kind. Lizzie had spotted him with a woman whom he was clearly having an affair with, and after some detective work had found out where she lived and then broken the news to Prue a few months ago.

Prue put down her teacup. 'Not in so many words. I've hinted to him that I'm suspicious about his Sunday meetings in Norwich, and it was enough to get him to back down when he was objecting to us giving a home to some evacuees. He got the message.'

Lizzie laughed. 'I'm glad to hear it. It's not something that Victor would want to get out and become public knowledge, is it?'

Prue nodded, smiling with satisfaction. 'And that's exactly what makes it such a good leverage point.'

'Are you ever going to tackle him about it properly – tell him you know all about it?' Thea asked. 'Or throw him out?'

Prue took a currant bun off the cake stand and placed it on her plate. 'I'm biding my time. I don't want to do anything while Alice is still living at home, but I will when the right time comes, and in the meantime the information is very useful.'

Thea picked up her teacup and held it high. 'A toast in tea then, to Lizzie's new job and to Prue keeping Victor in check!'

Her sisters gladly raised their cups in salute.

CHAPTER 30

'Down a bit,' Hazel said, waving her hand in the air as she gave directions. 'There, that's it!'

Evie was standing on a chair in Library Ward stringing up paper chain decorations, under the direction of Hazel, who was determined to get them looking as good as possible.

'How's that?' she asked, having secured the end of the paper chain.

'Perfect.' Hazel stood back, hands on her hips, nodding. 'Yes, that will do very nicely.'

'Honestly, you two!' said Corporal Tanner, one of the recently arrived bed-bound patients, who was smiling at them. 'You'd think you were decorating Trafalgar Square the amount of care you're taking.'

'Well, we want to make it look nice,' Evie said, stepping down off the chair and looking round the decorated ward.

Now that Christmas Eve had arrived, Matron Reed had finally given her permission for the wards and the men's recreation room to be decorated. Decorations had already been up for a few days out in the hallway after a large

Christmas tree, which had been grown on the estate, had been brought in. Evie loved the way it filled the air with the delicious scent of pine, which made a welcome change from the pervading disinfectant smell of the hospital. It also looked beautiful. Lady Campbell-Gryce had personally decorated the tree using some of her family's colourful, sparkling decorations. Every time Evie went past it, the sight of it filled her with Christmas joy and made her itch to decorate the wards as well.

At this morning's briefing, Matron had given Evie and Hazel the task of decorating Library Ward using the decorations the men had made over the past few days as part of their recreation. Made from just strips of newspaper joined together with flour and water glue, the paper chains now hung in graceful swoops above the ward, along with paper lanterns which dangled from thin cotton thread while cut-out intricately patterned snowflakes hung in the windows. The simple home-made decorations might lack colour and sparkle, but their creation, and now their display in the ward, was giving a welcome boost to the men stuck here in hospital over Christmas rather than at home with their families.

'I think it looks marvellous,' Hazel said, approvingly. 'It's given the ward a festive look, and now we're all set for Christmas.'

'Are you on duty tomorrow?' Corporal Tanner asked.

'We both are, but we'll be happy to be here,' Evie said, glancing at Hazel who nodded her agreement. 'It will be a lovely day. We hear that a fine lot of plump cockerels have been delivered for the dinner, and there's plenty of fresh vegetables from the walled garden. It should be quite a Christmas feast.'

'Sounds good to me.' Corporal Tanner leaned back against his plumped-up pillows. 'I'll look forward to it.'

Leaving him to rest quietly, Evie and Hazel headed to the nurses' sitting room for their tea break.

'I've never been away from home at Christmas before,' Hazel admitted as they walked past the pine-scented Christmas tree in the hall. 'It's going to feel strange, but I'm not complaining. I'm glad I'll be here tomorrow.'

'It will be my first time away as well,' Evie said. 'But it will be fine, I'm sure. I'm quite looking forward to it actually.' What she didn't say was that this Christmas working in a hospital would be a vast improvement on her Christmases of the past few years. Even if she were to be put on bed pan duty tomorrow, it would still be better than those.

'You all right?' Hazel said, stopping outside the door of the nurses' sitting room and looking at Evie. 'Only your face has gone pale.'

'I'm fine, just ready for a cup of tea after wobbling about standing on that chair.' Evie gave herself a mental shake. All of that was in the past now – this was a fresh, new life and none of that could hurt her any more – could it?

Usually in the evenings, once tea was finished and before the men had their supper of cocoa and a biscuit before bed, Matron liked an air of calmness and quiet to gradually settle over the wards to prepare the men for a good night's sleep. But not tonight. With Christmas Day only hours away, there was no settling being done.

Instead, it was as if an air of expectation hovered over the hospital, Evie thought. She, along with the other staff on duty, from nursing to kitchen staff, were gathered here in the hall by the Christmas tree. Mobile patients were also here, either standing or sitting as their injuries allowed, while those who were still bed-bound had been carried in their beds to the doorway of the wards so that they too could join in.

As Mrs Platten, the Quartermaster, began to play on the piano which had been pushed in from the recreation room, the familiar notes brought a hush over the hall. The carol needed no introduction, it was well-loved and one they'd all known since childhood. Instinctively at the right point, and as one, they began to sing *Once in Royal David's City*.

A shiver travelled down Evie's spine — it seemed as if she could almost reach out and touch the feeling of Christmas magic swelling in the room. She wasn't sure if it was the music or the singing. Perhaps it was the soft candlelight which was reflected manyfold in the decorations hanging on the tree. Whatever it was it made her grateful to be here, to be part of this place and with these people.

CHAPTER 31

Christmas Day began early for Thea when she was woken from a light sleep by her bedroom door creaking open. Feeling for the torch she kept on the stand beside her bed, she switched it on and shone it towards the door and saw two little faces peering in at her.

'Is it Christmas?' Betty asked, tentatively pushing the door open wider and taking a step into the room, her face alight with excitement. 'Only Father Christmas has been.' She held up one of the stockings the children had hung on the end of their bed last night – a pair of Thea's thick woollen socks, the sort that she wore under her rubber boots outside.

Thea glanced at the time on the clock beside her bed – it was a few minutes after six o'clock – so definitely Christmas Day, although still early.

'Yes, it is.' Thea said.

'We hoped it was.' Betty advanced further into Thea's room, coming to stand beside the bed, with George following silently behind her, his stocking clasped firmly in his arms, his eyes shining with excitement.

'Although it's only a little after six o'clock, much earlier than you normally get up.' Thea forced herself to keep a straight face, remembering the intoxicating feeling of sheer excitement and joy that she'd felt as a child on Christmas morning. She could see it in Betty and George's faces, although tempered with uncertainty that they were in a new place and with people who they'd never spent Christmas with before. At home they'd probably have burst into their parents' room and jumped on the bed. 'But since it's Christmas Day I think it's fine to get up early.' Thea smiled happily at them. 'So what has Father Christmas brought you then?'

'We don't know,' Betty said. 'We haven't peeped inside.'

'We have felt them,' George admitted.

Thea laughed. 'Oh, I used to do that when I was small. My brothers, sisters and I used to love feeling the outside of our stockings trying to work out what the shapes might be. Do you want to look inside now, or wait till later?'

'Now!' Betty and George chorused.

'Let me light the candle first so you can see what you're doing.' Thea quickly lit the candle she had in the candle holder beside her bed and the room was bathed in a soft glow, making their shadows dance on the wall.

Thea moved over in her bed and patted the top of the eiderdown where there was space. 'Climb up and let's see what Father Christmas has brought you.'

Once both children were sitting on her bed, Thea watched as they delved into their stockings, their faces lit with expectation and excitement. Their joy was infectious, making Thea feel more excited about Christmas than she had for a long time.

'Oh, look at this!' George exclaimed as he pulled a wooden toy aeroplane out of his stocking, and began to fly it above the bed, swooping his hand up and down. 'It's a Spitfire.'

Watching him playing, completely caught up in his game, Thea's heart swelled with joy that she had the chance to share Christmas with the children. Reuben had made the plane for George, knowing how fascinated the little boy was by the planes flying across the skies which were a common sight these days, and it was clearly a big hit with George.

'I have doll, and she's beautiful. Look at her dress – it's the same as mine!' Betty held up a rag doll to show Thea.

'I'm glad you like it.' Thea smiled warmly at the little girl, who like her brother was thrilled with her home-made gift. The doll had been made by Marianne who'd used some scraps of material from a dress she'd made for Betty to make the doll a matching one. 'What else have you got?'

Putting their toys to the side for a moment, the children delved into their stockings once more and were delighted at their gifts – some chocolate, nuts, a pencil and notebook and right at the toe of each of their stockings a precious orange. Lizzie, who'd come to stay for Christmas, had managed to buy two oranges from Norwich Market after a box had come in, and she had wanted the children to have them.

'Good morning and a Merry Christmas to you all,' a cheery voice called from the doorway making them all turn to look.

'Merry Christmas Hettie.' Thea smiled at her friend who was wrapped in her warm dressing gown.

'Look what Father Christmas brought us,' Betty said waving her doll for Hettie to see.

'I've got a plane,' George said thrusting his wooden plane towards Hettie as she stepped closer to have a look.

'You two have obviously been good children to have such lovely presents from Father Christmas.' Hettie said, admiring the plane and rag doll in turn.

'I'm glad he knew where to find us,' Betty said.

'Oh, don't worry, he always knows where you live,' Hettie

said. 'Right, I need to go and get the cockerel in the oven and then we'll have some breakfast, shall we?'

'I'll come and help,' Thea said.

'No need, we prepared the bird last night – I just need to stoke up the range and put it in the oven,' Hettie said. 'I'll give you a shout when the porridge is ready.'

~

'Christmas is different when there are children in the house,' Lizzie said plunging another plate into the bowl of hot, soapy washing-up water and starting to clean it.

'It certainly is, I've not been so excited about Christmas myself for years.' Thea wiped the plate she was drying, thinking what a warm glow this Christmas had brought her. In the days building up to it there had a been a variety of festive events that she'd been to because of the children – she'd watched them in a nativity play at school, been carol singing with them at the church, and to a Christmas party for the evacuee children put on by The Mother's Day Club. Betty and George's growing excitement had been infectious, and every adult at Rookery House had been buoyed up by it making this Christmas feel wonderfully different to the previous one.

Thea knew Betty and George were missing their parents today, but they had been delighted with the gifts their mother had sent to them, which Thea had placed under the Christmas tree for them to open after breakfast. Their mother might be living back in London again, but she hadn't forgotten her children, and was no doubt missing them today more than ever.

'Reminds me of when we were young.' Lizzie glanced at Thea. 'Makes me almost wish I had a husband and children.'

Thea stared at her sister, her eyebrows raised. 'Really?'

'I said *almost*! I'm happy as I am, Miss Freedom and Independence that's me.' Lizzie put a clean plate on the drainer and reached for another one to wash. 'But it's lovely to come here and join in with Christmas, thank you for having me come to stay, Thea.'

Thea put her hand on her sister's shoulder. 'It's good to have you here, even though you're having to sleep on a camp bed in the dining room. Anna would have had to do the same if she'd come home too, but the school asked her to stay on to help look after the girls who weren't going home for Christmas. At least it saved her from an uncomfortable bed.' Thea picked up another wet plate and dried it. 'You know Evie offered to give you her bed for your stay, which was kind of her. I told her no – she needs a good night's sleep when she's working and on her feet all day.'

'That was generous of her. I must thank her.' Lizzie stacked another clean, dripping plate on the drainer. 'It's a shame she can't be here today, but hospitals need nurses regardless of whether it's Christmas Day.'

'Evie told me at breakfast that there was going to be a special Christmas dinner at the hospital today, so at least the day will be different than usual there.'

'When will she be back?' Lizzie asked.

'Not till after eight tonight. With starting at half past seven each morning, it makes for a long working day.'

'Nursing is not a job for the faint-hearted.' Lizzie scrubbed at a dried-on piece of Christmas pudding in a bowl. 'Evie's clearly dedicated, she seems nice, too, what little I've seen of her. Where's she from – she sounds posh?'

'London, but clearly not the East End. But to be honest I don't know that much about her; she's quite reserved and hasn't talked about her family much or what she did before the war.' Thea frowned. 'Although she did tell me about how she was caught out in an air raid and after seeing another young woman killed, it made her decide to do what she'd been wanting to do which led to her coming here. It made her grab at life. But...'

'But what?' Lizzie asked looking at Thea.

Thea gestured with her hand. 'I get the feeling there's a lot more to Evie than she's let on, I don't know what, but her past is a mystery.'

'Then why don't you just ask her?'

'Because she's a private person – if she wanted to tell me then she would. Not everyone likes to tell their history to people.' Thea stacked the bowl she'd just dried on the pile of clean ones on the kitchen table. 'If she wants to talk about her past she will.'

'You're more patient than me!' Lizzie grinned. 'But then you always were, my steady, kind and patient older sister. The calming influence between me and Prue.'

Thea laughed. 'Well you both needed it. I'm glad to see you two getting on better these days. Since you found out what Victor's up to and told Prue, it's built a bridge between the pair of you.'

Lizzie nodded. 'Poor Prue, she should have kicked him out – I would have.'

'But you or I would never have married him in the first place,' Thea reminded her.

'Indeed.' Lizzie placed the last clean bowl on the drainer and poured the water out of the bowl. 'Why don't you put the clean things away and I'll finish the drying?' She took the tea towel out of Thea's hands and nudged Thea towards the stacks of crockery on the table. 'Then we can go and put our feet up.'

CHAPTER 32

'That was a smashin' Christmas dinner,' Nancy said. 'One of the best I've ever 'ad.'

Prue smiled warmly at Nancy, whom she'd come to regard as a friend since she'd arrived here. 'It was delicious, wasn't it? We might have rationing, but it doesn't affect us so badly in the countryside where we can provide more of our own food than in the cities.' It had been a tasty meal, Prue thought, the cockerel reared by Thea, and the vegetables coming from Prue's garden. Everything fresh and home-grown.

The pair of them were sitting opposite each other in comfy armchairs either side of a roaring fire. The room was decked out for Christmas with swathes of ivy and holly draped over the mantlepiece, and a pine-scented Christmas tree was festooned with glass baubles which prettily reflected the flickering light of the fire.

Alice and Nancy's two daughters, Marie and Joan, were sitting on the floor playing a game of snakes and ladders, giggling each time one of their counters was sent sliding down a snake.

Everyone was full of Christmas dinner and happy. The only other person who was in the house but missing from their happy gathering was Victor, who as soon as his dinner was eaten had disappeared into his study again. Prue was quite happy with that. Last year, she and Alice had left him sleeping off his Christmas dinner by the fire to go to Rookery House for some festive cheer. This year, with Nancy and her girls living here, the house was once again filled with Christmas joy – and that made Prue happy.

'You look thoughtful,' Nancy said, studying Prue's face. 'Are you all right?'

Prue nodded. 'Yes, I'm fine. Just thinking what a difference a year makes.'

'In what way?' Nancy asked.

'Well last year it was just me and Alice here with Victor. It wasn't as nice as today has been.' Prue's gaze met Nancy's. 'Edwin had moved into Thea's and was working for her before he left to join the Friends Ambulance Unit for his training.' She paused, remembering how Victor had refused to even allow Edwin to come home for Christmas Day, his bigoted attitude to his son being a conscientious objector over-riding any sense of family. 'Jack was away in the army, so Alice and I ended up going over to Thea's after Christmas dinner – it was much more cheerful there.'

'I can imagine.' Nancy gave Prue a sympathetic smile. 'Last year I'd never 'ave imagined we'd be living 'ere out in the countryside one year on. But I'm glad we're 'ere. I couldn't 'ave stayed in London with the girls, not how it is now.'

'Do you miss it?' Prue asked, as she put another piece of wood on the fire.

'Of course, but I like it here, it's different but it feels like a another 'ome to us now. I wonder 'ow things will have changed by this time next year?' Nancy said, casting a look at her girls who were laughing as Alice made a theatrical show of moving her counter down a snake on their games board.

Prue leaned back in her armchair. 'I try not to think that far ahead these days. So much is out of our control and it's fruitless to try and second guess what might or might not happen. All we can do is do our best each day and take things as they come.'

Nancy's face broke into a wide smile. 'You're a wise woman, Prue. I don't know what us evacuees would 'ave done without you looking out for us. We all 'ave a great respect for you and all you've done for us.'

Prue's cheeks grew warm – she wasn't used to such praise. 'I'm glad to help, I really am. It keeps me out of mischief!'

CHAPTER 33

January 1941 was proving to be bitterly cold, with an icy wind blowing in from the north. Evie was glad to have it at her back as she pedalled along the dark lane towards Great Plumstead Hall Hospital, her way lit by the thin beam from her bicycle lamp. She always enjoyed cycling to and from the hospital, the bicycle which Reuben had found for her was perfect, from its basket at the front to the shiny, black paintwork.

Hettie had said snow was likely to fall today, and as she'd dished up a bowl of warming porridge for Evie at breakfast, she warned her that the roads could be tricky on her way home tonight. Even now, a few flakes of snow were starting to fall, melting coldly on her face, and catching in the light from her bicycle lamp.

She was glad to reach the Hall, and as usual parked her bicycle in one of the old stables around the back and hurried inside, her cheeks smarting from the cold despite having had a scarf wrapped over them.

'Good morning!' Hazel's cheery voice greeted Evie as she went into the cloakroom to take off her coat and put on a clean apron, cuffs and veil. Hazel was standing in front of the mirror, battling with her own veil – making sure that the small red cross on one side was positioned correctly in the middle of her forehead – before she began the lengthy, and arm-aching, task of pleating the material, so she could pin it into a stiff butterfly bow at the back.

'It's freezing out there,' Evie said peeling off her outer garments and hanging them on a hook.

'It feels like it's going to snow,' Hazel said.

'It's already started falling, just a bit now, but no doubt there's more to come.' Evie slipped on her apron and tied the strings neatly around the back.

'Then it's a good job they brought the new patients here yesterday.'

'How many arrived?' Evie asked. It had been her day off yesterday, so she hadn't been there to help settle them in.

'There's four of them: one amputee, a stomach injury, another recovering from appendicitis and one with eye injuries. They seem a nice bunch.' Hazel pushed the final pin into her finished veil and stood back, turning her head from side to side checking her reflection in the mirror. 'There that should do it.'

Evie was now wrestling with her own veil, her cold fingers making it hard to fold the material as neatly as Matron would expect. 'Oh no, not again!' she groaned as another pleat came loose in her hand.

'Here let me help you.' Hazel took hold of Evie's veil and shook it out ready to start again. She held it up, positioning the red cross in the centre of Evie's forehead. 'Right, you hold it in place there and I'll sort out the rest.'

'Whoever came up with the idea of VADs having to wear this ridiculous head gear probably never had to put them on every day,' Evie muttered.

Hazel laughed as she expertly folded the material into neat pleats. 'I'm with you there. A simple cap would be so much better. There you go. That's done.'

Evie checked her reflection in the mirror. 'Thank you. I'd have been here waiting for my fingers to thaw out otherwise and been late on duty – Matron would have been on the warpath after me.'

'She can't complain about our veils this morning, they look very smart – so come on then, let's go and see what our jobs are for today.' Hazel linked her arm through Evie's, and they headed off for their morning briefing with Matron Reed.

Evie had been given the task of changing dressings on Library Ward, and was happy with that as it had given her the chance to meet the new patients who'd all been assigned to this ward. The three whose dressings she'd already changed were a cheerful bunch despite their injuries, probably glad to have been moved to a convalescent hospital. The grand surroundings and quieter atmosphere of Great Plumstead Hall, compared to the general hospital in Norwich, was usually a welcome change for their new patients, helping them recover.

The last of the new patients, still waiting for his dressing to be changed, was sitting quietly in his bed at the far end of the ward. As Evie pushed her trolley towards him, she observed the bandages around his head – from the top of his forehead down to the tip of his nose just above his nostrils – completely covering his injured eyes. Changing that dressing would be relatively straightforward she thought, much easier than the one she'd just done for the soldier whose lower leg had been amputated.

Before she approached him, Evie picked up the clipboard hanging at the end of his bed to check the soldier's details. As she read his name, something jolted at the edge of her memory but skittered away before she could grasp it. Shrugging it aside, she replaced the clipboard and went to the head of the bed.

'Good morning Private Blythe.' Evie laid her hand gently on his shoulder. 'I'm Nurse Jones and I'll be changing your dressing for you.'

He turned his head towards her. 'Good morning, nurse.'

'I hope you're settling in well?' Evie said as she began to prepare the dressings that she'd need for him. 'You got here just in time – it's snowing out there and it's getting heavier.'

'It seems nice… from what I can hear,' Private Blythe said. 'Much quieter than where we came from.'

'It's a lovely place, beautiful spacious rooms. Right, I'll talk you through what I'm doing, so you'll know what to expect,' Evie explained, knowing that the men always watched what she did when she changed dressings, often as not, to prepare themselves for any discomfort that might happen. But in Private Blythe's case, he couldn't see what she was doing, so it would help him if she talked as she worked. 'So the first thing I'll do is remove your current dressing.'

Evie moved to stand by his right-hand side, slightly behind him and gently unravelled the soft bandage from around his head. When his ear was revealed she had to stop herself from gasping. It had a V-shaped nick in it about half an inch above his earlobe – and she'd seen it before. Stared at it before. Evie's stomach plummeted like a stone into her black lace-up shoes as memories of those times came rushing in.

'Nurse?' Private Blythe turned his head towards her.

Evie realised that she'd stopped and forced her shaking hands to move again and finish removing the dressings.

'Is everything all right?' he asked, his voice worried.

'Absolutely.' Evie forced her voice to not betray the way she was shaking inside. 'It's snowing heavier than ever out there – it just caught my eye, like huge feathers coming down now. I'll just get the clean dressings.'

Glad of the chance to step away from him for a moment, and taking far longer than necessary to pick up the new lint pads and bandage, Evie knew what her memory had nudged her about earlier – the name Blythe. She'd heard that many times before. This man was part of her past, the past that she'd thought she'd escaped from but hadn't because here it was colliding slap bang with her present. What was she going to do? She needed to think, but first she had to do her job. At least he couldn't see her and identify her – for now anyway.

'This won't take long.' Evie forced a note of cheerfulness into her voice as she applied the new dressings over his closed eyes, then carefully wound the bandage around Private Blythe's face, covering the eyes that could lead to her downfall.

After she'd finished, Evie took the dressings trolley back to the storeroom, using all her determination to hold herself together. After quickly dealing with the trolley, not daring to leave it without cleaning it first, she fled to the nurses' bathroom. Luckily no one else was in there, and she leaned against the cold, porcelain sink gulping in deep breaths to calm her racing heart. Why here? Of all the places, why did he have to be sent here? She was happy in her new life, but now it could all crumble away. If Private Blythe's eyesight returned, as Matron had said it should at the morning briefing when she'd talked about the new patients, then he would recognise her. Her secret would be out. Then it would only be a matter of time before *he* found out and came to find her...

An urge to run, escape, surged through her... but Evie

didn't want to leave – she was happy here. She loved her new home at Rookery House with Thea and all the others. She didn't want to move on. Perhaps she wouldn't have to if Private Blythe's eyesight didn't return… although she couldn't wish that fate for him, that would be cruel.

Evie turned on a tap and splashed her face with cold water. The tingling sensation from the chilly water was a welcome distraction, momentarily making her feel better. There was nothing to be done for the moment, she reasoned – she needed to wait and see how things played out. In the meantime, it would be best to avoid having much to do with Private Blythe in case he recognised her voice. It was unlikely, as it was some time since she'd last seen him, and she'd never spoken that much to him before. So there was at least some hope.

~

'Matron wants to see us in the nurses' sitting room,' Hazel announced coming into the surgery in the old Butler's pantry a little before three o'clock that afternoon. 'She wants to see all of us nurses who live out.'

Evie turned around from where she was checking through the linen stores in one of the cupboards lining the walls. 'What about?'

'She didn't say, only that we should go there promptly!' Hazel raised her eyebrows. 'It's probably about getting home tonight; it could be tricky with all this snow. It hasn't let up snowing all day and now that the wind has picked up, it's started to drift as well.'

'We'd better go and find out what's going on.' Evie put down the clipboard with its detailed list of linens and followed her friend.

The two other nurses who lived out, both lodging with Mrs Platten at the Grange, like Hazel, were already in the nurses' sitting room when they arrived and Matron appeared moments later.

'As no doubt you are aware, the weather conditions have been worsening all day. Now the wind has increased it's causing the snow to drift and could make the roads impassable in places. The decision has been made for you *all* to stay here at the hospital rather than attempt to go home, both for your own safety and to ensure that we have adequate staff on duty tomorrow.' Matron paused for a moment, her eyes raking over each of them, as if daring them to challenge the decision. 'You will have to bed down in the Night Nursery and Day Nursery Wards, which fortunately do not have patients in them at present.'

The thought of staying here wouldn't have bothered Evie at any other time, but with Private Blythe's presence, she'd been looking forward to retreating to the safety of Rookery House at the end of the day. Now being told that it couldn't happen was a blow, but since Evie lived closer to the hospital than the other three nurses, perhaps she *could* get home.

'Rookery House, where I live, is on this side of the village – it's not so far away as the Grange. I'm sure I could make it home tonight and back again in the morning,' Evie said, the words bursting out of her before her mind could filter whether it was wise or not.

Matron pursed her lips, her gaze falling on Evie. 'Even that far is unwise. One of the orderlies has been out to check and the snow is more than a foot deep and now drifting, making travelling difficult. Staying here really is the *safest* and most *sensible* option.' Her tone made it clear it wasn't up for negotiation.

'But they'll be expecting me,' Evie said, thinking if she didn't arrive home then Thea would be worried.

'Do they have a telephone?' Matron asked.

Evie nodded. Rookery House was one of the few homes in the village which did have a telephone.

'Then you can ring them and let them know.' Matron looked at Hazel and the other two nurses. 'I have already informed Mrs Platten that you'll be staying here tonight. I'll leave you all to sort out which ward you'll be sleeping in; you don't need me to tell you.' With that, Matron swept out of the room.

'There are three beds in each of those wards, so how about we share the Night Nursery Ward, Evie?' Hazel suggested. 'And you two share the Day Nursery Ward?' she said to the two other nurses.

Evie nodded. 'All right.' She didn't really care where she slept, though at least if she was sharing with Hazel her cheerful chatter would help keep her mind off Private Blythe and what might happen if he recognised her.

Hazel beamed. 'Good, then we'll all have company, and no one will be left out. It will be fun, staying over. I always thought it was a shame you weren't lodging with the rest of us nurses.'

Evie pasted what she hoped was an agreeable smile on her face. As much as she liked Hazel, she preferred living at Rookery House away from the rest of her colleagues – not only because it gave her a break from being with the same people all the time, but because it was like living with a family. A warm, happy family which was something that Evie had never had in her life up until she had arrived in Norfolk. It had become precious to her and she didn't want it to end — which was what she feared would happen if the truth about her past was revealed.

CHAPTER 34

After a night of heavy snow, the clouds had cleared, and Sunday morning had dawned with the world blanketed beneath a layer of sparkling white over which arched a crisp, blue sky. It was beautiful Thea thought, as she carried a bucket of still-warm creamy milk back to the house, stepping in the footprints she'd made earlier going in the opposite direction. Although the snow was causing a disruption to their normal routines – Thea had kept Primrose in the byre after milking this morning as the grass in the meadow that the cow usually grazed was buried under a foot of snow, or more in places where it had drifted. At least Primrose seemed happy to remain inside – after poking her nose outside briefly, she'd returned to contentedly munching from the full hay rack instead.

Reaching the door of the scullery, Thea opened it and placed the bucket inside for Hettie to collect and then headed off to see to the chickens, her breath pluming in the freezing cold air. Like Primrose, the hens weren't keen on going out in the snow either. Following a quick venture outside after Thea had opened the hen coop door, most of the chickens hurried back inside where she'd put plenty of food and fresh water.

'I'd stay in there if I was you,' Thea said. 'Your poor feet will be frozen.' Her own feet, encased in thick woollen socks inside her rubber boots, were tingling from the cold, so the chickens' bare feet on snow must be painfully icy.

She cleared a small area around the coop, for those chickens who did want to wander around, but she noticed their feet were looking much pinker than usual, the chill taking effect quickly.

With the animals seen to, Thea headed back to the house in need of a hot drink to warm her up. Apart from making sure the animals were fed and watered, and milked in Primrose's case, and bringing in plenty of wood for the fires, there was little that could be done work wise outside today. Now the children were here, it was a good excuse to have some fun in the snow instead, just as she'd loved to do as a child.

'There, how does that look?' Thea stood back and looked at the large snowman, which she'd just pushed two fir cones into to make eyes.

'Good,' George said, his cheeks rosy from the cold.

George, Betty and Thea had worked together to build the snowman, starting by rolling a ball of snow along so that it gathered snow and grew until it was as big as they needed. Then they'd repeated the process making a smaller ball, which they'd placed on top of the bigger one for a head.

'He needs a scarf,' Betty said, unwinding her own and standing on tiptoes to put it around the snowman. 'That's better.'

The sound of barking caught their attention and they turned to see Bess bounding towards them, her leaps slowed by the deep snow. Behind her came Reuben, carrying something in his arms.

'Look what I found in one of the sheds.' He held up a wooden sledge with metal runners.

'I'd forgotten about that,' Thea said. It had been left hanging up on a shed wall by the previous owners of Rookery House. 'Is it still sound enough to use?'

Reuben nodded. 'I've checked it over and put some new rope on it to pull with – it just needs someone to ride on it. Is anyone here interested in a sledge ride?'

'Me!' Betty and George chorused.

'Climb aboard then.' Reuben put the sledge down and the children clambered on, Betty sitting at the back, George just in front of her, their legs sticking out in front.

'Hold on tight,' Thea said.

As Reuben took the strain on the rope and began to pull them along, the children beamed with happiness, giggling as Bess bounded along beside them.

Thea laughed, she loved seeing the children so happy – and it was a delight to see Reuben enjoying himself as well. George and Betty's arrival at Rookery House hadn't just changed the children's lives, it had also made a difference to everyone else who lived here too.

At Prue's house in the village, Nancy and her two girls, along with Alice, were playing in the back garden, enjoying the snow. They'd made two snowmen and were now having a snowball fight, laughing loudly as their poor aims failed to hit a target.

Prue had been outside earlier and joined in with making the snowmen but had now come indoors to heat up some soup for dinner as everyone would need something warming after being outside. She was watching them through the kitchen window, which looked out into the back garden, smiling at their giggling and shrieks of delight as they played, unaware that someone else had come into the room.

'I'm trying to do some work!' Victor's harsh voice made her jump. 'Tell them to be quiet.'

His presence, tone of voice and his overall demeanour was a sharp contrast to the fun and enjoyment being had outside. When was the last time Victor had laughed with joy or had fun? Prue wondered. Had he even played like that as a child? Victor had been in a bad mood all morning, his usual Sunday routine of going into Norwich for his so-called meetings impossible today because of the heavy snow interrupting the train service. Prue knew it wasn't the meeting he was missing but visiting his mistress.

'They're just having a bit of fun,' Prue said. 'They'll be in for dinner soon anyway.'

'It's that evacuee woman and her brats that's causing the trouble.'

'Alice is out there as well, and they are just enjoying themselves, Victor.'

'I knew we should never have had them, they come here causing trouble, interrupting our work.'

Prue turned to look at him, shaking her head. 'It's Sunday today, not a day of work, and they're having some harmless fun. That's all. Just enjoying the snow.'

'Hmmph! If it wasn't for the snow, I'd be able to get to my meeting.'

'I doubt very much the meeting will have happened today,' Prue said. 'It would have been difficult for everyone to get there. Why you have to have a meeting every Sunday afternoon I don't know.'

Victor folded his arms and stared at her, his ice-blue eyes cold. 'There's a war on Prudence, and responsible businessmen and councillors like myself have a lot to organise. It's not easy you know.'

'I'm sure it isn't, I do plenty of organising for the war effort myself,' Prue said, meeting his stare. She was so tempted to say that she knew all about the meetings he went to every Sunday and that they weren't about helping the war effort – only about Victor helping himself to something he shouldn't. But now wasn't the time. 'You'll be able to go again next week.'

Victor nodded, turned on his heel and headed back to his study, without saying another word. Was his conscience suddenly pricking him? Prue wondered.

Noise from the porch attracted her attention, the stamping of feet to knock snow off rubber boots – they were coming in and would be ready for their dinner. At least Victor couldn't complain about the noise any more, and with any luck would keep out of the way in his study for the remainder of the day. In fact, Prue decided, she would take him his soup in there on a tray. It would be a relief to not have him at the kitchen table glowering as they ate. They would enjoy their meal all the more for his absence.

CHAPTER 35

Evie had just spent her third night staying over at the hospital as heavy snow showers had continued to sweep in between occasional breaks of startling blue sky. Each snowstorm added another layer to the white blanketing the outside world, and Matron Reed had deemed it necessary for all staff who lived out to remain staying over at the hospital. Normally this wouldn't have bothered Evie, but that was before Private Blythe had arrived – his presence here had changed things, leaving her feeling unsettled and jittery. His potential to blow apart her new life was like a ticking timebomb.

'We might be able to go home tonight,' Hazel said sitting down next to Evie at the table in the nurses' sitting room, where they were having their breakfast. 'I just spoke to the gardener down by the kitchen, and he reckons the snow's passed over for now – there won't be any more falling for the time being, although it's still bitterly cold. Once they've cleared the road we can get home.'

'That's good,' Evie smiled at her friend in relief. She couldn't wait to get back to the safety of Rookery House after being stuck here at the hospital. Although she'd have to return to the hospital for her duty each day, but escaping home would provide some relief and a chance to think about her future. 'I've missed it.'

Hazel helped herself to a bowl of porridge. 'But it's been fun sharing a room, hasn't it? Chatting before we went to sleep.'

Evie nodded. 'Yes, rather like boarding school.'

Hazel stared at her. 'Oh, you never said you went to boarding school – what was it like?'

'Some parts were fun, others not so. I didn't like the French lessons and maths...' Evie pulled a face. School had been a break from home and had taught her how to adapt and survive, which she supposed had put her in good stead for what was to come. She glanced at her watch. 'We'd better hurry up and finish breakfast. Matron's briefing starts in ten minutes.'

It had been a busy morning on the ward — Matron had given out a long list of tasks for the nursing staff to complete. Now, while the men had their midday meal in the servants' hall, Evie was washing the top of the locker that stood beside the bed of the amputee patient, when she became aware of Matron Reed standing watching her. The older woman had been in and out of the ward all morning, keeping an eagle eye on what was going on.

'When you've finished here, I want to see you in my office, Nurse Jones.' Matron turned and left the ward, not waiting for a reply.

Hazel was cleaning a bed frame nearby and caught Evie's

eye. 'What's that about? You haven't done anything you shouldn't have, have you?'

Evie frowned. 'Not as far as I know. I haven't sat on a patient's bed again that's for sure.' She forced a smile, her stomach clenching at the thought of facing Matron.

'Perhaps she's got a special job for you,' Hazel suggested.

'Let's hope it's not bed pan duty again!' Evie said, trying to sound cheerful.

~

Standing outside Matron Reed's office a short while later, Evie smoothed down her apron and knocked tentatively on the door.

'Enter,' Matron's voice called.

Evie went in, closing the door quietly behind her. She stood in front of Matron's desk, her hands clasped tightly together behind her back.

Matron regarded her for a moment before speaking. 'I've noticed over the past few days that you are *avoiding* one of the patients, Nurse Jones.'

Evie's stomach dropped. She'd thought she'd been careful, but clearly nothing got past Matron. What should she say? If she admitted it, then Matron would want to know why and she could never tell her.

She frowned. 'Not intentionally, who do you mean?'

'Private Blythe.' Matron raised her eyebrows, her shrewd eyes studying Evie's face. 'I noticed that Nurse Robertson was doing his dressings this morning when I had given *you* the task of changing dressings on the ward, *not her*. So why didn't you do his?'

'I was running late, it took longer to do the dressings on our amputee patient, and it was almost time for the men's dinner,' Evie said, not admitting that she'd started the task of changing dressings later on purpose, specifically so that she could ask Hazel to help with Private Blythe's.

Matron's eyes narrowed and she folded her arms across her ample chest. 'Then you need to allow plenty of time for your given task, not ask others to step in when they have their own jobs to do.' She paused for a moment, her lips thinning. 'I haven't seen you talking to him as you do with the other patients either... My intuition tells me that you are avoiding him for some reason – is it his injury that bothers you, that he can't see you?'

Evie shook her head. Quite the opposite, she was *glad* that he couldn't see her! The thought made her feel guilty. 'No, not at all.'

'I expect *all* of my nurses to extend their care to *every* patient in this hospital. No exceptions or favourites, each man should receive your attention and time – do I make myself clear?'

Evie nodded. 'Yes, Matron.'

'Good, because I shall be watching you very closely. You can start by taking Private Blythe for a walk around inside this afternoon – he needs some exercise. You can be his eyes for him. In fact, that is a job you can do for him every day. Make sure that you do, and that I don't have to speak to you again about this matter.' Matron picked up a pen and began to write in the large ledger she kept on her desk, their meeting over.

Evie turned and went out, shutting the door quietly behind her. Outside, she leaned against the wall for a moment, her heart racing, and her legs shaky. So much for her plan to avoid Private Blythe – she'd now got the job of spending time with him *every* day – the last thing she wanted to do.

~

'There's another step going down here, it's just a shallow one,' Evie said, guiding Private Blythe towards the long corridor in the servants' part of the hall.

With his arm linked through hers, Private Blythe tentatively put one foot forward feeling with the toe of his slipper for the lower floor level, and, touching it, moved forward more confidently to step down onto it.

'That's it, well done,' Evie said. 'It's all one level from here, and this leads down to the kitchen and the back door. The old servants' hall is off to the side – it's where the mobile patients have their meals now.'

'I'm more used to this part of a grand house than the library,' he said as they walked slowly along the passageway. 'I was a chauffeur before the war.' Evie's stomach clenched – she didn't want to talk about that time. 'If my eyesight doesn't come back then I won't be able to drive anyone around ever again.'

'We can't be sure yet, so let's hope it does come back,' Evie said, trying to sound cheerful. She couldn't wish that he would spend the rest of his life in darkness, not even if it meant he recognised her. 'Anyway, you might not want to work as a chauffeur any more – after being in the army you have more experience and would perhaps prefer a different sort of job.'

Private Blythe shrugged. 'We'll see. Who knows how long the war will go on for and who'll win, it's not over yet by a long way.' He stopped walking and turned his head towards her. 'Your voice reminds me of someone, have we met before?'

Evie had to smother a gasp. 'No, I don't think so.' She forced her voice to not betray the way she was quaking inside. 'You've probably got me muddled up with someone else.' She knew that her voice was considered plummy compared with his and the other nurses, but it was like all the other girls she'd been at boarding school with who belonged to families like hers. There was nothing about her voice to make it stand out, she thought.

He nodded. 'It's just when you can't see, you listen that bit harder... Maybe you're right and I'm mixing you up with someone else, never mind.'

'It's fine. How about we stop off in the kitchen for a cup of tea?' Evie suggested, thinking the other staff in there would be able to chat to him as they worked, and provide some distraction. It was clear that Private Blythe did slightly recognise her voice, but thankfully not enough to pinpoint where he knew her from. 'And if we're in luck, they might have some freshly baked buns for you to sample.'

He smiled. 'That sounds good to me. I'll feel right at home there.'

CHAPTER 36

Thea headed downstairs after tucking Betty and George in bed for the night, having read several chapters of their current book. As usual, they'd asked for more, but they were tired and needed some sleep – what happened next in the story would have to wait until tomorrow night. Thea also had things to do – her plan for the coming year needed to be worked out.

Going into the kitchen, where Hettie sat by the range knitting, Thea fetched her notebook from the dresser and sat down at the table.

'Are they settled for the night?' Hettie asked.

'Yes, George could barely keep his eyes open for the last chapter. I'm sure he was asleep before I left the room.' Thea opened her notebook and began jotting down her ideas for expanding the range of foods they produced at Rookery House.

'You look busy,' Hettie said. 'What are you up to?'

'Planning the garden for this year and working out my plans to expand.' Thea looked up at the older woman, who was watching her but still knitting, her fingers knowing what to do without her having to look.

'What's the plan then?' Hettie asked.

'Well, we've got the land, so I want to put more of it into food production, grow more and raise some meat. I've decided to keep rabbits and get some weaner pigs to fatten up.'

'It would be nice to produce our own pork and cure our own ham and bacon.'

'It certainly would.'

'And we can make sausages as well.' Hettie stood up and pushed the kettle on to the hotplate of the range to boil. 'Prue was talking about setting up a pig club at the WI, using any waste food and vegetable peelings from around the village to feed the pigs – perhaps we could work with them.'

'Possibly,' Thea said. 'I'll talk to her about it. It would be a good way to turn waste into food. Feeding rabbits isn't such a problem as feeding pigs – once the spring comes there'll be plenty of plants to gather to feed them on. I'll…' Thea paused at the sound of the back door opening. 'That must be Evie back.'

The hospital's secretary had telephoned from the Hall earlier to say that nurses who lived out were no longer required to stay over because of the weather, so Evie would be coming home tonight after her duty ended at eight o'clock.

'I'll get her tea out.' Hettie reached for the potholder and took a covered plate out of the warming oven at the bottom of the range, where she had put Evie's evening meal to keep warm, as the rest of them had eaten theirs earlier.

'Welcome home!' Thea said, with a warm smile when Evie walked into the kitchen. 'It's nice to have you back again.'

Evie returned her smile. 'Thank you – it's good to be home again. Though I had to walk back pushing my bicycle. I didn't dare ride it as it's freezing hard out there, and the road's icy.'

'Here sit yourself down and get this into you,' Hettie said putting the plate of stew and mashed potatoes on the table. 'It will warm you through.'

'Thank you.' Evie sat down at the table opposite Thea.

'How are things at the hospital?' Thea asked.

'Busy, as usual. We had some new patients arrive the day before the snow – they've settled in well.'

'They got there just in time then,' Hettie said, pouring hot water into the teapot to make a fresh brew. 'The snow's pretty to look at, but it plays havoc with getting around. Still the snowplough's been through, and the roads are clear now as long as there's no more snow. Although this lot's going to linger while it's still so cold.'

'How are things here?' Evie asked, scooping up a forkful of stew.

'Fine, the children have been enjoying the snow,' Thea said.

'And you and Reuben too.' Hettie chuckled. 'Both of you have been playing outside with George and Betty. It was lovely to see.'

Thea laughed. 'I must admit we've enjoyed ourselves as well.'

Marianne came into the kitchen. 'Oh, hello Evie, it's good to have you back.'

'We all missed you,' Hettie said, setting out cups for each of them on the table. 'I know you haven't been here that long, Evie, but it didn't feel right without you.'

'I missed being here too,' Evie admitted. 'But Matron was insistent that we stay there at the hospital.'

Hettie nodded. 'She was right – the way the snow was coming down you could easily have got lost in it. Still, you're back now and all is as it should be.'

Thea noticed a look of despair flit across Evie's face. Unless she was very much mistaken, there was something not quite right with the young woman. Perhaps she was just exhausted from being at the hospital for three solid days, never having the chance to escape from it as she normally would. Or had something happened there to upset her? From what she knew of Evie, the young woman would not thank her for asking her now if there was anything bothering her. Thea would watch and wait, and if it was something other than just tiredness, then hopefully Evie would eventually talk to her about it.

~

Thea woke up with a start. She'd dreamed that she was in London while it was being bombed.

Now, wide awake, her memories catapulted her back to real-life London at the start of the Blitz — she'd been there that evening when squadrons of enemy bombers had appeared in the sky over the city. She'd gone to London in an attempt to get Anna released from imprisonment as an enemy alien. While she was there, Thea had also taken the opportunity to visit Edwin and had been with him when the air-raid siren had gone off, and then had spent the night helping in the hospital where he worked, carrying in casualties from the ambulances as they arrived at the hospital.

Only in Thea's dream, she'd been out in the streets desperately searching for Edwin while the planes roared overhead, bombs landing with sickening crumps and bangs. She'd finally found him lying staring up at the sky through sightless eyes and the horror of it had woken her.

Lying still as her heartbeat returned to its normal pace, Thea was relieved that it was only a dream, but it had played upon her fears for her nephew in London. And for her friend

Violet as well, who'd be in the thick of it at the East End ambulance station she was in charge of.

Turning onto her side, she forced herself to think of something else instead, something positive – her plans for the coming year – in the hope that she'd soon drift off to sleep again. She began to go over what she'd noted down this evening, thinking through where the new vegetable plots would go and what needed to be done before the rabbits and pigs arrived. Rather than distracting herself and bringing sleep closer, her thoughts rattled around her head and the chance of falling back to sleep became more remote.

It was no good, Thea decided, she'd get up and go downstairs for a drink of water then perhaps come back and read for a little while. Slipping on her dressing gown and slippers, she quietly opened her bedroom door, using the small torch she kept by her bed to light the way, and trod softly across the landing and down the stairs. Going into the kitchen, Thea closed the door behind her and jumped when her torchlight lit up a figure sitting at the table – it was Evie.

The young woman stood up. 'Thea!'

'I didn't know you were here. Are you all right?'

'I couldn't sleep.' Evie slumped down into her chair again.

'Same here.' Thea lit a candle and placed it in the middle of the table, the soft light from it throwing their shadows on to the walls. 'How about some cocoa – it might help us sleep.'

'Yes, thank you. I'll help.' Evie went to stand up again.

'No need, you stay there.' Thea busied herself making the cocoa, giving herself time to think while taking occasional sideways glances at the young woman who sat with her elbows on the table, her head in her hands, looking like she had the weight of the world on her shoulders.

'There you go.' Thea placed a mug of cocoa in front of Evie.

'Thank you.' Evie lifted her head and gave her a wan smile.

Thea sat down opposite Evie and took a sip of her own cocoa wondering how best to proceed. Despite Evie having lived here since last October, Thea hadn't got to know her as well as she had Marianne or Anna. It was partly because of the long hours that Evie worked at the hospital, but also due to the young woman's reticence – it was as if she had a protective wall around her. She was always pleasant and polite but kept her distance. The only time that Thea had seen her show emotion was after the young soldier had died of pneumonia. But tonight, something was clearly wrong with Evie. Was she in trouble? Did she need help? There was only one way to find out and if Thea left it to Evie to tell her, then she suspected she would be waiting a long time.

'Evie, I know you're a private person, and I respect that, but I can see that there is something wrong, that you're distressed.' Thea reached her hand across the table and gently touched the young woman's arm. 'I'd like to help you.'

Evie looked down at her hands which were clasped tightly around her mug of cocoa, her knuckles white against her skin. She sighed heavily and looked up at Thea, tears glistening in her eyes. 'You can't. Nobody can.' Her bottom lip trembled, and the tears slid down her face. 'It's just a matter of time before…'

'Before what?'

Evie dropped her gaze as her tears continued to fall, plopping onto the table, making dark splashes on the pale wood.

'What's going to happen?' Thea probed gently. She waited, the kitchen silent except for the ticking of the clock on the dresser.

Evie dropped her head in her hands again, elbows leaning on the table. Thea could see that Evie was fighting to control her emotions by the way her shoulders heaved, her breath coming in shuddering gasps. Eventually the young woman raised her head and gazed at Thea, her face etched with fear and anguish.

'Before he can see me and will know who I am,' Evie blurted out.

'Who?' Thea asked.

Evie leaned back in her chair and shook her head. 'Private Blythe. He'll recognise me and then it's just a matter of time before...' She hesitated. 'Before my *husband* finds out where I am.' She hung her head looking utterly wretched.

The news that Evie had a husband was a shock to Thea. There had been no mention of him by Evie, she didn't wear a wedding ring and no letters had ever arrived from him as far as Thea knew. Although Evie had been vague about her past, being married wasn't something anyone would forget to mention – unless of course they *wanted* to.

'Do you want to tell me about Private Blythe and what he has got to do with your husband?' Thea asked gently.

Evie nodded and took a deep breath. 'Private Blythe is one of the new patients who arrived just before the snow, his eyes are injured and are hidden under bandages. I recognised him, but thankfully he hasn't been able to see me... yet. But the doctors believe it's only a matter of time before his eyesight comes back and then...' She bit her bottom lip, her anxious eyes meeting Thea's. 'He'll recognise me.'

'Is he a friend of your husband's?'

'No!' Evie gave a harsh bark of laughter. 'My husband would *never* consider such a man as a suitable friend – he's too much of a snob. You see Private Blythe was the chauffeur for Douglas's parents. Blythe, as he was known, comes from a family who've worked for Douglas's family for many years, his father is head gardener, and his father's father was before him.

Private Blythe joined the same regiment as my husband — the Blythe family are loyal to their employers. And once Private Blythe sees me, he's sure to tell his parents who will be duty bound to pass the news onto Douglas's family and then my husband will find out and he will...' Evie's voice trembled. 'He'll come for me... He'll find me and...' Evie closed her eyes, tears seeping out from under her lids and running down her cheeks.

'Where does Douglas think you are?'

Evie opened her eyes and stared at Thea. 'He thinks I'm *dead*.' She paused for a few moments and then added, 'I faked my own death.'

Thea gasped, putting a hand to her mouth. 'But why?'

Evie thrust her chin forward. 'To escape. Douglas was not the man he pretended to be to other people. When it was just us, he was a bully, controlling, threatening... he hurt me. He even caused me to have a miscarriage... shoved me so hard I fell over and lost the baby. I was only a couple of months along, but I wanted that child so badly.' She fiddled with her long auburn plait, biting her bottom lip.

'I'm so sorry.' Thea reached for Evie's hand and held it.

'When I told my mother what he was really like, *begged* her to help me she...' Evie's voice cracked. 'She wouldn't believe me, even when I showed her my bruises and told her about the lost baby. She was more interested in my having made what she called *a good marriage* to a husband from a wealthy upper-class family, even though he was a brute. Everything I did was controlled by him. So when he joined the army and left home and I hardly ever saw him, I was delighted. Even more so when he was eventually sent abroad. The last time we were together was when he had embarkation leave last June.' Evie managed a shaky smile. 'I'd trained in secret to become a VAD and neither Douglas, nor any of his family or my mother knew what I was doing. My full name is Genevieve Hamilton-Jones. I used a different name when I did my training so no one would know me – shortening it to Evie Jones. I like that much better.' She took a deep breath and then went on. 'Remember I told you about how last October I got on a bus and sat next to the young woman who was about to join the WAAF, but who was killed by a bomb on her way to the underground?'

Thea nodded. 'Yes, and you were with her but went back to the bus to get your suitcase.'

'Afterwards, while I was sitting out the air raid in the underground, I started to think that it was as if I'd been given another chance. I asked myself, *Did I want to spend the rest of my life married to someone who treated me so badly?*' Evie bit her bottom lip, her eyes flooding with tears once more and it was a few moments before she managed to speak again. 'My answer was no! So I went back to near where the woman was killed, handed my handbag in to a policeman, telling him that I'd found it, then sneaked back to my flat, took what I needed and fled. Douglas would have been told that I'd been killed but there was no body left to identify. I know it was wrong... but I was *desperate* to escape.'

Thea squeezed Evie's hand gently. 'I'm not judging you for what you did – I'm only sorry that your marriage was so awful that you had to do it. Do you think Private Blythe will definitely recognise you?'

Evie nodded, her face bereft. 'Yes. He chauffeured Douglas and me around many times while we were staying with his parents. He even drove me to the church on my wedding day.'

'And you think he would pass on the news so that Douglas's family would be informed?'

'I would imagine so. His father still works for the Hamilton-Jones. Although if his sight doesn't come back then

I'm safe, but I can't wish for that to happen, for him to spend the rest of his life blind just to save me. Perhaps I should leave and go somewhere else, only I *love* it here with you all – it's the first proper, kind and caring home I've known.' Evie's voice was hoarse. 'My mother is uncaring, she's more interested in a person's social standing than how they behave towards her only daughter. And I like working at the hospital too.'

'We wouldn't want you to go either,' Thea said in a heartfelt tone. Her gaze met Evie's. 'There's too much uncertainty about the situation to go and throw away something you love. I think you should wait and see what happens, whether Private Blythe regains his sight enough to recognise you or not. If he does then perhaps you should tell him the truth. Once he knows what your marriage was really like, he might not reveal where you are to Douglas's family.'

Evie nodded, her face looking hopeful for the first time. 'You're right, I should wait and not panic. It's just the fear of what will happen if Douglas finds out and comes after me.'

'Where is Douglas?' Thea asked.

'I'm not sure exactly, his regiment was being posted abroad but he couldn't tell me where. I left before I got a first letter from him.'

'Well unless he's returned to this country, even if he does find out about you, there will be time to decide what to do.' Thea squeezed Evie's hand again. 'You are *not* alone in this. I will help you and will *not* let Douglas lay a finger on you ever again. We will all help you.'

'Thank you.' Evie's eyes filled with tears again. 'You have shown me more kindness and understanding than my own mother ever did. Please don't tell anyone about what I've done, not yet. I don't want Hettie or Marianne to think badly of me.'

'They wouldn't do that. But I promise I won't say a word to them,' Thea reassured her.

It was no wonder Evie was so reserved, hiding herself behind an invisible wall after what she'd been through, Thea thought. She would like to have a word with Evie's mother. Imagine not helping your daughter when she came to you for help, ignoring her bruises and distress. And as for Douglas... well he was nothing but a bully and the sort of man Thea wholeheartedly disliked.

CHAPTER 37

'Is it good news?' Nancy asked, as she sliced carrots sitting opposite Prue at the kitchen table where they were preparing the evening meal.

Prue looked up from the letter which had just been delivered and nodded. 'The best – Edwin's coming home next week for a few days leave.'

Nancy smiled at Prue. 'That *is* good news. How long is it since you last saw him?'

'Too long!' Prue frowned. 'Not since last summer after he finished his training, just before he was posted to London.'

'The girls can move in with me while he's here so he can have his room back.' Nancy put the carrots she'd sliced into the casserole dish to cook in the rabbit stew for their evening meal.

'There's no need – Edwin won't be staying here.' Prue sighed, picking up a knife and starting to finely chop an onion, the smell quickly permeating the air, making her eyes water. 'But thank you for thinking of it anyway. He'll stay at Thea's.'

'Why?' Nancy asked. 'Don't you want him 'ere?'

'Oh, *I* do, but Victor won't have him in the house.' Prue glanced at Edwin's letter lying on the table, wishing that it could be different and that her son would be coming back here. 'After Edwin registered as a conscientious objector Victor was furious and threw him out, disowned his own son. He said he's not to come here again.'

'The man's a fool!' Nancy reached across the table and patted Prue's arm. 'Can't Edwin stay here anyway and just ignore what Victor decrees?'

'Can you imagine how that would be? It would spoil Edwin's visit and I don't want that.'

'If you don't mind me saying so, it's your 'ome as much as Victor's.'

'But Victor owns it, not me. As much as it galls me to not have Edwin stay here, I know it's for the best, really, Nancy. Victor was so horrible and cruel to his son, and his attitude to Edwin hasn't changed since then. I'm not going to even suggest that Edwin stay here. He can come here during the day while Victor's at work if he wants to, but they shouldn't meet. I doubt Edwin wants to see him anyway.'

Nancy frowned, studying Prue's face. 'What are you doing married to a man like him?'

Prue stared at the younger woman for a moment, taken aback by her forthright question, but she liked that about Nancy. 'You're not the first one to have asked that – you should talk to Thea about it. She tried her hardest to persuade me not to marry him in the first place.'

'But you did – why? Or was he different then?' Nancy probed, starting to peel a potato.

'Not really, Victor has always been… difficult! I foolishly thought that I might be able to change him.' Prue shook her head. 'And I desperately wanted to be a mother to his two motherless little boys. There were so many men lost in the Great War I knew it might be my only chance to have a family. I thought it was worth the risk. And it has been wonderful to be a mother to Jack and Edwin and to have a daughter of my own, too.' She glanced out of the kitchen window where she could see Alice and Nancy's two daughters out in the back garden, where they were attempting to build a miniature igloo from the snow that remained.

'But now... well you don't even share a room,' Nancy said. 'And I ain't ever seen Victor show you any affection since I've been 'ere.'

Prue forced a laugh, and she tipped the chopped onions off the chopping board into the casserole dish. 'No, that stopped a *long* time ago. Not that there was much to start with.' These days he was showering his affection on his mistress, but she wasn't going to tell Nancy that. 'He told me not so long ago that marrying me was more like a business arrangement as far as he was concerned – he needed someone to look after his children. A wife was cheaper than employing someone to do it.'

Nancy gasped. 'Miserly bugger!'

Prue nodded, her eyes meeting Nancy's. 'Yes, he is.'

'So why do you *stay* married to 'im?' Nancy asked. 'Those two little boys are grown men now.'

'I'm biding my time. I don't want to upset things while Alice is still here, but that won't be for much longer. I think she'll want to go off and do something like her brothers are doing. And when that happens, I'm free to make changes.'

'I'm glad to 'ear it.' Nancy sliced the potato she'd just peeled. 'You're too nice a person to be saddled with someone like Victor.'

'Thank you.' Prue loved Nancy's straightforward honesty. It made a refreshing change in the house after years of tiptoeing around Victor.

CHAPTER 38

'Is there a lot of snow left?' Private Blythe asked as he and Evie walked, arm in arm, along the terrace at the back of Great Plumstead Hall Hospital.

'Yes, and especially in places where it drifted,' Evie said, her breath pluming in the icy cold air.

Walking on the terrace was safe as all the snow had been cleared from it to provide an outside space for mobile patients to get some fresh air. Matron Reed was keen for them to get outside and exercise whenever possible. So now Evie's daily walks with Private Blythe had branched out from walking around the long corridors of the servants' quarters to walking outside, providing he was well wrapped up in warm clothes against the biting cold.

It was over a week since Evie had broken down and confessed her past to Thea, and since then she'd managed to maintain a steady, professional façade but all the while feeling like there was a ticking timebomb waiting to explode. The question over whether Private Blythe's sight had returned could be answered this afternoon as he had an appointment with the doctor. Evie was trying hard not to dwell on it and the what ifs for now, doing her best to enjoy their walk.

To Evie's surprise, she'd come to appreciate and even look forward to her walks with the young soldier whom she'd discovered was an intelligent and witty person, who shared her love of books. Their mutual enjoyment of reading had been revealed when Private Blythe had asked her to read to him, and she'd taken *Oliver Twist* from the selection of books available for the men in the recreation room. Now Evie read to him whenever she got the chance.

It had led to discussions about the story and characters, along with talk of many other books they loved. If it hadn't been for the fact that Private Blythe had the potential to reveal who Evie really was, then he would have been a well-suited companion for her. He might not have been to the expensive schools which Douglas had, but Private Blythe showed far greater intelligence and cultured knowledge than her husband – most of which he'd gained from his innate desire to learn and by reading books borrowed from libraries.

'The air smells cold and crisp.' Private Blythe breathed in deeply. 'It's waking me up – I hardly slept last night.' He gave a heartfelt sigh. 'I couldn't get the thought of this afternoon out of my mind. What do you think will happen – do you think I'll be able to see again, nurse?'

It was a question that Evie had asked herself many times, and the answer was always the same, despite what consequence it might have for her.

'I hope you will.' She squeezed his arm, knowing that this afternoon might be when she would find out one way or another.

He halted and grabbed hold of her hand, turning to face her. 'I'm scared.' He swallowed hard, and she could see he was fighting his emotions, a muscle twitching in his jaw. 'Will you be there with me?'

Evie was glad he couldn't see her face because no doubt it showed her dread at such a prospect.

He must have sensed her hesitation. 'Please.'

'Very well, but only if Matron allows it,' she agreed reluctantly. 'She's the boss.'

He nodded. 'Thank you. I'll ask her.'

They began to walk again towards the far end of the terrace where a robin was singing its cheerful song from the top of a nearby shrub. They stopped to listen, Private Blythe cocking his head to one side as if to focus on it more intently.

'Birdsong sounds sharper than it used to,' he said. 'I hope I'll be able to see birds singing again, not just hear them.'

'Why don't we go inside, and I'll read you some more of *Oliver Twist*?' Evie suggested. They would normally have spent longer outside, but she desperately needed some distraction from the way her mind had started to twist and turn, worrying about what direction her fate would take this afternoon. Losing herself within the words of a much-loved book would be a balm, a temporary refuge before the storm hit – books had given her respite and escape so many times before.

'Are you trying to distract me, Nurse Jones?' Private Blythe asked, a smile playing at the corners of his mouth.

'Indeed I am, you've caught me, red-handed.' Evie replied lightly.

'Then I would welcome the distraction – thank you.'

As Evie led him indoors, she thought how this afternoon could be a turning point for Private Blythe as well as herself. Her heart squeezed for the man whom she'd grown to like – hoping that he would be freed from his sightless world, despite what it would mean for her. Once he'd been just a silent chauffeur, driving her and her husband around, someone who'd barely been acknowledged by either of them. Douglas would never have considered Blythe to be an intelligent, well-read person, his inbred snobbery meant he regarded servants as lesser people. The irony that such a person might have the power to reveal his wife's deception to Douglas was not lost on Evie.

The blackout blind had been put in place in the window of the Butler's pantry, blocking out the pale winter's afternoon sunshine and plunging the room, which was now used as a surgery, into gloom. It was relieved slightly by the lit candle which Matron Reed held as she stood behind Private Blythe, watching as the local doctor unwound the bandage from around the young man's head.

Evie wished she were elsewhere as she watched the last piece of bandage fall away leaving just a pad of lint over each eye. Standing beside Private Blythe, she had a clear view of proceedings, the young man's wish for her to be here having been granted by Matron. She couldn't even step back into the shadowy edges of the room, as Private Blythe held on tightly to her hand, his fingers squeezing hers so hard that she could feel the rapid beat of his heart which matched her own.

'Keep your eyes closed after I remove the lint until I tell you to open them,' the doctor instructed.

Once the lint was gone, the doctor nodded at Matron who shielded the flame of the candle with her hand, further dimming the light in the room.

'Right, when you're ready, slowly open your eyes,' the doctor said.

Private Blythe took several deep breaths, flickered his eyes open briefly then snapped them shut again, before repeating it several times. Evie held her breath. Could he see?

'Try again,' the doctor said, holding up his hand in front of Private Blythe.

The young man haltingly opened his eyes again and a look of disbelief passed over his face. Evie's stomach knotted – what could he see?

'How many fingers am I holding up?' The doctor waggled three fingers in the air.

'Three! I can see three fingers,' Private Blythe's voice was gruff with emotion. 'I can see!'

'Excellent!' The doctor smiled. 'We'll need to assess how well your vision has returned once you're used to light again. You'll need to wear these dark glasses during daytime for a week and keep indoors. I'll come back and check how you're doing in a week's time.' He handed a pair of dark glasses to Private Blythe and watched as he put them on.

'I'll make sure Private Blythe does as instructed,' Matron Reed said. 'I'm pleased with this outcome – it's good news.' She laid her hand on the young soldier's shoulder for a moment. 'Nurse Jones if you'll escort our patient back to the ward.'

'Yes, Matron.' Evie felt as if she were in a nightmare, just waiting for the blow to fall. She couldn't recall leaving the surgery and it was only as they were walking along the corridor leading from the servants' quarters, that she realised Private Blythe hadn't said anything else since the doctor's swift dismissal. He was walking with his arm through hers, perhaps through habit or maybe for security until he was used to seeing again.

'Are you all right?' she asked.

He didn't reply for a few moments, and when he did his voice was strained. 'I'm shocked. I'd got it into my head that when I opened my eyes it would just be nothingness. Seeing the doctor's fingers waving at me...' He shook his head, a smile spreading across his face. 'I couldn't believe it.'

'I'm so pleased for you,' Evie said, completely meaning it. It was marvellous for him – but not her. Had he recognised her yet amidst all the shock and delight at finding his future was not going to be lived in darkness?

'I want to go and have a lie down,' he said, his voice suddenly weary. 'I'm exhausted.'

'A good idea. Just remember you need to keep those dark glasses on when you're awake or Matron Reed will be after you,' she said, forcing jollity into her voice.

'I don't want that! I'll have a good look at her soon – see if she looks how I imagined.' He turned his head to look at Evie as they walked along. 'Thank you for being in there with me. It felt better knowing you were there by my side. I hope I didn't squeeze your hand too hard.'

'You're welcome and my hand will recover! Let's get you back to the ward and you can rest.'

Had he realised who she was? she wondered, as they carefully headed back up the stairs to the ground floor. Evie desperately wanted to know and yet at the same time she didn't.

It was almost the end of Evie's shift as she slipped quietly into Library Ward to check if Private Blythe had woken up. After she'd taken him back to the ward, he'd laid on his bed and fallen into a deep sleep and hadn't woken up since. Looking at him now, there was no change, he continued to sleep on, his mind and body exhausted from the day's anxious event. She would have to go home still not knowing whether he had recognised her. The question of whether his eyesight would return might have been answered, but her other pressing worry had not.

'Matron said Private Blythe has been asleep for hours,' the nurse who'd just come on duty for the night shift said, coming over to Evie. 'Not surprised, he was awake most of last night. It's good news about his eyesight though, isn't it?'

Evie nodded. 'Yes, it is.'

With a final glance at Private Blythe, she turned and left the ward, heading for the cloakroom to fetch her coat before bicycling back to Rookery House. Tomorrow was her day off, with a chance for some respite before she had to return to the hospital and find out if her past would be revealed, along with her deception. She had no way of knowing and that uncertainty was hard to bear. Her fate was well and truly out of her hands.

CHAPTER 39

'You're doing a great job there,' Thea said looking over Betty's shoulder, as the little girl added to her picture of London buildings that she was drawing on the welcome home banner they were making for Edwin's return this afternoon.

'I drew the barrage balloons.' George pointed to the egg shapes in the air above the London skyline which Evie was helping them draw.

'It makes it look very real.' Thea put her arm around the little boy's shoulders and gave them a squeeze. 'I'm sure Edwin will be delighted.'

Thea looked across the kitchen table at Evie whom she'd roped in to help with the banner, thinking it would help to distract the young woman from her worries. Evie had told her last night, after she'd come home from her shift at the hospital, that Private Blythe's sight had returned, but that he hadn't said anything about recognising her – yet. But that didn't mean he hadn't, and understandably Evie was terribly anxious about it.

'Thank you for helping with this, Evie.'

'I'm glad to.' Evie smiled at the children. 'We're enjoying doing it aren't we?'

'Yes!' Betty beamed, briefly looking up from her drawing before returning her attention to her work.

'It reminds me of home and me mam,' George said solemnly.

'Perhaps you can draw the London skyline for her in your next letter,' Thea suggested. 'Your mam would like that.'

George looked at her and nodded, then returned to the drawing adding another barrage balloon.

Thea's heart squeezed for the little boy, who she knew missed his mother dreadfully but dealt with it stoically. She made sure that the children wrote to their mother every week with her help, keeping that vitally important link between them going. Thankfully their mother was as good a correspondent in return, not forgetting her children now that she was back in London with her husband. Jess Collins was a good mother who'd sacrificed being with her children for their safety, and Thea was grateful for the chance it had given her to act as a surrogate mother to them.

'When you finish the banner, we'll hang it up on the dresser so that Edwin can see it when he comes in,' Thea said. 'And everyone will be able to admire it at tonight's celebration.'

They were having a celebratory tea at Rookery House to welcome Edwin home. Hettie was cooking a special meal of Edwin's favourite food, and Alice and Prue would be there along with Reuben. Thea was looking forward to it.

Prue looked happy, Thea thought as her sister walked in through the back door of Rookery House later that afternoon, closely followed by Edwin and Alice. Having her son home again, even for a few days, was an enormous boost to Prue who worried about him working in London, but at least for now he was here, and he was safe.

'Edwin! Welcome home!' Thea hurried across the kitchen and pulled her nephew into her arms. He was thinner than the last time she'd seen him, she thought as she hugged him, no doubt the effects of his job and rationing taking its toll.

'It's good to be back,' Edwin said, putting down his suitcase and returning her embrace.

After Edwin had been greeted and hugged by Hettie, Marianne and Reuben, and introduced to Evie and the children, and the welcome home banner much admired, they sat down at the kitchen table for their tea. It wasn't a fancy meal, but one that Edwin loved – good home cooking prepared by Hettie's skilled hands.

'Oh, this tastes delicious! Thank you, Hettie.' Edwin gathered up another forkful of herby wild rabbit stew and dumplings. 'I don't get food like this in London.'

Hettie beamed at him across the table, her blue eyes shining with delight. 'It's my pleasure to make it again for you lad. And there's apple crumble and cream for afters. I wanted to make your favourites for you.'

'You spoil me, Hettie.' Edwin returned the older woman's smile.

The talk around the table filled Edwin in on the latest goings-on in the village and up at the Hall now that it was a hospital. It was only after the apple crumble had been eaten, George and Betty had gone to play in the front room with Marianne and Emily, and Evie had excused herself and gone upstairs, that Hettie cracked open a bottle of her infamous but delicious blackberry wine and poured out glasses for the remaining adults who lingered at the table. The warm cosiness of the kitchen, soft light from the lamp and full stomachs after a tasty meal, made for a contented, happy atmosphere, Thea thought.

'What's it like in London now?' Reuben asked. 'I don't know if what they say on the news on the wireless or print in the newspapers is the truth.'

'It's better than it was – the bombers don't come back *every* night like they did last autumn.' Edwin twisted his glass of blackberry wine around between his hands. 'And that's good, although the wondering and waiting can be a strain because there's always that expectation that they *might* arrive each night, but everyone's thankful when they don't.'

Thea glanced at Prue who she knew would be thankful for every night the bombers didn't target London.

'What do you do on nights when they don't come?' Hettie asked, her cheeks rosy from the glass of wine she'd drunk.

'If we're not needed out giving first aid in an air raid, then we work at the hospital doing whatever's necessary – acting as porters or orderlies on the wards. As long as I'm doing something useful, I'm happy.'

'Do you get scared when you're out in air raids?' Alice asked.

Edwin looked at his sister and nodded. 'Sometimes, I'd be lying if I said otherwise. Everybody does. But it's not all doom and gloom, there's funny things as well, things that make you smile, like the little dog who's part of an ambulance crew. She's a pretty little thing with golden fur, although I've seen her looking grey when she's covered with dust after digging in rubble for buried casualties – Trixie's her name and she's always a welcome sight.'

'Oh, I've heard of her! She's from Ambulance Station 75,' Thea said, smiling at Edwin. 'Violet's written about Trixie in her letters, told me how the little dog was dug out of a bombed-out building in which her owner was killed. Winnie, one of the ambulance drivers, rescued Trixie and she's become part of her crew. I'm glad you've seen her, Edwin. According to Violet, Trixie's made quite a difference to Station 75 as well, providing a bit of lightness in tricky times.'

'She sounds like a lovely little dog, a smart one as well,' Reuben said.

'The war's a lot worse in London than it is here,' Alice said. 'Sometimes it feels like we're so removed from it in this village, it's hard to believe what's going on in other places like London.'

'There's been plenty of changes in the village because of the war,' Hettie said, leaning back in her chair. 'We've got Marianne and Evie here because of it, the Hall's now a hospital, there's rationing and planes flying over all the time. You should be thankful we haven't got much bombing here in Norfolk.'

Alice's face flushed. 'I am. It would be awful if what's happening in London happened here. It's just sometimes I think I should be doing something else to help like Edwin and Jack are.'

'But you *are* helping,' Prue reminded Alice, her face earnest. 'You're growing food here and that's important. Thea needs your help.'

Thea understood Alice's feelings – she'd felt the same herself during the Great War, wanting to do something more involved, escape the confines of village life and broaden her horizons. And she had – it had been difficult and scary, but one of the best things she'd ever done.

'If you want to do something else, Alice, then you must.' Thea glanced at Prue who was frowning at her. 'I can always get help from somewhere else, perhaps part-time from a land girl.'

'You're only seventeen!' Prue reminded her daughter. 'You've got plenty of time to do something else. I don't think the war's going to be over for some time yet.'

'Think carefully about what you want to do, sis,' Edwin advised, putting his arm around Alice's shoulders. 'Like Ma said, you've got time, and there's no rush.'

Alice nodded. 'I will, don't worry.'

CHAPTER 40

Evie wasn't sure whether to be relieved or disappointed to discover that Private Blythe wasn't in Library Ward as she pushed an empty wicker laundry hamper in there after the morning briefing. He, like all the other mobile men, had gone to have his breakfast in the old servants' dining room. Evie knew that it was only a matter of time before she did see him and had hardly slept last night for worrying about whether he would recognise her — or had already.

'Come on, slowcoach,' Hazel chided her, parking the hamper of clean bedding that she'd wheeled into the ward by the first bed. 'We need to get these beds changed or Matron will be after us.'

Evie and Hazel had both been assigned the job of changing the beds as their first task of the morning.

Grabbing a pillow, Evie quickly removed the pillowcase and threw it into the laundry hamper. 'Don't worry, we'll get it done.'

'I've heard there might be some more socials organised soon. I'd love it if they had a dance in the village,' Hazel said cheerfully, as she removed the bottom sheet from the bed they were changing. 'Wouldn't it be wonderful if they did, and we could go – I love dancing. It would be especially good if a dance coincided with my day off.'

Evie took a clean sheet from the hamper of fresh bedding and with a deft flick of her wrists spread it over the mattress. 'Where did you hear that?'

'From Mrs Platten; she was told by Mrs Wilson – she's the sister of Thea where you live, isn't she? She said the first social was a great success and that they'd like to hold more of them.'

'It was a lovely afternoon, everyone enjoyed themselves.' Evie carefully tucked in the sheet, making neat hospital corners on her side of the mattress while her friend did the same on the other. 'But I haven't heard anything about another social or a dance. So don't go getting your hopes up just yet!'

'You never know, so I'll keep on hoping.' Hazel giggled. 'Matron might allow some of the patients to go, and if we happened to be on duty, perhaps we could go too to look after them. It's ages since I went to a dance.' Hazel looked wistful.

They finished tucking in the top wool blanket and Evie checked everything was neat and up to Matron Reed's exacting standards, before they moved on to change the next bed.

'You don't seem so keen on going to a dance, don't you like dancing?' Hazel asked tossing a used sheet into the laundry basket.

Evie looked across the bed at her friend. 'I do, but there's been nothing organised yet.' And she might not even *be here* for any more village socials or dances, she added silently. She dreaded to think what Matron Reed or Lady Campbell-Gryce's reaction would be if they found out that she wasn't exactly who she said she was, and even worse that she'd faked her own death. She doubted very much that she would have a job here any more.

'We'll just have to hope for the best then.' Hazel smiled at Evie, her optimistic nature shining through.

By the time some of the men returned after they'd had their breakfast, Evie and Hazel had finished changing all the beds and were pushing their wicker laundry baskets out of the ward into the hallway.

'Good morning,' Hazel and Evie greeted them.

'Morning nurses,' the men chorused back, smiling at the pair of them.

'You been doing our room service?' Corporal Tanner, who could now walk with crutches, asked nodding towards the laundry baskets.

'Yes, your beds are all freshly made up. You won't get better service at the Ritz Hotel in London,' Hazel retorted.

'We are *not* running a hotel here, but a hospital,' Matron's authoritative voice said from behind the men, the woman having quietly appeared and overheard their banter. 'And if you're running short of tasks to do, Nurse Robertson, there are plenty more jobs that I can assign you. Have you finished everything I gave you to do this morning?'

Hazel's face flushed scarlet. 'No, Matron. Sorry, Matron.'

'Then what are you doing gossiping in the hallway? Go and get on with your work. Nurse Jones before you go, I'd like a word.'

Evie's stomach clenched. Had Private Blythe spoken to Matron about her? But if he had, then surely she would already have been hauled into Matron's office.

Matron waited until Hazel had headed off in the direction of the laundry room, and the men had scattered, either in to the ward or to the recreation room.

'Nurse Jones, I want you to continue your daily walks with

Private Blythe – he might be able to see, but we don't know yet how well his vision has returned. I don't want to risk him falling and hurting himself. And remember it must only be indoors until after he's seen the doctor again, and always make sure he's wearing the dark glasses – he's been fine with it so far, but he might forget as the days go on.'

'Yes, Matron.' Evie was relieved that was all Matron Reed had to say for now, although it did mean that she'd continue to spend time with Private Blythe.

❧

It was mid-morning by the time Evie, having finished the list of tasks that Matron had given her, went in search of Private Blythe. She found him in the recreation room, which had been the Campbell-Gryce's drawing room before the Hall was converted into a hospital. Now, it was patients who played the grand piano standing in the corner of the large room or lounged on the sofa and in wing-backed leather armchairs.

Private Blythe was sitting in one of the armchairs with a large book on his lap, slowly turning the pages which were richly illustrated with pictures of plants and animals. He was doing as the doctor had ordered and wearing his dark glasses.

Evie took a deep breath before approaching him. She'd enjoyed their many chats about the books they'd read and would miss them if she had to leave, even though he'd be responsible for her going.

'Good morning, Private Blythe.' She smiled tentatively at him as he looked up at her. 'What are you reading?'

He returned her smile. 'Morning, Nurse Jones. It's a book about British fauna and flora.' He held it up so she could see the cover. 'Can't quite read it properly but I'm enjoying looking at the pictures.'

'That's good. Hopefully with time you'll be able to read the text again, or you might just need some reading spectacles to make it clearer.'

'That wouldn't bother me now, not when I could so easily have been unable to see anything. I'm just grateful that I *can* see.'

'I've come to take you for a walk, only inside I'm afraid. Matron instructed me to go with you to make sure you don't fall over,' Evie said.

Private Blythe put the book on a nearby table and stood up. 'She's probably right, and besides I always enjoy your company.' He put out his arm and Evie hooked hers through his as they'd done on previous walks.

'You slept a long time after you saw the doctor – you were still asleep at the end of my shift,' Evie said as they headed across the black and white chequered floor of the Hall towards the servants' area.

'I was so tired, what with hardly any sleep the night before and the worry about what would happen. When I woke up, I was scared it had only been a dream until I opened my eyes and saw it wasn't.'

'You put your dark glasses on then, I hope.'

He nodded. 'Of course. The nurse on duty was there and made sure I did. Don't worry, I'm not going to take any risks. I'll be patient and wait.'

They'd walked the length of the long corridor running through the servants' area and had turned around and were retracing their steps when Private Blythe came to a halt, pulled his arm out from hers and turned to face Evie.

'Is anything wrong?' she asked.

'I wanted to ask you something.' He looked in each direction along the corridor as if checking that they were alone before continuing, 'Are you Douglas Hamilton-Jones' wife?'

Evie felt the blood draining from her face and her heart skipped a beat. *He had recognised her.* Should she try and bluff her way out of this, pretend she had no idea what he was talking about?

'Only when I couldn't see, I thought I'd heard your voice somewhere before, and now I can see your face, I think you might be Mr Douglas's wife, or if not, then you look and sound very much like her... you've got the same colour hair, that beautiful auburn colour and such blue eyes. I thought so when I first saw you after the bandages were taken off, only I wasn't sure and didn't like to say.' He hesitated. 'But then I wondered if I was imagining it in the excitement of seeing again.' He paused and Evie knew from the tilt of his head that he was studying her face, although his eyes were hidden behind his dark glasses. 'When you came into the recreation room just now, I thought: I remember driving that lady to her wedding.' He frowned. 'Only I'd heard that Mr Douglas's wife was killed in the Blitz...'

Evie bit her bottom lip fighting back tears of anger, frustration and disappointment that the happy home and job she'd carved out for herself here was over. Part of her wanted to run, escape to where no one knew about her and what she'd done, but another part wanted to explain, be honest with someone whom she'd come to like and had enjoyed spending time with.

'Nurse Jones?' Private Blythe's face was full of concern. 'Are you all right?'

'Not really.' She exhaled loudly, her legs feeling shaky. 'I've been *dreading* you recognising me from the moment I realised who you were. I recognised your ear when I was changing your dressing.'

He touched the V-shaped nick about half an inch above his earlobe. 'You mean this?' he asked. 'It's the result of messing about with some gardening tools as a child.'

Evie nodded. 'I used to focus on the back of your head when you were driving us around and I noticed it. Looking at you was far better than listening to Douglas.' She put a hand over her mouth to stifle a sob as memories of the many times Douglas had belittled her as they'd been driven along came back to her. As always Douglas had saved his criticism and cruelty for when they were alone, playing the role of a charming, attentive husband when in company. Of course they hadn't been quite alone while Private Blythe chauffeured them, but Douglas would never have considered that one of the servants mattered, or that he need conceal his real character in front of them.

'Why didn't you say something when you recognised me?' he asked.

'Because I didn't *want* you to know who I was.' Tears filled her eyes. 'I'm supposed to be dead – killed in the London Blitz. But clearly I'm not.' Her voice wavered and she hung her head, unable to stop her tears from falling.

Private Blythe reached out and gently touched her arm. 'I'm glad you weren't killed in the Blitz, but I don't understand why people think you were and yet you're here… And very much alive.'

Evie pulled a clean handkerchief out of her pocket, wiped away her tears and looked at him. 'I…' She hesitated for a moment. 'I faked my own death because I had to escape. I couldn't go on living the life I was any longer. A future as Douglas's wife was intolerable. He's a cruel man. He hurt me with words and fists. I even miscarried after he pushed me over. But no one would believe that of him, coming from such an upper-class family. My own mother wouldn't believe me, even when I showed her my bruises.'

'*I* believe you,' Private Blythe said. 'Mr Douglas's character is no secret to the servants. I heard the way he spoke to you in the back of the car. The man's a bully.'

Private Blythe's acknowledgement of how Douglas had treated her brought fresh tears to her eyes. And he believed her, having witnessed some of it himself. Not the physical attacks, just the verbal ones, but enough to know what sort of man hid behind Douglas's upper-class, smooth exterior. It was such a relief that Private Blythe knew Evie was speaking the truth about her husband.

'I've been terrified that word would get from you to your family and then to Douglas's family. If Douglas knew I was alive he'd come for me,' Evie admitted.

'Don't worry, they won't find out from me. You had good reason to escape and I'm not going to tell *anyone*, least of all Mr Douglas's family.' He gave her a sympathetic look. 'I promise you; your secret is safe with me.'

Evie nodded, putting her hands to her face to stem the emotion that threatened to overwhelm her. She'd been so scared. 'I thought... with your family's loyalty to Douglas's family... that you'd feel duty bound to tell them.'

Private Blythe frowned. 'You mistake the need for a job and living in a tied house with true loyalty. Some servants might live that way, but not me. And especially not for a bully like Douglas Hamilton-Jones. I have no intention of going back to work for his family.'

'But your father's the head gardener there at the hall.'

He pushed his shoulders back. 'That's up to him. But I want a different life, not one reliant on someone else putting a roof over my head and who can just as easily take it away again when they're done with me or I'm too old to work. I promise you,' he placed his hand over his heart, 'I will not tell a living soul.'

'Thank you.' Evie grabbed hold of his hand and squeezed it.

'What are you planning to do?'

'Stay here and carry on nursing.'

'I mean after the war,' he said.

'I'm not sure yet, only that I'm *never* going back to Douglas. I'll move far away where there's no chance of anyone recognising me.' She took a deep breath and lifted her chin. 'Now, Private Blythe, you're supposed to be getting some exercise, not standing chatting.' She offered him her arm and he took it.

'I'm sorry that things were so bad that the only way out was to fake your death,' he said as they walked along. 'What made you do it, if you don't mind me asking?'

'Sitting next to a young woman on a bus,' Evie began, and told him what had happened on that fateful day last October which had changed the course of her life.

Evie bicycled home through the dark after her shift had ended with a much lighter heart than she'd had on the way to the hospital that morning. With the question that had haunted her for the past few days answered, her attention was more focused on her surroundings than her inner worries. She marvelled at the way the almost full moon bathed the world in a milky greyness sending shadows of trees across the road and how the cold night air nipped at her cheeks as she bicycled along. It was wonderful to feel free of her worries.

Turning into the gateway of Rookery House, Evie jumped off her bicycle and pushed it to the shed around the back where the bicycles were kept. She noticed a glow of light coming from Primrose's byre – Thea must be in there checking on the cow as she did each night.

Quickly putting her bicycle away, Evie made her way over to the byre, eager to share her news with Thea who'd been so kind and supportive when she'd confessed her secret to her.

'Hello,' Evie called as she approached the open door of the byre and went in.

Thea was standing beside Primrose stroking the underside of the cow's neck, which Evie knew the animal loved.

'Hello. How was your day?' Thea asked, looking over at Evie.

'Private Blythe knows who I am, but it's all right he isn't going to tell anyone. He's promised.' She spoke quickly, the words spilling out. 'He'd heard that I'd been killed in the Blitz.'

'Did you tell him *why* you had to escape – and were driven to fake your own death?' Thea asked.

'Yes. He understood because he knew what Douglas was capable of, he'd heard the way he talked to me in the back of the car while he was driving us. It seems that the servants who work for Douglas's family are aware of his double character, the way he treated me when he considered us to be alone. He didn't even try to hide it from them because he doesn't count the staff as people.' Evie sighed. 'I think half the time his whole family don't even see the servants who look after them, they just expect to be waited on hand and foot with never a word of thanks.' She shook her head. 'Anyway, it means Private Blythe knows that I'm telling the truth about Douglas. *He* believes me when my own mother didn't.'

'And you're sure he won't tell his family who could pass on the information to Douglas's parents?' Thea probed.

'Yes, Private Blythe might have worked for the Hamilton-Jones, but he doesn't have undivided loyalty to them, and he certainly doesn't like Douglas. I trust him not to say anything.

So...' She smiled. 'I can stop worrying now – I'm safe here in my new home and can carry on at the hospital. Everything is going to be all right.'

Thea gave Primrose a final pat and unhooked the Tilley lamp from a hook in the roof. 'It's good news, Evie. I'm pleased for you – I know how worried you were.' She put a hand on Evie's arm. 'It's worked out well *this time*, but what happens if someone else recognises you in the future. Someone who *will* inform your husband or his family about you – it could happen.'

Evie's stomach tightened. She knew that was a possibility and the reality was that she'd always be looking over her shoulder, worrying that someone might recognise her and that word would get back to Douglas and he would find her and then... 'I know it could, so after the war I'll take myself off, somewhere a very long way away from England. Move to another country where the chances of anyone ever knowing who I am are far less.'

Thea nodded. 'But what if you ever wanted to get married again one day? Not all men are like Douglas. You wouldn't be able to while you're still legally married to him.'

'I can't imagine that ever happening. Douglas has put me off marriage for life.'

Thea's gaze met Evie's. 'I hate to say this, but you will *never* be totally free of him while you are still legally married. Even if you are thousands of miles apart, you'd still be legally bound to him, and it would stop you marrying again *if* you ever wanted to. Perhaps you should just ask him for a divorce,' Thea suggested, tentatively. 'Make a clean, legal break from him and his family.'

'I can't do that! He'd know I was alive and find me and then...' Evie's voice wavered. 'Douglas wouldn't take kindly to me running off. It's safest to just carry on as I am, then after the war when it's safe to travel I'll move to Australia or New Zealand, go far away where no one will recognise me.' *I hope*, Evie added silently to herself.

Deep down, Evie knew that Thea was right when she said she'd never totally be free of Douglas and the fear of being recognised and him finding her, but that was the lesser evil compared with asking him for a divorce. Not only was divorce scandalous, but Douglas would hate the idea of someone he'd dominated suggesting such a thing. Douglas's life was mapped out the way *he* wanted it, and the thought of how he'd react to being challenged terrified her.

Thea nodded sympathetically. 'I understand, although I hate that you can't be fully free of him. But you know him, and I don't, so you must do what is right for you. I hope that you can go on to live a happy life.'

'Thank you. I'm going to try and forget about Douglas and carry on. I love living here, I feel that I've finally come home – it's the best home I've ever had. What I had before is firmly in the past, and that's where it's staying,' Evie said, forcing her voice to sound firm and confident. 'Douglas has ruined enough of my life. I'm not going to let worrying about him spoil any more.'

Thea put her arm through Evie's. 'I'm glad to hear it. You're a strong young woman and deserve to be happy. Come on, Hettie made a delicious pie for tea and has kept yours warm for you, you must be hungry after that long shift.'

'I am, and after today's good news, my appetite's returned!'

CHAPTER 41

You need to keep busy, Prue told herself blinking back tears as she fished in her handbag for the key to the village hall. She'd allowed herself to shed a few tears after waving Edwin off at the station a short while ago, but now she really must pull herself together.

It never got any easier seeing either of her sons off at the station, never knowing when she'd see them again – and she suspected that was how it would always be for her. Prue's mothering instinct was a strong integral part of her, and as proud as she was of the fine young men they'd grown into, it was this part of her that wanted to keep them close by, keep them safe.

'Morning, Prue,' a voice called as Prue unlocked the village hall door. She turned around and saw Hettie leaning her bicycle against the wall.

'Hettie, you surprised me – you're early!' Prue said, hoping that her recent tears weren't evident on her face.

Hettie raised her eyebrows, her gaze meeting Prue's. 'And so are you by my reckoning.' She looked at her wristwatch to confirm it. 'I guessed you'd come straight here after seeing Edwin off and thought you might appreciate some company.'

Prue managed a wan smile. 'You know me so well. I decided to come in a bit early: get organised, keep busy.'

'It's the best way. Did Edwin get off all right?' Hettie asked, unstrapping her wicker basket from the back carrier of her bicycle.

'Yes.' Tears pricked Prue's eyes again and she dropped her gaze to the ground.

'Come on, let's go and put the kettle on and make some tea and then we'll get organised for the knitting bee.' Hettie put her arm through Prue's and led her inside the village hall. 'We've got plenty to keep us busy today, and the sooner we get started the better.'

After her shaky start this morning, Prue was feeling much brighter by the time the members of The Mother's Day Club filed in to begin their knitting bee at ten o'clock. As usual, there was a good turnout: a mixture of women who'd been evacuated here as expectant mothers, the more recently arrived mothers who'd moved here after being bombed out, along with some village members of the Women's Institute. Between them they should be able to produce a lot of knitting today.

'Good morning, everyone,' Prue said once they were settled, sitting around several small tables that she and Hettie had set out, with balls of wool, needles and knitting patterns placed on each one. 'Welcome to another of our knitting bees, turning the wool bought from salvage collection funds into garments for our servicemen and women.'

'Where there's muck there's brass, my granny always used to say,' Gloria said, making the other women laugh.

'Exactly!' Prue smiled at Gloria who exuded enthusiasm and positivity and was a stalwart member of The Mother's Day Club. 'So today is all about knitting. It's up to you what sort of garment you make – there's a need for scarves, socks, gloves and balaclavas. Everything you'll require is on the tables in front of you and if you want help, ask Hettie…' Prue turned and gestured towards Hettie who was sitting at a table next to Nancy. 'She's an expert knitter and will be able to help you if you get stuck.'

Hettie nodded, smiling round at the group of women.

'We ain't expected to get whatever we make finished today, are we?' Nancy asked.

'Of course not,' Prue said. 'The plan is to make a good start here, then take your knitting home and finish it there. I'm planning to send a load of finished items at the end of next week. If everybody gets off to a good start today and knits whenever possible at home, five or ten minutes here or there, it will all mount up and we should be able to do it.'

'You can count on us, Prue,' Gloria said, reaching for some wool and needles from the table in front of her. 'Let's get knitting ladies!'

Once everybody had selected their wool, chosen a pattern and cast on their stitches, the hall settled into a hive of activity, the rhythmic clicking of needles and chatter of women permeated with frequent bursts of laughter. This was just what she needed, Prue thought, as she worked on the ribbed top of a sock, knitting two, purling two, in a pattern round and round her three needles.

'Ask Prue,' she heard Gloria say from her table at the other end of the village hall.

Prue looked over to where Gloria was sitting next to Grace

Barker from the shop, who was also a member of the village Women's Institute. 'Is everything all right?' Prue asked.

'We were just wondering when the next social gathering is going to be,' Grace said. 'Is there anything planned? The one we had before Christmas was a great success and it would be nice to do something else.'

Prue could see that the other women were listening, their conversations halting for the moment. 'Well, it would be good to do something else, all that snow made it difficult to have anything for a few weeks, but now the weather has improved…' She pondered. 'Although we need to keep raising funds for doing things like this – there's only so much time to do things in.'

'We could combine fundraising and something sociable,' Nancy suggested.

'We could have a dance! A Valentine's dance!' Gloria said, enthusiastically. 'Valentine's Day is coming up soon, we could decorate the hall with hearts, charge an entrance fee to raise funds – it would be marvellous. What do you think Prue?'

Prue considered for a moment knowing that all eyes were on her. She nodded. 'I think it's an excellent idea. It will be fun, sociable *and* raise funds. Although we've only got just over a week until Valentine's Day to get organised. Can we do it in time?'

'Definitely if we all pitch in.' Nancy looked around at the women. 'Raise your hand if you're willing to 'elp.' A sea of hands went up. 'There you go Prue, we've had the idea, there are plenty who will 'elp, so let's hold a Mother's Day Club Valentine's dance.'

'Very well then,' Prue agreed. 'The villagers of Great Plumstead are in for a treat.'

CHAPTER 42

Evie was in the storeroom cutting up lengths of lint dressings ready to be packed into metal drums for sterilising. It was one of the many essential jobs that needed doing to keep the hospital running smoothly – and she was grateful for the chance to sit down while she did it. It had been a busy morning, Matron Reed having instructed the nurses to give the wards a thorough cleaning on top of their usual tasks.

Absorbed in her work, Evie jumped when the door opened, and Hazel came in.

'There you are, I've been looking for you.' Hazel sat down opposite her at the table, picked up some gauze from the pile waiting to be dealt with, and began to cut it into dressing-size pieces. 'Private Blythe wants to see you when you have a moment – he said to tell you he's had a letter arrive in the afternoon post. What's that all about?'

Evie's stomach tightened, wondering if the letter could have something to do with her. Had he gone back on his word and betrayed her secret?

She forced herself to smile at Hazel. 'Oh, he probably just

wants me to read it to him – you know his eyesight hasn't fully recovered and until he gets some spectacles he's unable to read properly himself.'

It was over a week since Private Blythe had told her that he'd recognised her and she'd confided in him, telling him what she'd done and why. Since then, Evie had walked with him every day until his assessment with the doctor, when he'd been given the all-clear to not wear dark glasses indoors any more, although he still had to wear them outside for a further week. Unfortunately, Private Blythe's vision hadn't fully returned to how it had been before in both of his eyes, and he'd soon be medically discharged from the army.

'Where is he now?' Evie asked.

'He's probably outside – Matron was insisting mobile men should go outside and get some fresh air.' Hazel's eyes met Evie's. 'Why don't you go and find him? I'll carry on in here. Perhaps Private Blythe's taken a fancy to you, you two have spent a lot of time together.' She grinned mischievously.

'I don't think so.' Evie stood up and pushed her chair in under the table. 'We just share a mutual love of books, that's all. Thanks for taking over here, I won't be long.'

Evie quickly grabbed her coat from the cloakroom and headed outside. Stepping out onto the terrace at the back of the hall, which was bathed in pale winter sunshine, she spotted some of the men walking up and down, but none of them were Private Blythe. She walked to the top of the steps leading down onto the lawn and saw a lone figure standing looking over the large ornamental pond – it was him.

Hurrying down to him, her stomach doing somersaults at the thought of what he might be about to tell her, Evie desperately hoped her faith and trust in him hadn't been in vain.

'I heard you were looking for me,' she said as she reached him.

Private Blythe turned and looked at her, his eyes hidden behind his dark glasses. 'I've had a letter from home.' He held up his hand, palm towards her. 'And before you ask, don't worry I haven't told anyone about you, I gave you my word and I will always honour it.'

'Why did you want to see me?' Evie asked, relieved that he hadn't revealed her secret.

'I think you should sit down.' He patted the stone edge surrounding the pond and Evie did as he asked. 'The letter is from my mother, and she writes of upset in the Hamilton-Jones household...' He paused for a moment, frowning. 'There's no easy way to say this, so I'll just say it straight – Douglas has been killed in action in North Africa. Your husband is dead.'

A shiver ran down Evie's spine as she stared at him, the words slowly sinking in.

He nodded and put his hand on her shoulder. 'He can't ever come after you any more – or hurt you.'

'Are you sure?' Evie asked in a shaky voice.

Private Blythe reached into his pocket, took out an envelope and offered it to her. 'Here, read it for yourself.'

Evie took the envelope, pulled out the letter and read the words penned by his mother. It was indeed as Private Blythe had said, Douglas Hamilton-Jones, her cruel husband, had died fighting for his country – and that made her a widow. She was free of worrying about him ever finding her again. The relief was immense. No matter how much she'd loved her new life, the niggling worry that someday he'd discover she was still alive and come to find her had been lurking at the back of her mind.

'Are you all right?' Private Blythe asked kindly. 'It must be a shock.'

Evie stared down at the letter in her hands. 'I'm not happy that he's dead...' she said softly, a frown knitting her brow. 'I didn't want him to die, only to leave me alone. His parents must be devastated like your mother says.'

'I know you didn't wish him ill, you're not like that. But it does mean that you're out of danger from him – you could go back to London again if you wanted. You don't have to hide away here any longer.'

She nodded, realising that what Private Blythe had said was true. There had been many aspects of her previous life as Douglas's wife in London that she'd never wanted again, but there were things that she missed which she'd had to abandon when she'd fled... her precious books for instance. Now she could go back for them.

'You could tell your family that you're alive,' he suggested tentatively. 'They must have been upset when they were told that you'd been killed.'

'I suppose so, but there's only my mother and she never supported me when I asked her for help – she wouldn't believe that Douglas did those things. He charmed my mother with his good side: she never saw his dark one, just the bruises on my arms.' Evie sighed. 'I'll need to think about it.'

She stood up. 'I'd better get back to work. Thank you for telling me.'

Private Blythe nodded. 'I'm glad I found out before I left. Matron told me earlier that I'll be leaving on Friday.'

'We'll miss you.' Evie touched his arm. 'At least you'll be out of the army. What are you going to do?'

'I'm not sure, only that I won't be going back to chauffeuring again. I'll work something out.'

Evie gave him a smile and then headed back into the Hall, her mind in turmoil. The news of Douglas's death was a lot to take in and its impact on her future was going to take some thinking about.

CHAPTER 43

Evie was used to the comings and goings of patients – it had been part of her nursing career from the start. Although coming to work here at Great Plumstead Hall Hospital had allowed her to care for each patient far longer than she had in London. Back there, patients were moved out to safer hospitals in the countryside as soon as possible because of the danger of bombing, so there was never the time to get to know them well.

This morning's imminent departure of Private Blythe felt bittersweet to Evie. Her time caring for him had triggered a spectrum of emotions in her – from shock and fear to friendship. He had held her fate in his hands and yet proven to be a decent, honourable and most trustworthy man, helping to restore her faith in men. They weren't all like Douglas.

Standing by the door of Library Ward, Evie watched as Private Blythe went around saying his goodbyes, shaking the hands of the bed-bound patients, who cheerily wished him well. Fellow patients leaving was always a time of good cheer, and especially in this case as Private Blythe would be medically discharged from the army because his sight hadn't fully returned to a necessary standard in one eye after his injury.

'Is Private Blythe ready?' Matron Reed asked coming to stand next to Evie. 'The transport is ready to take him to the station.'

'Almost, he's just saying his farewells,' Evie replied.

'Come along, Private Blythe,' Matron called to him. 'You don't want to miss your train now do you?'

Private Blythe turned to look at them standing in the doorway. 'I'll be right there, Matron.'

'Well Private Blythe, our time caring for you is over, a job well done, I think,' Matron said ushering him towards the front door. 'I wish you well for your future. Don't forget us, will you? I'd like to hear what you do next.'

Evie followed them, not having had a chance to say her goodbyes to him yet.

'I'll let you know how I'm getting on,' Private Blythe said halting by the open front door, where one of the orderlies stood waiting, having brought the hospital car around to the front of the Hall ready to drive him to the station. He held out his hand to Matron. 'Thank you for all your care, I appreciate it very much.'

Matron shook his hand. 'I'm glad that your sight has returned – it's what we hoped for.'

He nodded. 'Everyone here has been so kind and caring.' His eyes fell on Evie who stood just behind Matron. 'Thank you, Nurse Jones for your great patience and kindness looking after me when I couldn't see. And for reading and talking about books with me. It helped pass worrying times.' He held out his hand to her and Evie stepped forward and took it. As they shook hands, he gently squeezed her fingers.

'I'm glad that I helped,' Evie said. 'I won't forget our talks.'

Her eyes met his and a silent message passed between them, both of them knowing that those talks hadn't just been about books. 'Do let us know how you get on.'

Private Blythe smiled. 'I will, I promise I'll write to you, I always keep my promises!' He winked at Evie and then went out of the front door and climbed in the passenger door of the car.

Matron and Evie stood in the doorway and waved him off, watching as the car disappeared down the long driveway.

'Another job well done, wouldn't you say, Nurse Jones?' Matron said turning to face Evie. 'I commend you on your care and patience with Private Blythe. I know you went out of your way to help him, reading to him during your breaks at times. I was impressed by your commitment.' She smiled and put her hand on Evie's shoulder. 'You're a fine member of our nursing team. Very well done.'

'Thank you.' Evie was taken aback by Matron's words; coming from her, it was praise indeed.

Matron smiled warmly at Evie. 'Now back to work for the pair of us – we've still got patients to care for.' She gave a nod of her head and strode off towards Dining Room Ward.

Evie stood for a moment watching her, thinking that she'd come a long way from her first days here at the hospital. Then closing the front door, she headed for the Butler's pantry, where she had the latest stack of clean laundry to check through and put away.

CHAPTER 44

'Can I talk to you? I'd appreciate your advice,' Evie asked.

Thea closed the range door after banking it up with fuel for the night to keep the kitchen warm, and looked at Evie, whose face was anxious. 'Of course.'

The pair of them were alone in the kitchen at Rookery House, Marianne and Hettie having retired to bed a short while ago. Thea sat down in one of the chairs that had been pulled up beside the range and gestured for Evie to sit down in the one opposite where Hettie had been knitting before she'd gone up to bed.

'How can I help you?' Thea asked. 'Private Blythe hasn't told anybody has he?'

Evie shook her head. 'No, he's kept his word. And he left the hospital this morning to be medically discharged from the army. The thing is, earlier this week, he had a letter from his mother with news about Douglas.' Evie dropped her gaze down to her hands, which were clasped tightly in her lap, for a few moments before looking up, her anxious blue eyes meeting Thea's. 'Douglas is *dead*. He was killed in action in North Africa.'

Thea stared at Evie. 'Are you sure?'

'Absolutely. Private Blythe showed me the letter. His mother said that the Hamilton-Jones family are naturally upset at the news. It's not something she would make up. That means that I'm now a widow and I don't have to worry any more that he'll find me.' She sighed tremulously. 'I'm free! Completely free. I don't need to be scared any more.' Tears glistened in Evie's eyes.

Thea reached across and took hold of one of Evie's hands and squeezed it gently. 'That's quite some news. What are you going to do now?'

'I've been thinking of nothing else for days, ever since Private Blythe told me,' Evie explained. 'I didn't want to say anything to you until I'd decided what the best thing to do is, and I have – I think. But before I do it, I'd appreciate your opinion in case it's a ridiculous idea.'

Thea smiled at Evie encouragingly, listening attentively.

'I've decided to write to my mother, explain everything and ask her to meet me in London. I want to be able to go back there freely with no more hiding. I'd also like to collect some of my things from the flat which I had to leave behind when I fled – that's if it hasn't been bombed.' Evie bit her bottom lip. 'Only I have no idea how my mother will react, but I need to be honest with her so that I can move on and live my life freely, with no more lies, no more hiding. What do you think, Thea? Am I crazy to stir things up, or should I just leave things as they are?'

Thea leaned back in her chair and regarded the young woman who'd carried such a heavy burden on her shoulders. 'I understand your need to be honest with your mother, because if you don't try then it may haunt you for the rest of your life. I think it sounds the right thing to do, although it won't be easy. How do you think she'll react?'

Evie gave a slight shake of her head. 'I don't know. After her lack of sympathy when I showed her what Douglas had done to me, I really don't know what she'll say when she finds out that I faked my death to escape him.'

'It was a drastic action to take – surely your mother will realise how bad it was for you to do that.'

Evie gave a weak smile. 'I thought showing her bruises where Douglas had beaten me, telling her I'd miscarried her grandchild after he shoved me over would have spurred my mother into action… made her believe and support me…' She shook her head and then straightened her shoulders. 'Like I said I'm going to ask her to meet me. I was wondering if you'd come with me. Please?'

Thea didn't hesitate. 'Of course I will. I'll do all I can to help you.'

'Thank you, I appreciate that. My mother might not want to see me, but if she does, having you there will help me face her.'

'By my reckoning your mother should be ashamed of letting you down when you went to her for help.' Thea leaned forward and touched Evie's arm. 'If she agrees to meet you, I'll be there with you, you don't have to face it alone.'

Evie nodded. 'Thank you. And can I ask you not to tell Hettie or Marianne about what I did. I will tell them, but not yet.'

'I understand, and I promise I won't say anything. When are you going to write to your mother?'

Evie stood up. 'I'll go and do it now, get it over with.' She bent down and kissed Thea's cheek. 'Goodnight and thank you for everything.'

Thea sat by the warm range for a bit longer, thinking

through what they'd just been discussing, the kitchen quiet except for the ticking of the clock on the dresser. She hoped that Evie's mother would have the decency to see her daughter and, importantly, apologise for failing to support her when Evie had gone to her for help. News that Douglas had been killed was a blessing in disguise for Evie, bringing her freedom. She hoped that now the young woman could start to relax the barriers that she'd understandably built up around herself.

CHAPTER 45

Evie stared out of the train window at the passing countryside. She and Thea had caught the early train and were on their way to London where they might be meeting Evie's mother. After which she'd return to the flat where she'd lived with Douglas for one last time to collect some things. Today was to be a flying visit to the city, touching briefly with her past and setting things straight for her future – and it had made a tight knot settle heavily in her stomach.

'Are you all right?' Thea asked, looking at Evie across the width of the compartment from where she sat opposite, a newspaper on her lap.

'I'm nervous,' Evie admitted. 'I have no idea whether my mother will turn up and I'm not sure whether I want her to or not, to be honest.'

The long letter Evie had sent to her mother explaining what she'd done and importantly *why* she'd done it, had received a swift reply from her mother, who clearly was shocked but relieved that her only child was still alive. Her mother's letter had explained that she hadn't fully appreciated how awful things were for Evie when she'd asked for her help.

In response, Evie had written back telling her mother that she would be at the Lyons Corner House on the Strand at midday today if her mother wanted to meet her. Evie had deliberately chosen this venue knowing that her mother would not normally frequent such a place, much preferring somewhere like the Dorchester, but going there would have reminded Evie of visiting it with Douglas.

'You've done all you can, you've been honest with her and it's out of your hands,' Thea said sympathetically.

Evie nodded. 'I'm glad you'll be there with me whatever happens. Facing up to mother has always been difficult for me.'

Thea reached across and put a hand on Evie's arm. 'You are a brave young woman. Don't let anyone ever put you down again.'

Sudden tears pricked Evie's eyes. 'I'll try not to.'

She turned her gaze to look out of the window once more, where open countryside had now given way to the outskirts of London and evidence of enemy bombing raids was clear to see. There were gaps in the rows of houses, like missing teeth, and piles of rubble and blackened brickwork scorched by flames.

'It's shocking to see,' Thea said, staring wide-eyed out of the window. 'I've heard about the raids on the wireless, read about them in the newspapers, but seeing so much damage is heart-breaking.'

Evie nodded. 'The war has come to London in a far more horrifying way than in Great Plumstead.'

'I'm grateful that Jess Collins had the strength to leave Betty and George in the village so they could come and live with us. Imagine if she'd brought them back to this...' Thea paused, her face pale. 'And every time the bombers come back it gets worse – more people injured and killed.'

'She did the right thing. Betty, George and I have all been lucky to come and live at Rookery House,' Evie said, her gaze meeting Thea's.

'The place wouldn't be the same without you all,' Thea said, warmly.

Evie sat facing the entrance so that she had a clear view of when her mother arrived at the Lyons Corner House... *if* she arrived. It was now five minutes past midday, and there was still no sign of her.

'We should give her five more minutes and if she hasn't turned up, then we must order,' Thea said.

Evie nodded. They'd already had to ask the Nippy waitress to wait before she took their order, explaining that they were expecting another person, but it was busy in the restaurant, and they couldn't sit here for much longer taking up a table without ordering.

Every time the door opened and more people came in, Evie looked up to see if it was her mother, part of her hopeful, another relieved when it wasn't. And then suddenly her mother was there, standing by the door looking around her. She was immaculately dressed as always, more suited to the Dorchester than here, but she'd come. Evie waved to her and was surprised at the look of delight on her mother's face when she spotted her.

'She's here!' Evie stood up to greet her mother, who was weaving her way between the tables to reach them.

'Genevieve!' her mother said softly, pausing to look at Evie for a moment before kissing her daughter's cheek, her familiar floral perfume scenting the air. 'I'm so happy to see you.'

'Hello Mother. You came.' Evie's voice came out gruff with unexpected emotion.

Her mother's eyes met hers 'Did you doubt that I would?'

Evie lifted her chin. 'I wasn't sure.'

'But you're *my daughter*, of course I came. I'm late I know, and I apologise, the train was delayed up from Sussex.' Her mother turned to look at Thea who'd stood up, quietly watching their exchange.

'Mother, this is Thea Thornton who I live with in Norfolk. Thea, this my mother,' Evie introduced them.

Thea held out her hand, which Evie's mother took. 'How do you do?'

'Hello, Miss Thornton. Thank you for giving my daughter a home,' Evie's mother said in her plummy voice.

The appearance of the waitress again asking if they were now ready to order distracted them for a few minutes as they checked the menu and decided on what they wanted.

Now seated beside Thea, her mother stared across the table at Evie, while around them the chink of cutlery on plates and hum of many conversations went on. Evie's stomach somersaulted as she waited for her mother to speak, to make the first move... to possibly extend an olive branch.

Her mother's face looked uncertain, nervous even and Evie noticed the deep breath before beginning to speak in a soft voice. 'Since your letter came last week, I have spent a great deal of time thinking about what you did, and importantly *why* you were driven to such extreme measures...' Her mother's voice wavered, and she paused, composing herself before continuing, 'I remembered the day you came to me and showed me the bruises on your arms and told me how Douglas treated you in private. How you'd lost a baby...' She dropped her gaze to her hands, which were clasped tightly in her lap, for a moment before looking up and meeting Evie's eyes once more. 'I am *desperately* sorry that I didn't listen properly, that I didn't help you as I should have done. I didn't want to believe such things about Douglas simply because I'd always thought he was a fine husband for you to have. So charming and caring of you, or at least that was what I saw. Only I was very much mistaken and when you tried to tell me, I didn't listen.'

Evie stared at her mother. In the many times she'd thought about this potential meeting in the past few days, she'd not expected her mother to declare her mistake and apologise so freely.

'I was scared to tell you,' Evie admitted, looking her mother straight in the eye. 'It took a long time for me to pluck up the courage to speak to you about it. I know all you saw was Douglas being charming and apparently the perfect husband, but that was a show – he wasn't like that in private, quite the opposite.'

'I didn't know!' Evie's mother said.

'Not until I told you and showed you what he'd done to me – and they weren't the first or the last bruises he gave me. And it wasn't just physical either, he belittled me, ordered me around – he was in charge of me and my life.'

Evie's mother bit her lip, fighting tears that filled her eyes. 'I *wish* I had listened to you, Genevieve. If only I could turn back the clock…'

Evie held up her hand. 'He's gone, Mother. Douglas can't hurt me any longer.' She glanced at Thea who'd sat quietly supporting her, letting her and her mother talk, but who she knew would step in if needed. Thea gave her an encouraging smile. 'I'm happy with my new life, with my work and where I live. I've made good friends and don't want to look back. I'm glad you came today, I really am.' She straightened her shoulders and smiled at her mother, feeling lighter, as another heavy weight from her previous life slid off her shoulders. Her mother's heartfelt apology meant a huge amount to her.

Evie's mother dabbed at her eyes with a neatly pressed handkerchief that she'd taken out of her handbag. 'I'm glad that you have found a new life... That you're happy – that's the most important thing. Thank you for writing to me and for meeting me today. I know you didn't have to – you could have never contacted me again and I would have gone on believing that my daughter had died.'

Evie nodded, tears suddenly filling her eyes. She was grateful for the arrival of the waitress carrying a tray with their order. Once everything had been unloaded and distributed to who was having what, she had regained her composure.

'I'd like to go to the flat this afternoon to get some of my things that I want from there,' Evie explained as she picked up her knife and fork ready to eat. 'The rest of it – the furniture and Douglas's belongings – his family can do what they want with. Douglas chose all the furniture anyway.'

'I know his parents kept the flat on after you...' Her mother hesitated. 'After you left, so Douglas had somewhere in town when he came back.'

Evie was relieved to hear that. The flat belonged to Douglas's parents and thankfully they hadn't rented it out to anyone else.

'It's up to them what they do with it now, but if they haven't done anything yet and my books and things are still there, then I'd like to get them.'

'I could come with you if you like, or perhaps Thea is already going with you to help,' Evie's mother suggested tentatively.

'I'm going to see a friend,' Thea said, pouring out cups of tea from the pot. 'Evie wanted to go there on her own, and we're meeting back at Liverpool Street station later to get the train home.'

Evie considered for a moment. Did she want her mother there? Going back to the flat was sure to rake up some unpleasant memories and perhaps it would be better to face them alone. Her mother's apology seemed like the start of a new, more grown-up and equal relationship with her, and Evie didn't want that tainted by anything this afternoon.

'Thank you, Mother, but I need to do this on my own.'

Her mother nodded. 'I understand. I hope you'll let me know how you get on.'

Evie smiled at her mother. 'I will.'

CHAPTER 46

Thea turned off the Minories and walked in under the arched entrance to Ambulance Station 75, where her arrival was greeted by barking from a small, golden-haired dog, who rushed out of one of the garages, her fluffy tail wagging from side to side.

'Trixie, what on earth is the matter?' A plummy voice called from the depths of the garage, whose doors stood open, the waiting ambulance parked inside ready to go. Moments later a willowy young woman with honey-blonde hair and pillar-box-red lips stepped out from the garage and spotted Thea approaching. 'Hello, can I help you...?' She paused, frowning, and then broke into a smile. 'Hello, it's Thea, isn't it? We met last year.'

Thea nodded, smiling warmly at the young woman who she recognised as Winnie. 'That's right, I was here the day the Blitz started.' She bent down and patted Trixie who'd stopped barking and rushed over to her, jumping up to put her front paws on Thea's leg, her tail still wagging furiously.

Winnie rolled her eyes. 'That's right. The day the Blitz

started, and it's barely stopped since. It's lovely to see you again – so what's brought you back to London? Have you come to join the ambulance service? The boss would be delighted to have you on board.'

'I'm afraid not, it's just a flying visit. I was hoping to see Violet... I mean Station Officer Steele.'

'Is she expecting you?' Winnie asked.

'No, I thought I'd surprise her.'

Winnie beamed. 'She'll be delighted; let me take you up to her office.'

Thea's first thought at the sight of her friend through the window in the office door, was that Violet looked tired. She knew that her friend had had flu a few weeks ago and fully recovering from that could take time. Combined with the ever-present risk of air raids, being in charge of an ambulance station and its crew was clearly taking its toll on Violet Steele, although Thea knew her friend would never admit to it or give in.

Winnie tapped on the door of the office, where Violet sat at her desk busy doing paperwork.

'Come in,' Violet called without looking up.

'Visitor to see boss,' Winnie said opening the door then stepping to the side and ushering Thea in.

Violet looked up and, at the sight of Thea, a wide smile lit up her face. 'Thea!' She sprang to her feet and enveloped Thea in a warm embrace. 'How wonderful to see you.'

'And you,' Thea said.

'Shall I make you some tea?' Winnie asked lingering in the doorway.

Violet smiled at the younger woman. 'Yes please, thank you

Winnie.' Returning her attention to Thea she asked, 'What brings you to London – you haven't had any more lodgers arrested have you?'

Thea shook her head. 'No, but I did come to support another lodger with some family business. We just came for the day and while she's finishing what she has to do, I thought I'd come and see you.'

'Well I'm delighted you have.' Violet gestured for Thea to take a seat and sat down by her desk again. 'So how are you? And how are your young evacuees?'

Violet knew all about Thea giving a home to Betty and George as they wrote to each other regularly.

'It's going well,' Thea said. 'I was worried about it at first wondering if we'd manage, but between Hettie, Marianne and myself, there's always somebody there to look after the children. I must admit that it's fun having them living with us, it's brought about a part of life that I never thought I'd experience.'

'Mothering you mean?' Violet asked, her brown eyes shrewd behind her tortoiseshell-rimmed glasses.

Thea nodded. 'I...' She paused as Winnie appeared with a tray holding cups of tea and a plate of biscuits which she put down on the desk.

'Here we are,' Winnie said, with a cheerful smile. 'Something to eat and drink while you have a good catch-up.'

'Thank you, Winnie,' Violet said.

'You're welcome.' Winnie went out, closing the door quietly behind her.

'What were you about to say?' Violet asked.

'That I know I'm not Betty or George's real mother, only a sort of temporary one, but it's given me the chance to experience what it's like, the worry and the joy. Awful as the Blitz is, it has unexpectedly led to this opportunity.'

Violet nodded, her gaze meeting Thea's. 'I remember when we were in France, how we used to talk about the families we hoped we'd have one day...' She sighed. 'But that was before we lost our fiancés.'

Thea reached across the desk and put her hand on Violet's arm. Like many women of their generation, they'd lost the men they loved, those they had been planning on spending their lives with, and the potential future families they could have had together.

'They're still in our hearts,' Thea said, softly.

Violet nodded. 'Always.' She paused for a moment looking thoughtful. 'I suppose with you being responsible for children now, there's no hope of me persuading you to come and join the ambulance service and work here, is there?'

Thea laughed. 'I'm afraid not, although as you know I do drive an ambulance as part of my WVS work now and then.' Thea took a sip of her tea. 'One of my reasons for coming to see you was to invite you to stay at Rookery House when you get some leave. Come and enjoy some fresh country air and home-produced food.'

Violet raised her eyebrows behind her glasses. 'That's very kind of you, and I'd love to accept, but I can't possibly take any leave while the Blitz continues.'

'It can't go on for ever though, can it?'

'I sincerely hope not!' Violet took a biscuit from the plate and nibbled at it.

'When it does stop, then you have an open invitation to come and stay – just let me know so we can have a bed ready for you.' Thea hoped that she'd be able to welcome her dear friend to her home in the not-too-distant future, when she'd be able to make sure she rested and recuperated.

The rest of her visit passed quickly, the pair of them chatting about their daily lives, while other members of the ambulance crew whom she'd met last autumn popped in to say hello – Frankie and Bella, Mac and Sparky. A variety of individual characters who together made up a strong team, of whom she knew Violet was immensely proud of and cared for deeply in her role as their Station Officer.

~

Violet walked out to the entrance of Ambulance Station 75 with Thea, their arms linked together, as entwined as their friendship which had lasted since the days of the Great War.

'I'm so glad you came to see me,' Violet said, coming to a halt as they reached the opening onto the Minories. 'It's been such a treat, a real pick-me-up.'

'It's been lovely to see you.' Thea put her arms around her friend and hugged her tightly. 'Look after yourself, Violet. You will, won't you?'

Violet took a step back and nodded. 'Absolutely! I need to be here to keep that lot in order.' She gestured back into the ambulance station with a nod of her head. 'And I have every intention of taking you up on your generous invitation, Thea. You've told me so much about Rookery House – I'd love to come and see it for myself, and spend a proper length of time with you of course.'

'I shall look forward to it.' Thea took hold of Violet's hand and squeezed it. 'Until we meet again, take care.' She smiled warmly at her dear friend and then set off heading for Liverpool Street station and home.

CHAPTER 47

Evie prised the loose brick out of the wall and was relieved to see that the key was still where she had left it when she'd fled her marital home. Back then, she'd never have imagined that she would ever return here again of her own free will, but circumstances had changed... she had changed. Now, coming back she was free to collect some treasured possessions that she'd been forced to leave when she'd made her escape.

Letting herself into the flat, Evie closed the door behind her and put down the empty suitcase that she'd brought with her. She took several slow steadying breaths to calm her pounding heart. As she did so, the faint scent of Douglas's cologne hit her. Even when he wasn't here, and had been gone for months, it had always lingered like some insidious presence watching over her. It was just a smell, Evie firmly reminded herself, *he* wasn't here and never would be again.

Squaring her shoulders, she walked along the hallway and into the sitting room where sunlight streamed in through the tall windows, highlighting dust motes dancing in the air.

Looking around everything was the same as when she'd last been here, although the place was covered with dust, and thick cobwebs were strung high up in the cornices of the ceiling. Clearly no one had been here since she'd left, which was no surprise to Evie as Douglas's parents had never once visited since she and Douglas had moved in after their wedding. Her parents-in-law preferred life in the countryside and now that Douglas was dead, they would probably just arrange for the flat to be cleared and rented out or sold.

Her eyes fell on the large, silver-framed photograph standing on top of a side table – it was from their wedding. Evie picked it up, wiped off the powdery dust with her fingers and stared at her smiling face as she stood beside her new husband. She'd had no idea what she was getting into, and had been happy, delighted to marry the charming Douglas. Evie had been amazed and thrilled when he'd shown interest in someone like her, not choosing one of the more vivacious young women who'd been part of their social circle for his wife. But those women were stronger, more confident than she'd ever been – they would not have allowed Douglas to dominate them. Looking back, she realised that Douglas had chosen her for her personality – her quietness, her lack of confidence, her ability to be moulded and dictated to. She could see that now.

Evie put the photograph down. Life had taught her many lessons since then – she wasn't that same innocent young woman any more. She glanced at her watch and seeing it was almost two o'clock, she knew she needed to get started as there was a lot to do.

Retrieving her empty case from near the front door, she carried it through to the bedroom where she'd kept her beloved books in a little bookcase. Douglas had refused to have them in the sitting room as they would *spoil the decor* in his opinion.

Evie got to work taking her clothes out of the wardrobe and chest of drawers, placing them in piles on the bed. There were a few items that she wanted to keep, but other garments she had no desire to ever wear again. They were the ones that Douglas had liked, often even chosen for her – she'd never liked them, worn them under his control. She ran her finger over one such dress, made from blue silk – it had been expensive, but she'd loathed it. She quickly folded it and added it to the pile to be donated to the WVS.

When she'd finished emptying her drawers and sorting her clothes, Evie took a large suitcase down from the top of the wardrobe and began to pack it with the clothes she wanted to keep. She kept some woollen jumpers to one side to put to use in the smaller suitcase that she'd brought with her, to act as padding around her books so that they didn't become battered on the journey back to Norfolk.

Turning her attention to the bookcase she removed the books, wiping off the layer of dust with a cloth, pausing every now and then to stroke the covers. Evie recalled the many happy hours of escape that these books had given her as she packed them carefully into the suitcase, relishing the idea of being able to read them whenever she wanted back at Rookery House.

By the time Evie had finished she'd packed both suitcases as well as several parcels of clothes which she'd wrapped in brown paper and tied up with string, ready to take to the nearby WVS centre which Thea had found out about for her. Then, once she'd delivered those, all she had to do was retrieve the suitcases, leave the flat for the last time and make her way to Liverpool Street station to meet Thea and get the train home.

Picking up the parcels, Evie smiled to herself, feeling lighter in spirit. Coming here had been challenging but now she could put the past firmly behind her – from here on, it was her future which mattered.

CHAPTER 48

Prue stood behind the refreshments table watching the dancers smiling and laughing as they moved to the toe-tapping music.

'They all look like they're having a good time, don't they?' Hettie said standing next to Prue, where she was helping serve cups of tea, glasses of her home-made elderflower cordial, sandwiches and currant buns.

'They certainly do.' Prue gazed around the hall which members of The Mother's Day Club had decorated for the Valentine Dance. Heart-shaped bunting had been made from newspaper and string, and looped around the edges of the village hall, and across the width just below the ceiling.

Lady Campbell-Gryce had loaned a magnificent gramophone player with a huge trumpet, along with a stack of records perfect for dancing to. Reuben had set it up on a table on the raised platform at one end of the hall, and kept the music coming, one song after another.

The dancers were all enjoying themselves, whatever their age. In keeping with previous social events, today's dance was open to everyone so that parents could bring along their children – the whole village community was welcome. It didn't matter who people were – if they'd only moved to the village a few months ago or had lived here all their lives, they were all having fun. And not only that, all the money raised from the entrance fee and sale of refreshments would be added to the wool fund – to keep future knitting bees going. Prue loved the way everything had come together – how they enjoyed themselves with a purpose. It really was the perfect combination in her opinion!

Thea had two dance partners – Betty and George. They'd both wanted to dance with her so the three of them had joined together and were enjoying their rather haphazard progress around the hall's dance floor. What they lacked in technique, they made up for in enjoyment.

They weren't the only unusual partners; Marianne was dancing with Emily in her arms, the little girl giggling as her mother twirled around to the music. Rosalind Platten was proving popular with the mobile patients from Great Plumstead hospital who'd come to the dance – and she looked like she was having a fine time, smiling happily as she was whisked around the dance floor. It was something that Thea would never have imagined possible remembering how Rosalind had been at the beginning of the war – but like so many people, she'd taken on a new role for the war effort, and it had changed her for the better, Thea thought. Everyone here had been touched by the war in some way. She certainly had, and it had brought her these two delightful children to care for, and that gave her great joy.

'It's a pity you're on duty today and had to come to the dance in your uniform,' Hazel said to Evie as they stood drinking glasses of elderflower cordial while having a break from dancing. 'I'm lucky it was my weekend off so I could wear a pretty dress.'

Evie looked down at her blue nurse's uniform with the crisp white apron worn on top, before meeting her friend's eyes, smiling warmly at her. 'It's fine. I'm happy to be here in my uniform and grateful that Matron allowed me to accompany the patients here.'

In truth, it was a delight to be able to wear her uniform out in public, Evie thought. She was proud to be seen wearing it because it was something she'd never have dared to do just a few short months ago. Back then, in London, she had hidden her work as a nurse, changing out of her uniform before leaving the hospital for fear of someone she knew spotting her and revealing her secret to her husband or his family. But that was firmly in the past – Evie would never hide herself away like that again. Hazel knew nothing of Evie's history and so couldn't appreciate just how much the simple joy of being here in her uniform meant to Evie.

'Nurse Jones, you promised me a dance,' Corporal Barkham said appearing by Evie's side. His leg was almost completely healed, and he was making the most of being mobile again. 'If you would do me the honour.' He gave a little bow.

Evie laughed and gave a small curtsy. 'I'd be delighted, thank you.' She placed her empty glass on a nearby table and took his hand, and smiling at Hazel, who grinned back at her, allowed him to lead her onto the dance floor.

'How was your trip to London?' Corporal Barkham asked as he led her around the floor, surprisingly light on his feet.

'It was good,' she told him, not wanting to elaborate. She'd already explained to him that she'd been to see family when she'd returned to the hospital after her day off.

'I hope you're not thinking of going back to nurse in London, are you?' he asked. 'Only you'd be sorely missed.'

'No, I'm not going back.' Evie looked around the hall, spotting all her friends who'd become so dear to her since she had arrived here – Thea and the children who danced by smiling and waving at her, Hettie serving at the refreshments table, Marianne chatting to another mother with Emily in her arms, and Reuben up on the little stage in charge of the music. They were like family to her now; this village and Rookery House had become her home.

Evie smiled happily at Corporal Barkham. 'I'm not going anywhere – it took me a long time to find such a special place to call home, and now I've found it, I'm staying.'

Dear Reader,

I hope you enjoyed reading Evie's story and spending time with Thea, Hettie and Marianne at Rookery House, along with other residents of Great Plumstead whom I first wrote about in the two *Mother's Day Club* books.

After finishing *The Mother's Day Victory*, I didn't want to say goodbye to Thea, Prue and Hettie and all the other characters of Great Plumstead and so this new follow-on series was born. I plan to write more books in this *Rookery House* series, following the characters through the war and meeting new ones who will come to live in or visit the village. There are lots of stories to tell! The next one in the series will be a novella called *A First Christmas at Rookery House*.

I love hearing from readers – it's one of the greatest joys of being a writer – so please do get in touch via:

Facebook: Rosie Hendry Books
Twitter: @hendry_rosie
Instagram: rosiehendryauthor
Website: **www.rosiehendry.com**

You can sign up to get my newsletter delivered straight to your inbox, with all the latest on my writing life, exclusive looks behind the scenes of my work, and reader competitions.

If you have the time and would like to share your thoughts about this book, do please leave a review. I read and appreciate each one as it's wonderful to hear what you think. Reviews also encourage other readers to try my books.

With warmest wishes,

Rosie

HEAR MORE FROM ROSIE

Want to keep up to date with Rosie's latest releases?

Sign up to receive her monthly newsletter at her website.
www.rosiehendry.com

Subscribers get Rosie's newsletter delivered to their inbox and are always the first to know about the latest books, as well as getting exclusive behind the scenes news, plus reader competitions.

You can unsubscribe at any time and your email will never be shared with anyone else.

IF YOU ENJOYED A WARTIME WELCOME AT ROOKERY HOUSE

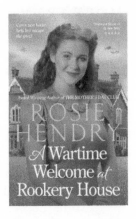

It would be wonderful if you could spare a few minutes to leave a star rating, or write a review, at the retailer where you bought this book.

Reviews don't need to be long – a sentence or two is absolutely fine. They make a huge difference to authors, helping us know what readers think of our books and what they particularly enjoy. Reviews also help other readers discover new books to try for themselves.

You might also tell family and friends you think would enjoy this book.

Thank you!

ACKNOWLEDGMENTS

Many people have helped me with my research into wartime Norfolk – a big thank you to the volunteers at Reepham Archive and Aylsham Heritage Centre and Archives for their support, Norfolk Library Service for supplying many research books, and the Imperial War Museum in London for access to recorded oral histories and documents.

My mum patiently answered my many questions about life in rural Norfolk in the Second World War – thank you.

Thank you to my editor Catriona Robb, cover designer Andrew Brown and photographer Gordon Crabb.

My fellow writers are a great support and I appreciate their friendship, company, wise words and listening ears. Thank you especially to Pam Brooks, Victoria Connelly, Elaine Everest, Fiona Ford, Jean Fullerton, Jenni Keer, Lizzie Lamb, Clare Marchant, Heidi-Jo Swain, Claire Wade and Ian Wilfred. Belonging to the RNA's Norfolk and Suffolk chapter and the Strictly Saga Group is a great joy – thank you all.

Finally, thank you to David, who listens and supports me in all I do.

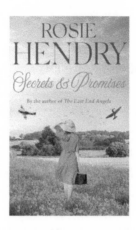

A poignant and unputdownable story of a woman who must finally acknowledge the secret she has hidden for a lifetime. But will it cost her all she holds dear?

England, 1944: With deadly doodlebugs terrorising London, **Bessie Rushbrook** agrees to give shelter to eight-year-old evacuee, **Marigold**, in her Norfolk home. However, the little girl is no random stranger, and Bessie must honour the promise she gave to Marigold's mother, **Grace**, and not reveal her connection to the child.

Marigold's arrival stirs up Bessie's memories from the past when the world was at war for the first time. She is forced to face her actions from those days, and question the haunting secret that she's long kept hidden.

When Grace is injured in London, Bessie makes the heart-wrenching decision to confess her secret, knowing that it could destroy everything she holds dear – her marriage, family and home. Will those who love her understand, and can they forgive her?

ALSO BY ROSIE HENDRY

East End Angels series

East End Angels

Secrets of the East End Angels

Christmas with the East End Angels

Victory for the East End Angels

Women on the Home Front series

The Mother's Day Club

The Mother's Day Victory

Rookery House series

A Wartime Welcome at Rookery House

Standalone novel

Secrets and Promises

Novellas

A Home from Home

Love on a Scottish Island

Rosie Hendry lived and worked in the USA before settling back in her home county of Norfolk, England, where she lives in a village by the sea with her family. She likes walking in nature, reading (of course) and when she has the time, even some dressmaking!

Rosie writes stories from the heart that are inspired by historical records, where gems of social history are often to be found. Her interest in the WWII era was sparked by her father's many tales of growing up at that time.

Rosie is the winner of the 2022 Romantic Novelists' Association (RNA) award for historical romantic sagas, with *The Mother's Day Club*. That book already has a sequel - *The Mother's Day Victory* — and Rosie has continued writing about the same characters in her new Rookery House series, the first of which is *A Wartime Welcome at Rookery House*.

To find out more visit **www.rosiehendry.com**

facebook.com/RosieHendrybooks
twitter.com/hendry_rosie
instagram.com/rosiehendryauthor

Milton Keynes UK
Ingram Content Group UK Ltd.
UKHW011811010923
427885UK00001B/4